For Maya

1. ABOVE

The reason Jamie moved away from the comfortable two-story brick nest he'd grown up in wasn't because a twenty-six-year-old ought not to still have his mother doing his laundry, cooking his meals, and chastising him for bedroom mess. In fact, those things (and even the same tired, ridiculous arguments replayed nightly between his parents), were an ideal tonic, with a sweet taste of normality. Comfortable, familiar. Stifling too, but so are bandages and splints.

He'd been through *something*, something not normal at all, but that was almost all he knew. Whatever it had been, no one in the world would believe it possible, except maybe those locked in mental wards (who may well be right about what they themselves saw and heard, for all anyone really knew). Whatever Jamie had been through had been real, actually real. It had changed and injured him, made the world and its reality a much less certain picture. The supernatural existed, he knew it in his bones. Maybe every tale about vampires and other dark things had some grounding in truth, safely hiding in plain sight behind "it's just a story."

To hear his father wailing in despair at the TV while his football team lost, like the TV itself were some unfair god which might show mercy and change the course of things . . . that was tonic too.

There were people, in fact most people, whose gravest concern was a scoreboard at a stadium somewhere, their receding hairline, a hated boss, money, and all the usual everyday junk. Whatever Jamie had been through had no place in their world, even though some of them—his parents certainly—had seen hints and clues: that night the cops picked him up in a clown suit with blood on the oversized red shoes.

No, that was not part of their world . . . and so Jamie tried to be like them. He grew outraged at bad movies and poor service, howled in grief with his father when certain sport teams lost, went to his job and got drunk on weekends, just like everyone else. And yet . . .

Just as a deep part of Jamie knew better, knew that *something* had happened, a part of his parents knew it too. A glance when he entered the room, home from work, a glance with doubt and suspicion flashing in his mother's eyes for just one moment. From his father, gazing over the top of his newspaper at breakfast, studying his son's profile, as if seeking the first hint of peculiarity surfacing . . . then back to the paper when Jamie noticed him watching. The whispered conversations falling to silence and awkwardness as he came within earshot, when they may as well have screamed at him from a megaphone WE ARE TALKING ABOUT YOU, OUR WEIRD SON. YOU ARE A PUZZLE WE ARE AFRAID TO SOLVE.

It all said pretty much one thing: *You did something, didn't you?*

Jamie knew as well as they did, beneath the thin veneer of strained normality: the answer was *yes*. Hell yes. He'd done something, all right. But what?

According to the phone calls—they had started out sporadically, sometimes three in a day, sometimes nothing for nearly a month— he was a murderer. The first calls were nothing but breathing, deep and angry breathing, presumably from the same caller who mysteriously hung up if anyone but Jamie answered the phone. With time the breather worked up the courage to talk, or more likely, worked up the blind fury to talk. "You killed him. You killed my boy. Where is my boy?"

Of course it was Mrs. Rolph, Steve's mother. The disappearing Steve. The problem of course was that for all Jamie knew, Mrs. Rolph was quite right—maybe he had killed him. "I wish I could help you," he'd told her the first time, then said what he'd repeated so often to disbelieving cops, investigators, psychiatrists, and the occasional journalist, so often that the words actually felt dishonest: "But I have no idea what really happened that night, or before that night. No memory at all, I swear. Maybe Steve's still okay, still out there somewhere. Maybe he'll turn up any day now. I wish I knew."

"Tell me what you know," the hoarse voice growled through the phone. "Where's my boy? You were with him. They found blood on you, blood on your clothes, blood all over you . . ." The growl dissolved into sobs and choking gargles.

"I'm sorry," Jamie said. "I wish I knew, but I just don't remember. I was . . . driving home from work, from the Wentworth Club. And then . . . headlights, by the road side . . . wearing a clown suit . . ." he trailed off, looking back to that night and seeing almost nothing. All that remained was the clown outfit, now neatly folded in a box at the bottom of a cupboard upstairs. And the little velvet bag which had sat in its pants pocket.

"Murderer," the growl hissed, sizzled, spat. "Murderer. Killer. You bastard. We'll never forget."

"I'm sorry," Jamie said, then did what he would do every other time that same caller called, accusing, begging, or just weeping. He hung up.

The day he knew he had to leave the nest at long last was when he picked up the phone one Friday, lusting for pizza, and heard his mother's voice on the other end of the line. She'd not heard the click of the upstairs phone being picked up and he hung on the line a second or two, instinct telling him he was being discussed.

"...and he wakes up screaming. No, not every night but often enough. Won't ever tell me what's wrong. Thrashing on the bed, you should hear it sometimes, those bed springs creaking. I had to check that he hadn't snuck a girl in there."

The other voice said, "Does your son have a relationship, Mrs. McMahon?"

"Only with his hand. And they're very close." Jamie winced. But it got worse. "When can you come and see him?" said his mother.

"Tomorrow," said the other voice, firmly.

"Oh, thank goodness."

"Whatever has caused memories to be repressed must be significant trauma. It's very unusual for an adult to block out memories like this. Is it just the dreams?"

His mother's voice lowered. "Well he's... since that time he disappeared then came back, he's different. It's hard to say why or how, just sometimes a look in his eye. Or it seems he's holding some private amusement, and occasionally he will make jokes that are just entirely inappropriate."

"There must be more to it than that," said the other voice gently. "You can't simply be concerned about bad taste jokes?"

"He never used to do this! I think of that clown suit they found him in—it's almost like sometimes he *is* trying to be like a clown. And that friend of his who vanished. I just don't know him anymore. There's someone else in there with him, I sometimes think."

Jamie shook his head in bewilderment, no longer able to wait for this conversation to end before hanging up. He eased the phone gently into its cradle. Fine, then. He would put the old girl—the old man too for that matter—at ease and get out of here, because he heard what she hadn't said: her son scared her.

Right away he texted Dean, an occasional drinking buddy from work and asked if he still had a room for rent. The reply came quickly: YEA. FURNISHED. BEER IN FRIDGE. MOVE IN!!!

In an hour, Jamie's stuff was almost completely packed and his parents were clued in over breakfast. "Oh," said his mother, sighing in disappointment but hiding—he knew it—no small amount of relief.

The counselor came and got no more from Jamie than resentment and the repetition of "I'm fine" and "I don't remember." She asked him about nightmares. He just shrugged and hid the weird disquiet that squirmed in his gut like a snake uncoiling. Nightmares? Oh, yes there were nightmares . . . somehow familiar harsh voices, threats and curses over a backdrop of demonic creatures snarling and biting at the ground their feet slashed and pounded, attacking the earth, each other, and all the while carny music playing sugar sweet, carny rides and games flashing colors gaudy and more obscene than blood red . . .

"Really, I'm fine," he said again. "I don't need counseling, I'm getting on with my life and you just stole half an hour of it. Bye."

Then his car was packed and he was headed for a high-rise apartment in the city.

It was a week later when Mr. McMahon—a light sleeper, as ten-year-old Jamie and friends had discovered when they snuck out to throw rocks at the neighbor's roof—stretched out of bed at 3:00 am, his body popping and groaning like a cantankerous machine. He emptied his bladder, yawned, and for no reason he knew went to the bedroom window, holding open the curtain and spilling in a beam of street light. The cul-de-sac beneath, bathed in white moon- and street-light, held its breath in stillness. Not a shrub or tree leaf fluttered in any ghost of a breeze. The parked cars, front gardens, mailboxes: all seemed to silently stare just like Mr. McMahon did at something unfamiliar and foreign. Something that hadn't woken the dogs and got them barking, the way any other lurking stranger would have done.

A clown stood at the top of the curving driveway. Mr. McMahon knew at once it was not his son, though his eyes checked to be sure. The horribly bright and mismatched colors of its wide suspender-held pants and its puffy shirt screamed with discordant cheer. Its white-gloved hand clutched what may have been an old pocket watch with a thin dangling chain. Under a pointed hat with bells,

7

whose tinkling faintly tickled Mr. McMahon's ears and got his flesh goosebumped and shivering, the white face with its black painted smile (over the top of the actual lips downturned and scowling) tilted up, passed over the house's façade, then gazed again at the pocket watch, if that's what it was. The head shook, maybe in annoyance, sending more sweet ugly bell chimes up to the window as the clown muttered some curse or other.

Behind Mr. McMahon, the bed groaned as his wife turned over and murmured thickly, "What is it?"

He looked at her, pondering: it would be a mean trick to tell her a clown had come to visit, meaner still to let her come and see it, and then to privately chuckle to himself as she lay awake in uneasy fear for the next two weeks. Mean, but fun. He opened his mouth to tell her, then he thought of the resulting short temper he'd have to deal with. "It's nothing, love," he said instead, dropping the curtain back and lowering himself to bed. He pecked his wife's cheek and within seconds was convinced he'd done a noble thing from sheer benevolence for her peace of mind.

About the clown he didn't much trouble himself; some idiot kid who'd heard Jamie's story in the news and wanted to see the house as if it were a piece of folklore. His goose bumps settled.

Ah, the embarrassment of it all was finally easing off: ever since Jamie was arrested in the Queen Street Mall for setting off fireworks, Mr. McMahon's co-workers had been giving him hell. Then when the dumb kid disappeared, they gave him sympathy, which was worse. It was all in the past, now. His mind soon filled again with football, the job, the lawn, garden, and neighbors.

It was kind of funny—Jamie had no memory of actually packing into his car the rectangular cardboard box which held the clown outfit they'd found him wearing "that night." Yet here it was, the last thing in his Nissan's trunk to be carried up the lift to his new life in the city. The outfit had been forensically pored over for DNA evidence before they returned it to him. He'd been tempted to throw the box into the big industrial bin in the car park. But in his hands now was a link, a clue. It found its home on the floor of his walk-in closet, along with the little velvet bag the police had not seen cause to examine once they'd decided it wasn't full of drugs.

Every day, dressing for work before the mirror, the corner of the box caught his eye. Each time he quelled a curious, mild urge to open it and just take a look at the bright gaudy clothing. No harm in looking, surely? Just to look at it, run his hand over the printed flowers, stripes, dots, puppy dogs chasing bright blue balls?

His new job basically involved moving boxes of files around in the bowels of the Department of Finance, and being yelled at by the woman who ruled that dusty forgotten tomb of manila folders and file cabinets. Some days a pile or box of files did a complete tour of the room and wound up back where it started; why Jamie or his boss was being paid a decent wage to do this was never clearly explained. He managed to keep her voice to a background abstraction and theorized it was all some kind of temperament test for duties higher up the ladder—if he'd tolerate this treatment without a nervous breakdown, he'd be useful to the government as a fall guy when shit hit fans for top ranked bureaucrats or even ministers, one fine day.

Some days he longed for nothing more than to throw an egg at the dumpy schoolmarm, seeing clearly how it would sound and look, the frenzy of her reaction. The urge grew with surprising power. If not egging her, he'd leave a cream pie on her seat, or tape sharp pins to the light switch, put a cane toad in her top desk drawer. While it did occur to him that these might be the responses a clown would come up with in a similar circumstance, that hardly seemed relevant.

His roommate Dean rescued him from this particular torment and threw him into another. Dean's job was to give talks to various government employees about their superannuation, but one Tuesday when holed up with one of his female admirers, Dean said over breakfast, "Good news! You're filling in for me today. I already told your supervisor. Here's my notes, just read them into the mic

9

then get out of there before they can ask questions. And enjoy the free sandwiches. It's easy."

"No way," said Jamie, but apparently it sounded exactly like "Sure, I'll do it gladly," because Dean clapped his shoulder and said, "Sweet, owe you one. Beers on me Friday." Dean pointed down at the not unimpressive erection tent-poling his blue boxers then nodded to his bedroom, making a none too subtle gesture with finger and thumb to indicate coitus would soon transpire. Given the way sound went through this apartment, Jamie didn't really need it spelled out—the words "Oh Jesus," "Cop it," "Give it to me," and "Oh no you don't, it's my pussy now," had periodically roused him from sleep.

So with just one terrified flashback of his last public speaking episode (Year twelve English. Discussion of *Lord of the Flies*. Some bastard—never found out who—wrote "I LOVE TAMARA" on his third palm card. He read the words out loud then tried to suck them back in an instant too late, for he had indeed loved Tamara, and her shell-shocked, horrified expression had ripped his heart out while the rest of the class laughed mercilessly), he thought about the prospect of being in front of people, the center of attention, and . . .

And, well, actually he didn't mind the idea. In fact, suddenly it seemed pretty good, got his blood tingling in a way that seemed both new and familiar. Why, maybe he could think of a few jokes and one-liners to toss in. And as it went, he spent more time thinking about jokes to tell his audience than he spent studying Dean's notes, a veritable spring in his step and an intoxicating fizz in his blood, which built and built until that damned slow clock let him have his moment in the spotlight.

The sixty or so janitors and school groundskeepers brayed with appreciative laughter. "My name is Jamie, and I'm here to discuss your super. Of course, you're all super to me." More laughs, laughs at the lameness of the puns, his cheesy grin, hammed up delivery and patronizing smile. He couldn't stop. They loved him and he loved them, their laughter especially, could drink it down all day, must have more, more! "I'll be with you for the next forty minutes or so, which means if you like the sound of my voice, you're in for a real treat." Laughter, precious laughter. How it filled him up and made him feel feather light. Why, he could bound across the floor, do a back flip off the podium . . .

The clearing throat of Dean's supervisor made him—with great effort—think more serious thoughts. Somehow he managed to read through the notes, restricting himself to one wisecrack every five minutes. It was tough. Slowly he worked his way to another fine intoxicating sound, the applause of an audience.

The supervisor approved, in the end. She offered him a new job doing such talks regularly and said, "A few opening jokes to engage them, that's not so bad. But we're discussing people's financial future, so don't turn the whole thing into a clown show, whatever you do."

Jamie coughed, choked on his own spit. He managed somehow to get out the words, "Oh yeah, sure, clown show. Wouldn't want to do that."

On Friday it was drunk time/woman hunting time with a small gang of chaps from elsewhere in the building, led by the master hunter, Dean (who bought Jamie's first four beers as promised). Dean was six-two, well built with a gymmed-up body, but by no means the handsomest thing in the bar, as far as Jamie or the rest of them could tell. Which didn't bother the ladies at all—when bored with poker machines or moping to them about the one ex he'd truly loved, he'd approach a likely target, speak with her as if he'd already known her for years, and within an hour he'd have his prey. Sometimes it only took a few minutes. Jamie and the others studied him at it, tried to work out what he actually did, but there was really no telling. Often as not his prey was someone's fiancée, wife, girlfriend. A cop's? A karate instructor's? A mob hitman's? It didn't much matter to Dean. And all the while, every day, Dean still moaned, sighed, and waxed depressed about the one ex who had actually dumped *him*, not the other way around.

"Oh yeah, the excuses man," said another of the gang, as poker machines trilled and chimed their insane music around them, now and then clattering up a vomit of coins. "He hated being with that ex when he was with her, was bored out of his mind. Out cheating on her every weekend, off at the casino playing blackjack while she stays home alone. Feeding her the most convoluted sitcom excuses you ever heard. One time, he got me to smack him in the face in the cubicles at work, so he could claim he'd been mugged and bashed, couldn't make their dinner date that night. He came out drinking with us, talked a stripper into bed, or actually into an alley, fucked her right in front of a homeless guy who was asking for money the whole time. So his ex, this Broncos cheerleader, finally had enough, ditched him, and now months later he's in crazy love with her."

They watched Dean take his new friend by the elbow, both of them laughing at a shared joke as he led her outside, surely headed for the room next to Jamie's. The other two drinking pals were both near age twenty, when getting laid is more or less the point of everything else in life. They studied Dean's every stride, facial expression, and movement as he gradually wove through the busy sea of people breaking like waves on the pub's bar. *Ding-a-ling, ching, chime*, the insane poker machine music played and played, all too much like carnival music. "I'm out guys," Jamie said. "I stay here much longer I'll be dreaming all night about happy robots."

"Ah, Jamie, you're such a clown."

It was like a slap—Jamie's head whipped back, eyes wide, stunned a moment before murmuring goodbyes and making an exit more clumsy and drunken than it should have been after his four beers. The other two drinking buddies/hunters of the elusive female watched him ping pong off door corners, seats, and people's shoulders. "Interesting," said the one who'd called Jamie a clown. "I wondered how he'd react to that."

"What? Why?"

"That whole circus thing. Didn't you hear about it? That was *him*. Right in the thick of it. They didn't even find the bodies. He denied all knowledge and they believed him. I hear he even passed a lie detector test."

"Wait, Jamie was that guy they found?"

"Dressed like a clown, yep. Man, I knew Dean had some balls, but living with that guy? Dean's got some *balls*. Already one person Jamie lived with vanished from the face of the planet. Gone. They didn't even find his body. Only some blood."

A brief awed silence ensued. "Does Dean know?"

"Doubt it. But I'm going to tell him to watch his back. And we better watch ours."

Perturbed, Jamie found his feet taking him not home but on a veering detour, past an excited group running toward George Street where apparently some idiot was trashing a bunch of cars right in front of the cops. Jamie headed down through Queen Street, moving through packs of Friday night revelers, some whooping and laughing, while drunk teenagers new to all of this staggered by and gave him looks probably suggesting they were not to be fucked with, or something. He half expected someone to shout "That's him! It's that clown guy!" or maybe just "Murderer."

And here he was, in the quiet little arcade leading to the Wentworth Club. With some surprise he realized it was the first time he'd been here since . . . since returning to his life from some other place. But there was nothing here of interest, just the same high end clothes and shoe shops along the arcade, the eerie quiet that seemed by magic to repel any drunken youths from wandering through. No clues. Yes, that was why he'd come: to find clues. This place had been part of it, maybe where it had all begun. But now it told him nothing.

A tap on his shoulder cut off his thoughts. He'd not heard the club's glass door slide open, had been pacing up and down the arcade without realizing. He turned to see the smiling face of the current concierge beaming up at him from shoulder height. The smile was full of embarrassment; words came out of it: "Hello. Please. Go away."

"What? Why?" The smiley teeth veritably shone. This guy could sell toothpaste. Jamie said, "Hey, I used to have your job, you know that?"

"Oh, indeed. We at the desk have been given firm instruction to . . . and a picture of you, in case you should . . . several pictures, in fact, that in the event of . . . look, very important clientele, and . . . the management wishes to distance our establishment from . . . potential scandal, rumor, controversy."

"Scandal. Seriously, scandal? Wow. Listen to yourself. Our establishment, like you could take a part of it home if you wanted to. A real company man, aren't you. It's like you figure this job's got some kind of future."

"The police are to be . . . firm instructions . . . need I say it?"

Inspired by beer and rage, Jamie stepped closer, growled, "Listen, punk, I worked here and it happened to me. It could happen to you, too. Think about it. You think some of the late night crowd in here weren't involved? They are neck deep. Club management, the highest profile members, *all* of them. *Watch . . . your . . . back.*" He drank deep of the dawning terror on the dweeb's face then walked away, thinking: *Wow. This thing is really going to follow me around til the very end. Forever suspect.*

Back out in the mall, among crowds of scantily clad young women and their male orbiters. Drunken shrieks, laughs, staggering steps in high heels. The people out there were coalescing at some point mid-mall, which finally caught Jamie's attention. A big group had gathered like the excited crowds that flock to the school oval for fisticuffs and antler butting, but it had to be something else given all the howls of laughter. "Look at him!" someone hollered.

So Jamie ambled over, took a look over the heads of the outer ring of people, and froze. Part of him must have known what he'd see. Confused and panicking within the ring of people was a round-bellied, white-faced clown with the weirdest eyes he'd ever seen. One was slitted and frankly a little scary with some weird animal quality, the other boggled around at the people like it had never seen such creatures before. Its thick round head refused to turn at the neck; its arms stayed locked at its sides with the hands bunched to fists, spasmodically uncurling, then closing. It wore a ludicrous puffy shirt with bright colors shamelessly splashed over it. Pants that ought to be baggy were stuffed tight with thick jiggling flesh, pushing at the seams with each frightened half turn while it looked desperately for an escape route in the ring of spectators.

Jamie alone seemed to find it other than funny. It frightened him, but also he alone could tell its distress was real—it was not playing around, it wanted to be away from their gazes and shrieks of laughter. "Its eyes! Look at its eyes!" someone cackled.

The clown's hands slapped over its ears to shut out the noise. One of the more drunken and daring in the ring stepped forward, a wiry young man with a goatee who had parted with his shirt. He leaned forward, offered the clown a hand to shake, grinning ear to ear. The clown slapped itself in the face, hard, then harder. Some of the crowd laughed even louder, but the slaps went on and got harder, til they rang out like a mound of dough or side of beef being pounded with a baseball bat, and the first spray of blood flew from its lips, then cheek, then ear, then eye, spattering the pavement, spattering the clothes of those nearest . . . only then did some of them stop laughing.

The young shirtless drunk, not perturbed by this, said slowly "Are you lost? Do you need some help? Are you a bit special in the head?"

The clown's lips peeled back. A hissing sound of indrawn breath made its belly swell and grow, fuller and fuller until the shirt popped a button and the fabric tore, letting hang loose a glob of pink-white meat. "How do they *do* that?" said someone to Jamie's right. "Those special effects . . ."

All at once a high-pitched wail exploded from the circle's middle. Those closest clapped hands to their ears, ducked down to their haunches. On it went, far louder than a car horn. The circle shrank back, no one laughing anymore. The shirtless drunk lay writhing on the pavement, hands to his ears.

Jamie stood with the blood pounding in his ears and adrenaline surging. *You wanted a clue,* he thought, *and you just got one.* This clown, he had seen it somewhere before . . .

15

The clown ceased its noise. Slowly, inevitably, it turned his way. The eyes met his and narrowed. One step, two steps, it came in a jerking rush. *Crunch crunch*, its oversized shoes trampled the young man and sent out the sick crack of a broken femur and rib.

Jamie backed up a few steps, then turned and ran through the crowd of people, most of whom had turned to stare down the mall at the noise. He risked one glance back—he expected to see it coming, but if it was, it was lost in the movement of people.

For the rest of the half run, half walk home, he tried to do what normal people would do, to convince himself it was just a street performance gone wrong, that those were indeed just "special effects," and most of all that it had nothing to do with *him*. By the time he got home, he had almost succeeded in kidding himself, but he knew that's exactly what he was doing.

The apartment was basically one round wall, two-thirds the way up a high-rise overlooking the Storey Bridge. The Brisbane River wound sluggish and placid below, in no mood just now to flood the human filth put into it back across the streets as it had several times before and surely would again, sooner or later. A tall gang of similar buildings stood around them in all directions, their evening glow proud ornaments in the gorgeous Brisbane night light display. A young city, the sense of possibility was as palpable as the sense of history layered thick in other places. This town was a nearly blank page, waiting to be written.

The high-rises opposite had their share of exhibitionists, old and young, attractive and distinctly otherwise, partial to undressing with the lights on and blinds open, not to mention bouts of shameless rutting. To that end there sat a pair of binoculars on the sill, military grade. Some nights the entertainment was better than watching TV.

Jamie entered the place, which already felt like home, expecting to hear all manner of the usual Dean bedroom war cries, but the flat was silent, the lights off with only the twilight glow of outside light seeping in. He had an urge to find Dean and tell him about the clown from the mall, to get a dose of the common reality which so easily rationalized away the dark and strange. (That clown had looked right *at* him. Had come after *him*, out of all the people there, watching it. Had *recognized* him . . .) But a woman's giggling sounded faintly from Dean's bedroom followed by his low murmur. They were between festivities, then, and fireworks would soon ensue. Jamie sighed and went to his room, pulled back the blanket and screamed.

A knife lay on his sheets, which were rumpled and messed up. A few small but unmistakable spots of blood were sprinkled around it. A door slammed open. Dean rushed in, saw what he was looking at. "Oh, sorry. Forgot," he said, taking the knife.

"Yours?" said Jamie, relieved, then pissed off.

"Yeah. Sorry, bro. Hadn't changed my sheets yet, so me and Jodi had to start out in here."

"Why not change your own fucking sheets? Couldn't the sex have waited five minutes while you changed your sheets?"

"Got to seal the deal, bro. Take no chances. You'd be surprised how many deals get blown by an unflushed toilet or dirty sheets. Don't worry, mine are changed now."

"But . . . look, I'm no prude. But why a knife?"

Dean sighed. "This Jodi, what can I say. She's a crazy girl. Real intense."

"This is someone you just met tonight? About an hour or two ago?"

"Seen her around. The knife was her idea, she read some book and wanted to try it. Wanted me to wear a balaclava too, this fantasy about burglars? Hey if I get her in the right mood maybe you'll get an invite. Want me to ask? She likes redheads."

"Tempting." It actually was, upon reflection. "But no, not after the day I've had and not before having at least one conversation with her. Call me old-fashioned . . ."

"Suit yourself. Gotta go." There followed the coitus hand signal and Dean left as abruptly as he'd come. Jamie changed his sheets,

17

lay back with eyes closed as bedspring music began to play through the thin, thin walls.

What was all this? All these urges to do whacky, antisocial, clowny things. His mother had been right: in most conversations back home he'd been looking for the chance to make a stupid one-liner, often in poor taste. He'd never even noticed himself doing it. Now this new delight—nay, addiction to making a room full of people laugh, not through any real wit or cleverness but with cheesy delivery. He could draw a laugh at any time in those presentations, and if his supervisor weren't there to watch, he'd clown around for the entire thing.

Clown around. Clown.

"Tell my cock you love it," Dean's voice suddenly boomed through the walls.

"I love, love, love your cock," came the reply.

"Don't talk to me. Talk to the cock! Don't look at me. Look at the cock! Call it Ramrod."

"I love you Ramrod. Oh JESUS." The bed next door protested, staged its own earthquake. Jamie swore and turned on his stereo, cranked the volume high. "*And now, an oldie but a goodie from 'The Kinks. Death of a Clown!'*"

"Are you serious?" Jamie said. He almost laughed as the song filled his room. The box in his closet caught his eye, lit only by the stereo's little blue panel light. It called him, that box, beckoned him like Sauron's ring of power.

There was no fighting it. He stroked the hideously gaudy fabric, the red shoes. Undressed himself, and . . .

The clothes fit. Perfectly. Better than perfectly—he was made for these clothes. The rustle of cloth whispered encouraging things. The fabric caressed his skin with gentle loving touches. A feeling of deep glee stole into him, tickled him, made him squirm and laugh. He put on the big red shoes. They squeezed down over his feet and felt so right. He was lighter than air. He could back flip around the room, out the hall, off the balcony and land on concrete, only to bounce right back up here like a rubber ball.

And the mirror said he looked awesome, hilarious, even a little noble. And the mirror said, "Jamie, help me. They're bringing me back, they're gonna bring everyone back. I don't want to be a clown no more, Gonko's pissed at me, he's gonna—"

Jamie, wide-eyed, watched his reflection's mouth move as it spoke to him in his own voice, the reflection's pleading eyes fear-filled. He screamed for the second time that night, ran out of the room in time to see Dean burst from his own room, naked, to investigate. Dean's eyes went wide. "Holy shit balls. What the hell are you wearing?"

Jamie, scared and sweating, pulled the clown shirt off—or tried to. The shirt wouldn't come off. Nor the pants or shoes. They clung hard, seemed to fight back as he tugged at them. "Look, don't freak out," Jamie began, but Dean's door slammed shut and no more sounds came through the walls that night.

Saturday morning: Dean was all sexed out. That Jodi was pretty cool, and wild enough to be a regular, but of course she was no Emily. No one in the world ever would be. Now and then he'd catch a look at Emily in her cheer squad outfit on TV during a Broncos game, and it never failed to bring him to the brink of tears.

Jodi had ducked out to meet a friend and do that shopping thing women seemed to dig so much. There'd be no car park fights with husbands for him to worry about this time, another plus, although he'd actually made some pretty good friends out of those dudes once they'd blown off some steam.

He ignored the ringing landline phone, suspecting it was work calling, but Jamie woke and answered it. No clown suit this morning, and just what the hell that had been all about Dean did not care to ponder. A dress-up role-play thing would have made sense if the guy hadn't come home alone. You never really knew someone til you lived with them, he supposed.

Dean paused in his doorway as Jamie's voice rose in anger. "How did you get this number?" he yelled into the phone. "All right, Mrs. Rolph. You got me pegged. I am a murderer. I killed your son, okay? I rubbed his face with a cheese grater til his scream was loud enough to break glass, is that what you want to hear? Then I ran him over with a wheat thresher. Slowly. Fed his body to wild pigs, and they told me he tastes like shit. I kept the finger bones, and I have them in a little jar. Every full moon I take the bones out and rub them on my crotch. Happy? You call me again, and I will visit you next. Oh, you bet it's a threat. Oh, you're recording all this? Neato. Yeah I slipped up, huh? You're a real super sleuth. You do that, tell the cops I said hi. Bye bye now." Jamie slammed the phone down, slammed his bedroom door and went back to sleep.

Dean frowned. He would be lying to himself if he said what he'd just heard was not the cause for some concern. Jamie would surely explain when he next awoke. "Cheese grater?" he murmured.

Dean's mobile rang with his Beethoven ring tone (violin concerto in D-major, the only classical music he knew.) As always he looked hopefully for Emily's name on the caller ID, but it was only Paulie. "Sup?" said Dean.

"Man, I knew you had some balls, but I'm telling you, you have got some *balls*." Dean smiled, pleased—the conversation had started well. "Check this out," Paulie went on quickly. "Police hunt violent attacker clown. From the news dude, online. I'll text you the link. Check it out, a guy in a clown suit beat up like ten people last night, almost trampled this dude to death, put like three in hospital, smashed up some cars and maybe there's more than one of them out there."

Dean was not smiling now. He could not remember—had Jamie been wearing the clown suit when he walked in the door? Dean had to swallow before speaking. "What's this got to do with me and my balls?"

"Man, let me tell you something about your roommate." And so Paulie told him all he knew, and then all he guessed and suspected.

⊕

20

It was near evening when Jamie woke again, kitchen and coffee and possibly nightclub bound. Also he wanted to get online, look into community theater, see if a guy like him could just walk up and get a role in some comedy. Dean, sans shirt, stood by the window, and Jamie noted without much interest or alarm the baseball bat in Dean's hands. "Howdy," said Jamie in the cowboy accent they had been amusing each other with for a couple of days now.

"Okay, let's just keep this quiet and calm," said Dean. "Jodi's having a quick nap in my room. No need to go crazy."

"Keep what quiet? Go crazy why?"

"I had you committed."

It took half a minute for the words to actually register within Jamie's skull. When they did, he knew it was not a joke. "You WHAT?"

"Okay, I guess committed is a bit of an exaggeration. But they're sending people to talk to you. Medical people, mostly. From the hospital. Maybe there'll be police with them too—they were a bit iffy on that point." Dean hesitated. "Not that I, you know, emphasized that they should send cops to handle you. But it sometimes works out that way if the patient won't go willingly or seems real unstable or violent."

"The patient? Won't go? Willingly?"

"Hey let's keep this quiet. For myself? I personally don't doubt you're sane? Not for a minute. But then I'm not a professional medical guy. And it's like I told them, I never actually *saw* you do anything all that violent, not when I was around anyway. So stay cool and this should all go just great."

I will now kick this guy's teeth down his neck, Jamie thought. *He is dead. So very dead.* The knife rack caught his eye, sang a siren song. The rolling pin hung up on its stand looked a decent place to start. He grabbed it. It felt so natural in his hand.

Just then the front door burst open.

2. BELOW

The hated wooden building had taken a battering which had ripped like skin its cracked shell to show the secrets of its horrid flesh, and show the man who was its beating heart and scheming brain for years uncounted, every day doing secret things, terrible things the world just outside the house doesn't want to know of. Much less does the world far, far above want to know of the experiments, arts and pleasures of the man, and the often living flesh he uses as clay playthings. Nor does it want to hear the pain that is his music, conducted with pale twitching fingers. The Funhouse owner is known to some as, and loves to be called, "the Matter Manipulator." And how he loves the furtive queasy looks they give him, the way they hurry out of his path when he goes outside that battered wooden cage to ogle the flesh he may one day use for his projects.

Some repairs have been done to the Funhouse of course, for it has been nearly a year since the night of Kurt's rampage through the showgrounds, the night the proprietor was provoked at last into bursting out of his human form and devouring everything he could. Some planks were hammered over, cracks plastered, leaving only the glow of reddish light to bleed through slim gaps and cracks like unwelcome light seeping in through eyelids of waking sleepers. Just the occasional shuffle and moan can be heard by the gypsies and dwarfs now and then hurrying by that foul place . . . and of course, they tell themselves they'd not heard a thing, and refuse to remember that this or that old acquaintance had, long ago, been sent to that house for some breach of circus rules, never to return. There is much else to busy one's mind with. George Pilo, Kurt's brother and the new boss, has given his orders, barked and spat them like gunfire all about the place, apostrophized with the crack of that dreaded, hated lash. There is work to do, so much work repairing, resurrecting, cleaning, rebuilding. The world needs its distractions and entertainments, after all. It needs its circus.

Down to the circus's very foundation pulses a growing urgency, restlessness, and hunger. Yet like something injured it has held off, held off, not yet sure enough of itself to brave the rigors of its trade, troubled by premonitions of its own total doom, troubled that some of them *up there* know the circus is here, have seen it naked without its glamour to shield their eyes and memories. And it is nervous. Its collapse has left a gap in the world which will be filled sooner or later, by their show or by someone, something else's. This fear too gnaws through the showgrounds, so that little by little each day's activity grows more hurried: the *tap tap* of hammers, clang of tent pegs, flutter of unfurling newly woven canvas, the carny rats bustling around frantic to look busy and escape the lash.

But the circus needs performers—the show, as they say, must go on. And death in some of the world's secret shadowy parts is little more than an inconvenience.

Below the Funhouse, beside a sacrificial stone slab long unused, a tunnel twists into the showground's true depths, covered with a lid of wooden boards. It is not so very far down, in truth, despite being far from sight and mind. Its rock walls shine red and orange. Where that tunnel ends and meets the stone cavern floor, a pair of baggy clown pants sit in a crumpled neglected pile. Forlornly, half-heartedly, the pockets now and then bulge with magically conjured bits and pieces summoned in the vain hope of escape: a small parachute puffs out to catch a gust of hot wind; a climbing pick clangs uselessly to the floor, a white flag of surrender weakly flutters. In time, all of these things dissolve back into air.

The owner of these magic pants had been ripped away from them very soon after he was carried to this hidden place by the former circus proprietor: Kurt Pilo. Of that, Gonko has no memory. He only remembers a locked trailer, shaking to tip them out and George's shrill barking voice.

Both Kurt and Gonko have wandered the tunnels since, through labyrinths and catacombs of stone which now and then give like sponge and bend inward underfoot, as would the skin of something living. For nothing here is as solid or physical as it appears. Hanging clumps of rock burst into the motion of a million crawling insects eager to bite, only to seem stone again soon after. Kurt and Gonko avoid when they can the grasping hands and meat-reeking hot breaths of their tormentors, whose forms change but whose tastes do not.

Gonko hides now as he usually hides, naked in a dark small corner beneath a folded lip of stone, out of sight of giggling growling fiends who often prowl by, looking for sport. Kurt has found no good hiding spot yet. Each day Kurt's screams carry back to him, as do the whispers which seem to come from the stone itself. They speak of many things, the breathing stones, of many circus secrets. Gonko has learned much. Now and then he visits Jamie's dreams. Jamie's dreams and other people's dreams, where with pleasure he kicks around the furniture of their subconscious and makes as much mess as he can. Mostly he dreams himself, of escape. He has tried to climb out many times but it is not allowed and each time they catch him and make him hurt so very badly.

George Pilo is an angry man, has always been, and that is no secret. But a word has not yet been invented to describe the extent of poisonous murderous hatred that seethes through Gonko's veins like lava when he remembers George trapping him and the other clowns in the doomed caravan, that night. Gonko has dim and jumbled images of it all—falling from the caravan is the last thing he knows, so George is (as far as Gonko can tell) the one to thank for his being here, trapped below. He sucks his teeth and soothes his burns and hurts with a promise to himself: there shall be revenge.

"Gonko. Oh, Gonko?" a familiar voice, deep and cheerful, calls from somewhere in the depths. The stones whisper the same words back, mindlessly mocking. Snapping mouths form in their not-physical clay.

Gonko bunches up in his hiding place. *Scuttle thump scrape* come limp footsteps through the tunnel just to his right. "Gonko! Gonko, come, we must speak. Of many interesting things."

Kurt. Same old jovial cheer no matter what has happened to him just an hour before. Just like it had sounded in his trailer, the desk piled high with bibles and crucifixes. Gonko peeks out and sees him, a thin hunched blackened thing of bones, plates, and claws, taller than a man but all bent and hunched over. A human face is stuck on the head at an angle, Kurt's old face with its fat lips over teeth too big, round red cheeks, serenely smiling eyes. Gonko ignores his calls up until Kurt says, ". . . must speak, Gonko. I have exciting news for you. You have tasks, up above."

Wary, Gonko sits up. He whispers out into the corridor, knowing the stone will bend and play with the sound so it seems to come from all around Kurt. "I'm listening, boss."

"Oh, ho ho," Kurt laughs sadly. His *scuttle thump scrape* edges back along, back toward Gonko until the huge bent-over insect-like mess of bone and face stands just outside Gonko's hiding spot. Nonetheless Kurt does not look in at him, pretending—so it seems to Gonko—to be gazing around in search of him. "You must not call me 'boss,' Gonko. For now, I'm just an employee. Like you. Although you are clown boss, aren't you Gonko?"

"Guess I would be, if I had any clowns."

"Hmm. Yes. Well that's one thing we ought to talk about. I've had a word with . . . upper management."

"I heard the screaming, boss. Kurt."

"Oh ho. They like a vigorous chat. And they like to emphasize their points, with many unique methods of . . ." Kurt's face contorts, retches; the black glistening rib-like cages of bone all up his spine rattle and shake for a minute or two. "But one must now and then deal harshly with underlings who do not perform. Or who . . . how to put it . . . destroy the enterprise altogether."

Wasn't me who wrecked it, Gonko thinks, suppressing a burst of rage, *but I'm down here with you, Kurt, you big dumb shit puke.* Aloud: "Wasn't your fault, Kurt. Or mine. We got sabotaged."

"Hm, well the buck must stop somewhere. With you and me, it seems! Our superiors have many valid reasons for their . . . disappointment. Before all the unpleasantness, why, did you know that they were getting ready to expand? Oh my, yes, many surface operations they had in mind, and the time, the conditions, were nearly ripe! But now . . ." Kurt sighs sadly. "There's much to do up there, Gonko, to make things ripe again."

The first faint stirrings of hope mingle with Gonko's rage and fear. "Is that so?"

"Mm, indeed. More interesting to me, Gonko, was that our superiors have superiors of their own! My goodness, the chain of command just stretches up out of sight, doesn't it?" Kurt's head twists around, eyes darting. "Or down. Have you been to the farthest depths of these passages and chambers, hm? Just hiding here near the entrance, are we, with no spirit of adventure? Then, why, you'd not have seen the great back slab of metal, thick and high. I saw it, Gonko. It has hinges and a handle, and goodness me, it reminds me of a door. For so it precisely is. Only . . ." Kurt drops to a whisper, "they can't come through yet. Oh no, not yet. It takes a very long time before a world is ready, for *them.* Rather like, I dare say, waiting for one's bath water to reach an ideal temperature. Those down here? They want very much to go . . . up. This circus, Gonko, is but a foothold in the world for them, just a vestibule. They've been here a rather long time. So a little longer to wait, why, it's displeasing to them, but not . . ." Kurt's eyes gleamed. "Not the end of the world."

"I'm with you, boss," says Gonko. "Say. You hear anything about maybe getting me the fuck out of here?"

Kurt's smile pushes up blush-red cheeks. "As it happens, yes! I have indeed. You're to go up at once and do a few things. To help the show back to its feet. They are nervous, our superiors. The world above has heard of us. Knows a little too much rumour and gossip. There is a list of names waiting above. You are to tie loose ends, at your discretion. And you are to gather your clowns again for the eventual purpose of capering, delighting persons, and amusement causing. All persons deserve entertainment, don't you think, Gonko?"

"You know, boss, I happen to agree with that."

"Hm."

"Only thing is, the crew's dead. You might recall biting out their organs."

Kurt raises a claw like a thin twisted spike of metal. He'd be finger wagging, Gonko knew, if he had fingers. "Tut tut! The positive, Gonko. Never focus on the *may nots* and *could nots*. Scrape the remains of your clowns together and visit the Funhouse curator. He'll know what to do. In the meantime the show shall be run by my ... dear ... brother ..." Kurt's voice descends to the growl of something so hungry it can never be sated, "my dearest brother, George."

Gonko nods. Quickly, he debates in his mind, then risks it, whispers: "And say, Kurt. If it turns out George can't run quite as mean a ship as the previous boss did? Just supposing George's show don't turn out so great? What then?"

Kurt's head swings slowly, slowly toward him, and the big white eyes meet his for a long time. Gonko shrinks back, certain he's just blabbed his way out of any escape from these caverns. Kurt, whatever else he may be, is loyal to his bosses, and Gonko has just hinted at sabotage. On and on the gaze bores in.

At last Kurt speaks. "If *that* happened, why, I imagine the previous proprietor would be re-instated, Gonko. And I imagine he would have certain favored performers about the place, whom he would be extra nice to, every chance he got."

"I think we understand each other." Gonko feels no small relief when Kurt finally limps away, broken parts of himself trailing behind. The boss is peculiar enough that he may have quite innocently taken the question as purely hypothetical and detected no agenda there ...

But no one likes George Pilo, especially Kurt. And Gonko figures even fewer will like him after a stint in charge of this place. He crawls free of his hiding place, finds his shirt and shoes, gropes for the entrance, and puts on again his magic pants for the climb. From the pockets two climbing picks spill out. Here is where monstrous hands usually stop him and wrench him back down, but nothing inhibits his escape, this time. Weakened, thin, in pain, slipping on the rock, the climb is over with minimal fuss—all he has to do is imagine George Pilo's gloating grin just a foot or two ahead of him. "Bet you can't," imaginary George sneers at him, "bet you can't get up there, shit head." George's face is the wooden floor above, soon smashed to splinters as Gonko crawls back into the showgrounds, then collapses.

Gonko blinks at the artificial evening light of the carnival's fake sky, throwing over everything a purplish twilight. Blood and splinters sprout from his knuckles. His clown shirt is a tattered mess of candy cane stripes. Although evening was knock-off time in Kurt's day, there is still the frantic sound of assembling, cleaning, and tinkering from near and far. The odd toneless whistle and drunken dwarf shanty carries through the noise of the circus being brought back to life. A smell of buttered popcorn and cotton candy weaves through the air's chill.

Gonko dreads the moment he will come face-to-face with George, feels as if rage will explode from his skin like a burst of thistly vines he cannot control, which will strangle George and let him off far too easy. But Gonko remembers circus life now, and it is slow and winding time. Revenge this time must be nuclear and total. This is no mere acrobat-style feud. Gonko thinks of the shaking trailer again. Before all this is through, he will see George down that tunnel, will smile and wave cheerio from the top as the tiny body tumbles, legs flailing, to wrathful masters.

So, somehow, with these promises made, he keeps the red from his vision as George's hollering voice screams, "Polish those guns!

Get that line of ducks straight! They move too fast! You stupid ugly shits must be hungry, have a taste of this!" And the lash cracks. Gonko's teeth grind, his body shudders with purest hate as he staggers toward the sound.

Carnies are cunning folk. The circus is understaffed, rather badly in fact, but enough dwarfs, gypsies, and other assorted breeds collected over the ages survived Kurt's massacre to recruit more of their kind, stealing up now and then to the surface, stealing back with tied up bundles *mmph*ing through gags or masking tape. The new ones are given a taste of powder, taught the old ways, conditioned through certain rituals to their new life, and then they belong to George.

George expects no one to love his style of management, or he himself—in fact he'd not have it otherwise. He means to be a tyrant, a terror, loathed by all. Yet the very mention of Kurt still puts the fear in every single one of these wretches, even the new ones who have only heard the tale, and they know well that George doesn't have it in him to throw *that* kind of tantrum. However fondly they may look back on the more relaxed regimen of Kurt's time at the helm, they'll tell themselves they're better off now. George has a plan, in fact, to keep the memory of that massacre and their fears nice and fresh. But that's for later.

George has not been idle in the year since that day. The show will be different now, with more emphasis on rides and games than on performers—at least, that had been his plan, since after Kurt most of the original performers pretty much resemble mince. He's been anxious to get things underway immediately, a minimalist show with small trick crowds to farm a little soul dust and keep his hand-picked security detail, the lumberjacks, pampered and loyal. But then he moved into Kurt's trailer, and discovered the phone.

All this time, he'd never known exactly how Kurt got his occasional directives from Below. There in the second desk drawer, still half buried under a litter of rattling molars, premolars, canines, and incisors, a bright green telephone quietly rang the very moment he found it. He'd answered ("WHAT?") and a voice breathed winter in his ear: "Not yet," it said, and said no more. There was nothing for it but to hang up the phone, cancel next week's show, and find someone to lash to ease his frustration.

The phone rings every day at roughly the same time, the chilly voice every time: "Not yet." Once or twice he has tried to find out when the shows should start, or at least get the delay explained. He's even groveled, picked up the phone before it rings to plead, "Look, sir, the dust! We're running low and they're grumbling, I have to pay this sorry bunch of maggots or we'll have riots—"

"NOT . . . YET," came the answer on what he'd actually hoped was a dead line.

"Look, why not yet? I got rides up and running, got new acrobats trained and conditioned. We kidnapped some Olympic gymnasts and trained 'em. Clever, eh? My idea! I got a lion tamer and a magician. Look, I got everything but the fortuneteller and some clowns. Why not yet?"

"NOT . . . YET."

Every day. He got the damned point already—okay okay, enough! And yet, ring ring ring . . .

Three days ago George whined as the cursed phone rang yet again. Tears brimmed in his eyes. His own stash of powder saved over many years was long gone, and Kurt's was almost gone. He could stand no more. "Listen!" he screamed into the mouthpiece. "Do you want me to run this circus or—"

The voice interrupted. It sounded oddly cheerful. "Get ready. Shows begin soon."

George trembled. "How soon?" But the line clicked dead. And George hopped around his trailer gleefully, until the click-clack of a typewriter in another desk drawer got his attention. There had been no typewriter there yesterday, he was sure. Invisible fingers knocked down the keys until a sheet of paper emerged with the words: FOR GONKO followed by a list of names. *For Gonko?* George mouthed to the mirror opposite his desk (it was a funhouse mirror, warping his reflection so he appeared three feet taller.) "Why 'For Gonko?' Gonko's dead. All the clowns are dead! My show doesn't need clowns. We got rides."

The typewriter had no paper left, but George followed the keys' depressing to spell out the reply: "You will need clowns, George. And clowns you will have."

It is not then with much surprise that George spies Gonko staggering through the twilight toward him. An odd mix of triumph, amusement, malice, and something George would not recognize in himself as fear bubble through him like fizzy soda pop. George is riding on the back of his favorite new asset, a goon he has fashioned with the aid of the Matter Manipulator from an especially large lumberjack. A saddle is lodged in the unfortunate's back, with long nails drilled into his bones. A small machine is wedged as a control panel in the thing's head, ensuring total obedience and giving it the free will of a potato. In a more perfect world, George thinks, everyone would be as controllable through knobs, joysticks, and levers.

George still has nightmares about how close he'd come that night to a bullet in the back of his neck, just after it seemed the danger had passed with Kurt dropping to the depths of the Funhouse basement. A clown, one of Gonko's own men, plugged two shots into the trailer door right beside him. A lumberjack—no fool, a real forward thinker who saw the lay of the future ahead and sought at once to curry the new boss's favor—crash-tackled the old clown, named Watson or Winston or something, and wrestled the gun away. "Shoot!" George had cried, his pants wetted. The lumberjack obeyed, and the old clown became just another casualty of the night, while the lumberjack earned George's trust, gratitude, and the privileged position he now enjoyed. He was, of course, George's ride-on goon.

The goon stomps clumsily to Gonko, lash in hand. George dismounts, marches over, the typewriter paper bunched in his fist, but something in Gonko's shocking forced smile stops George short of assuming the position (head pressed into Gonko's navel, eyes glaring up.) Gonko's smile spasms, twitches, seems ready to

31

blow steam out his ears, so determinedly is it being held in place. But the eyes don't lie. Out it comes, raked over his teeth: "Hello there, George. I've missed you real bad."

George scoffs, tosses the bunched up paper from the typewriter, aiming for that smile but hitting Gonko's red clown nose instead. It makes a small *ding* like the shoot-a-duck game when a bullseye lands. "Your orders," George shouts at him.

Gonko spasms again, all over.

"That list has names on it. Get it? Names! You go up there and fetch like a good doggy. Priority one: fortuneteller. Get her back here. Then do whatever to the rest." George tosses a pass-out at him next, hits the clown nose again: *ding*. "No rush either," says George, backing toward the safety of his goon as Gonko's eyes go blood-red. "No clowns needed in my show. You're gonna run errands, you're gonna cook and clean, do outside jobs. No performing for you. Not til you earn it. Other clowns are buried out by the dung pit. Be careful who you bring back, Gonko. No room for traitors in my show."

George expects a pleasing outburst, maybe even some grovel-ling, but a thoughtful look comes to Gonko instead. "You name it, George," he says. "My clowns will just work themselves stupid to make this the finest show you'll ever run." And he bows, then topples over, collapsing.

"Eh, that works," says George, content enough, and rides his goon back to the trailer, working the controls to flip the lash at any carnies who get close.

When Gonko rouses from slumber, the taste of hot dog with mustard sings in his mouth, so sweet and good he chews down hard and bites off something a little more bony than expected. A shriek of pain follows and the dwarf falls back, clutching a hand which now drizzles blood everywhere. Gonko knows the dwarf, one of his old contacts from Sideshow Alley who used to report to him now and then with intel on the acrobats, back in the feud days.

He's called Curls, after the fire-red beard obscuring pretty much all his face apart from eyes and nose, the bushy eyebrows just an extension of the beard. Beside Curls is a plate of hot dogs, donuts and a paper cup of fizzy drink.

Gonko finds even the finger rather succulent, but he has no beef with Curls—he nibbles just a little meat from it and spits it out onto the dust. "You made it through the mess?" says Gonko, by which he means Kurt's rampage.

"Oh, yep," Curls grunts, pocketing the finger and wrapping a handkerchief around the stump. He grimaces but lays not a word of blame, which Gonko notes with approval. A decent dwarf, is Curls.

"So why you stuffing food in my mouth?"

"George's say-so. You were out nearly a whole day. George says you got stuff to do for him." Gonko's burst of George-rage wakes him up better than coffee. Curls reads his look. "Got something in mind?" he whispers, shifting back a little.

"Listen. How many chums you got? Trusted chums. Keep their gums stapled shut no matter what?"

Curls attempts a finger count, grimacing. "Nine," he ventures. "More if, you know, you dropped a nice thing in their pocket. George cut back pay from half bags to quarters, now he's paying by the grain. By the grain! But them lumberjacks is getting paid good, so they bust whatever heads George tells 'em to." Curls leans close. "Why, I tell you, if the shows wasn't about to start again, why, half of 'em would up and—"

"Shh," says Gonko, devouring the remaining donuts and hotdogs in a few wolfish gulps. "Gonko gets the picture, Curls. You get in their ears, my chum. Whisper this or that about secret missions up there." Gonko thumbs toward the sky. "Fresh air. Full-grown ladies all over the place. The techno marvels of whatever fucking century this is. Only to some real savvy trusted carny rats, you dig?"

Curls digs. "Will we get to see the ocean?"

"All five of 'em. Better pay too. I'm talking happy pockets here, chum. But first, go get us some shovels. We're going treasure hunting."

Curls runs off. Gonko feels the thing taking shape in his mind, going from an indiscriminate lust for payback into an actual plan. It'll be risky, it'll be bold, but it'll be curtains for George Pilo if it all comes off. Curls soon returns with picks and shovels in a wheelbarrow larger than he is.

All night they dig around what George called the dung pit, the patch of earth the gypsy cooks somehow get their meat from. There are hot dog plants and cotton candy shrubs, popcorn bushes and little sizzling pools of fizzy drink, burbling up like oil. It is some time before Gonko's pick strikes through what feels kind of skull-like. Up comes the pick, pulling a mound of soil along with Goshy's corpse. The head is preserved enough, the torso too, but below the waist there's liquefied mush that reeks of swamp gas. They scoop up all they can into the wheelbarrow, gagging, coughing, puking. Goshy's face, still as stone, looks surprised. "Ugly, ugly bastard," Gonko whispers at the quivering flesh pile. He wheels it to the Funhouse, spills the lot just outside the door, unmindful of the liquid gluey mess across his shoes, then slowly takes the wheelbarrow back to fetch the others.

By morning it is done, or close enough. He finds most of Rufshod, the top half of Doopy, and speaks to them while he wheels each one across the turf to the Funhouse, saying nice things about the days to come, how they'd frolic on stage like dolphins at sea. Their bodies join Goshy's in a hideous pile spreading across the ground at the Funhouse door.

Gonko does not go back for Winston—that there is trouble he doesn't need, he knows that without George's warnings. Nor does he search for JJ—according to the typed list, JJ is up on the surface world, hiding out. He remembers JJ's treachery in the trailer too, and although the resulting rage does not hold a candle to the supernova George has ignited inside him, there is no question a solid beat-down is called for. If JJ survives it, whatever of him is left will make a useful clown in the new act.

Gonko pounds the Funhouse door four times. Slowly it creaks open and an eye peers out the crack. "Yes?"

Gonko pokes the clown parts with his shoe. "Bring 'em back."

The door opens wider and Gonko shoves his way in. The Matter Manipulator's beak-like nose constantly sniffs, and his eyes betray the kinds of thoughts he has. He is taller than a dwarf but not by much, moon pale with a slicked-back wedge of greasy black hair. He has never had the chance to punish Gonko, so Gonko has no fear of him. The reddish light of the studio glows upon furniture made of human beings, all of them so preserved and lifelike Gonko wagers some of them *are* in fact alive. He wins his wager when the chair he pulls up—its legs actual legs—gives a soft groan of pain as he slumps down on it.

The Matter Manipulator rubs his hands together, nonplussed. "This procedure, reanimation, is difficult, is time consuming," he stammers.

When Gonko replies, the Matter Manipulator cringes back like a hand has been raised to strike him. "How long's it gonna take you? Shows start soon. And we got other work to do."

"Varies. The time since death, the age of the—the organism. Too long and it is impossible! The time the, shall we say, essence has had, to wander wherever essences go, once they escape the flesh." His hands flutter like birds and he laughs, nervous.

"Bring 'em back," Gonko repeats wearily.

"The, um, ah, payment?"

Now Gonko does rise to strike him and the Matter Manipulator leans eagerly forward, excited. "Orders," Gonko barks. "From George himself. And from *higher* than George. Geddit?"

"Ah!" Even more excited. "Any news of below?"

"Kurt says 'Hi.' And says, do what you're told. He won't be down there forever."

"Do as I'm told! Then, we shall see. Keep it hush! I shan't be pestered by all who have lost a friend or enemy, or I shall never cease reanimating. Other works, hobbies with the living, far more interesting . . ."

35

Gonko begins shoveling the clown remains inside, for passing carnies have paused out there to stare at the mess. They ought not see his crew in such a state, it's a bad look. The Matter Manipulator vanishes to a back room and returns pushing something resembling an electric chair. Wires in thick bundles trail across the floor behind it, spitting sparks. "How long?" says Gonko.

"Check with me in three days." The Matter Manipulator's a little petulant now, for Gonko has clearly distracted him from any number of projects.

"I'll check back in an hour. Then an hour after that. And you're gonna mind your P's and Q's and be real super hospitable and you're gonna work around the clock, or Gonko's gonna get a little antsy, and he's gonna hurt someone real, real bad."

A touch stunned, the Matter Manipulator recovers quickly, smiles. "Something wrong, Mr. Gonko?"

Gonko startles them both with the discovery of a tear in his eye, an exaggerated clown tear which is big as his fist and bounces when it hits the floor. "These are my . . ." he chokes off the words.

"Your underlings?" the Matter Manipulator ventures.

"Goddammit, they're mush now. Glue. Look at this filth." He kneels in said filth, clutching Doopy's discolored head by the hair bristles. "I'll bring you back, Doops. You'll see. Chuckle times ahead, Doops, you and your brother. We'll ride the cackle train to giggle town. We'll knock 'em dead, all of 'em, just like old times."

"Impassioned. Moving." The Matter Manipulator hustles about now, clearly seething at orders and threats, likely filing them away for when Gonko is sent here for punishment, which will surely happen sooner or later with George running things. He brings out a spatula, razor, a portable freezer holding lumps of human flesh, a sack heavy with rolled up skin, scissors, some pink gloop Gonko's never seen before. Composing himself, Gonko says, "They'll be the same, right?"

"Oh, more or less."

"They better be."

"Some enhancements, mayhap. Some minor defects." The Matter Manipulator pulls on stained gloves, assembles vials and jars of various colorful liquids. He measures out a large swath of skin, plugs in a machine with antennas and flickering dials next to the big wired-up chair. Its little screen shows a flat pulse line.

Gonko paces around the disgusting furniture. From various bits and pieces eyes follow him, silently pleading. "What's this?" he says, picking up what looks like lipstick.

"Lipstick," says the rather annoyed Matter Manipulator.

"For?"

"A variant of clown face paint. George is considering a kissing booth, lust being a . . . harvest mechanism, yes, the show has not used in some while. We'd need a female specimen of sufficient beauty, I suppose. The lipstick will enhance her further."

"It works?"

"Never tested." The Matter Manipulator straps on goggles and fires up a small flame welder. "Take it and try it, if it pleases you."

The lipstick is already in Gonko's pocket, along with what looks like mascara and eye shadow. He watches the horrid little man at work for a while sawing lengths of bone into carefully measured pieces but can stand only so much. "Hurry back," he whispers to his ruined crew.

Through the showgrounds Gonko wanders until he finds the old clown tent, now rebuilt, refurbished, and apparently used as a storing room for everyone's miscellaneous shit. Somehow the sight of old fridges, caravan doors, half-made tables, and brass backed mirrors pokes him in an unwelcome place, and the rage bursts forth. "George," he whispers, not knowing what he says, seeing only red with lightning forks of white lashed through. "George. GEORGE. GEORRRGE!"

The crash, shatter, thud, split, and boom carry across the showgrounds while broken things fly out through the tent doorway. Some come to watch Cyclone Gonko in awe. Most, more wisely, flee the scene.

Later, on his way back to the Funhouse, Gonko strolls almost lost through the new circus layout, where George's orders have all but robbed the place of its character. The tents are all the same size, the same distance apart, perfectly swept, and it's all sparkling clean, from the swept floors to polished poles. Signs are up all over, with George's face on them, only a more noble handsome version of George, peering down from high places with the words GEORGE IS WATCHING and TRAITORS BEWARE. Gonko is baffled that not a single sign has been defaced.

He stops by the acrobat tent, where to his astonishment another sign out front reads: GEORGE'S PET FAVORITES (for now!) In smaller letters: SUCK UP AND RAT OUT YOUR FRIENDS FOR YOUR CHANCE! Three sublime bodies laze about inside, dripping with sweat from rehearsal. The new acrobats laugh and sip iced tea. Gonko sifts through fuzzy memories of that night; it takes him a while to recall the old acrobats are gone, and that Curls said something about kidnapped Olympic gymnasts replacing them. But by the time he's remembered these things, Gonko has already picked up a clump of hard dirt, yelled "Hey, fuck face," and hurled it as hard as he could at the first one to turn around. The throw strikes its target in the throat. Eyes go wide, cough cough splutter and all that caper as the others rush to the aid of their fallen friend.

"You beast!" one hollers at him. All three are weeping. The casualty rolls around with (admittedly) beautiful catlike grace.

Gonko remembers at that point there's no actual feud (til now maybe). But the way the place has changed, some old familiar touches are plenty welcome. "What the hell?" he says. "Sven would have fly-kicked me by now. Don't you know how to acrobat?"

"We abhor violence!"

"So this is gonna be one easy feud, is what you're telling me?"

They run off crying, leaving Gonko to pace restlessly around the grounds. It's a long spell of time for him—he feels like an expecting father outside the delivery room. Word reaches him that the acrobats have tattled to George and that George is on the lookout for him, but George has plenty of others to scream at and lash, and Gonko (rightly) suspects George has got a whiff of the menace oozing from his pores and is in no real rush to find him. Nonetheless he plays safe, hiding out whenever the unsteady stomp-stomp of George's goon comes near.

Things have changed all right. Rumor has it that among the punishment options, George takes particular delight in seating squabbling performers for demeaning "reconciliation" sessions with some therapist he grabbed from the world above, the same way he grabbed that accountant from back a little while. Quarreling parties are made to discuss their feelings and resolve conflicts, sometimes before an audience of carnies. It sounds truly diabolical—Gonko has to hand it to him, he knows how to spoil the fun, old George.

Sparks hiss and fizz behind the Funhouse door whenever Gonko prowls by. Word spreads that something weird is afoot in there, weirder than normal even, for very few carny rats come near in those hours. Not real keen on the décor in there himself, Gonko waits outside as much as he can, but when he hears from within "Breathe! Breathe!" he dashes in.

The floor is a repulsive mess of off-cuts in discarded piles, bone pieces leaking marrow. Lumps of flesh and organs sit in buckets. There's a zap in the air which stands hairs on end, more richness of graveyard and garbage can stink than surely have ever existed in just one room before. But there in the chair, with a blank expression behind newly applied face paint, is Doopy. His head is big and round as a basketball, with black bristles sticking out here and there. He is short, pot-bellied, glancing apologetically at the entire world. Blinking, breathing. Alive.

The Matter Manipulator wheels about, hands rubbing together. "The first attempt succeeds! Most pleasing. He lives, in his way."

"G-G-Gonko?" Doopy stammers, whispers. He lurches from the chair, falls in a heap. A banana peel has felled him. Gonko yanks him upright. Doopy paws his shirt. "It's *cold* over there, Gonko. It's real cold, and, and they make you *do* stuff."

"There, there," says Gonko, keeping his relief and joy in check because the Matter Manipulator is peering at him. But another clown tear betrays him, bounces off Doopy's shoulder as he thinks to hell with it and embraces his fellow clown. "Get busy," Gonko snarls at the Matter Manipulator, whose smile is ugly. He hauls up on his medical stretcher a squarish slab of flesh, sharpens his cleaver, holds back a tear of his own. The truth of it is, he's not felt so moved in many long years.

It takes just a day and a half longer before the rest of the crew are back around the same old card table, passing around the same old cards. Gonko watches them closely to see how they've pulled up. Aside from the occasional staring-into-space silence, Doopy's screaming nightmares about something he calls "Mr. Bigbad," and in Goshy's case an errant limb coming half off when he moves too fast, he is satisfied they are the same clowns they were before.

Although he hasn't got the whole crew yet. "Lean close," he says when Doopy and Rufshod finally finish their battle for who gets the last pretzel. They lean close, and he tells them the grand plan. They don't seem to hear a word of it and go right back to fighting over the now eaten pretzel. Goshy stares about, baffled by everything in sight. All systems normal.

"Tonight," Gonko tells his crew after a day or two of letting them settle into life, "we go up. Ruf, I'm avoiding George 'cause of some acrobat drama. Go get us some pass-outs. Might take a while to find JJ, but we'll hit up the old haunts first. We'll split up but keep track of each other. If you spot him, find out where he's staying. Then it's beat-down time and we scare him real bad."

"Gonko, is, can I, is it," Doopy stammers.

"You may use the restroom, Doopy. And if you ask me again I'll bury you back in the sludge where I found you."

Doopy cringes. "Aw shucks, Gonko. It's *bad* over there, real bad, I just can't go back there, it hurts your eyes and they make you *do* stuff."

"I liked it over there," says Rufshod. "Made some friends."

Doopy takes off his already soiled pants and dumps them in the latrine, putting on a new pair but not before giving everyone along the way an eyeful of the poetic license the Matter Manipulator has taken with his remolding job. "Oh Christ," Gonko mutters in disgust. "Doopy, I want the extra dick gone by morning. Don't even want to know what that other thing is, but cut it off too."

"It's tingle itchy, Gonko. But when I rub it, it goes tingle ouchy."

"Oh, Gonkoooo," George coos from the tent doorway. From atop his ride-on goon—which evidently scares the bejesus out of Goshy, who runs stiff-legged from the room and squeals like a kettle—George beckons. Behind him stands the acrobat recently assailed, and so the clowns are delayed an hour and a half as, with George in the corner eating popcorn and now and then braying out a one-man laugh track, Gonko and Claudius (the acrobat) discuss their feelings with George's new toy, the therapist.

She is forty-something, dressed in soothing earthy browns and greens with frizzy hair, spectacles, and a long neck on which her head constantly bobs in perfect understanding. Gonko's hands throttle the arms of his chair throughout. Claudius at least seems to find it all of value. "I guess what I feel—when a clown attacks me?—is a sense of rejection."

The therapist nods understandingly. "And maybe Gonko when he threw the mud, or feces, whatever it was—was protesting against some rejection *he* has felt in the past?"

George in the corner almost dies laughing.

"It's great your proprietor cares enough to sit in on our session," says the therapist.

"I feel a little validated by that," says Claudius, "though also the frequent laughing? Gives me feelings of confusion."

The time crawls by slower than it ever has. At the end Gonko cannot remember his name or occupation for the rage has conquered all. He manages somehow to hug the acrobat when ordered to and to say something resembling "sorry." When the angry mist clears, he is standing ankle deep in the rubble of a wagon, with various aches indicating his own hands and feet destroyed it.

The other clowns gaze on respectfully, clapping. (Goshy claps by puffing out his cheeks and slapping them against his gums, which he will do on and off for the remainder of the night.) The gypsy wagon owners stand by, less impressed, and Gonko remembers the grand plan. "All of you, grab a piece of this wagon," he tells the gypsies. "We're taking it up. Fix it up there. You're coming with us. Secret mission. There shall be pay and perks aplenty."

"Up where?" says one of the gypsies. These are more Kurt survivors; some of them have been here so long the world above has become almost mythical.

"Come and Uncle Gonko will show you." Few who'd watched his display would disobey him so the gypsies reluctantly pick up the larger pieces of the wagon while the clowns gather up some of the rest of it. There isn't room in the lift for all of them plus the wagon parts so the clowns go up first. "Here is the grand secret plan," Gonko says, "and this time, listen." Already stuffed close, the clowns lean closer, the contact provoking a range of comic sounds from chiming bells, popping toast, to flatulence. "Our *own* show. Up above, in the place tricks come from. That caravan I trashed is the first part. We sneak out more bits and pieces, stash 'em somewhere til we're ready. Then we take a real long time to deal with this." He holds up the list of names George has given him. "We farm us some powder, see? We pay more than George is paying and bribe anyone we want to be part of the new show."

"But what if George wants us to be in *his* show?" says Rufshod.

"He don't. We'll be lower than gypsies down there—he said it with his own gob. And these orders come from higher than George." He rattles the list for emphasis. "So unless one of the bigbosses wants to crawl up that tunnel to tell it different, we make the rules up here, we do what we want. Which is whatever Gonko says. Got it?"

"Just clowns though?" says Rufshod. "I mean we're just clowns. What about a freak show and acrobats and lion tamers and shit?"

"In time," says Gonko.

"Gosh," says Doopy.

"And it gets better, my lovelies. In time we starve out George's show altogether. How? Ticket collectors. Geddit? We get our own people on that job. We make 'em send down to George only tricks we already entertained. Tricks who been sucked dry. No dust for

George. And in time, no circus for George, when no one's getting paid down below, and the boss-bosses ain't getting their cut neither. Think they'll put up with George for long?" Doopy, frantic, raises his hand. "Speak."

"I had this great idea, Gonko," and Gonko tunes out as Doopy relates everything Gonko has just said, which takes the entire length of the trip up.

They surface through the elevator to a port-a-john in a Brisbane City construction site, vacant now since it's night. The gypsies have to make four more trips for the rest of the wagon parts. Gonko tells the carnies to steal a truck, load the wagon parts in, and then head north before they fix it. They have no tools or anything, but carny rats fix shit like magic. Gonko will find them when the time comes, once he's found a good site for the new show.

The other clowns step cautiously from the lift, out into the crisp air of a winter Brisbane evening. Suddenly they are all silent and stand there in a daze, their faces mirrors of Goshy's perpetual surprise. "What's the gag?" says Gonko. "We got stuff to do."

Doopy points at the stars. "Wh—what are them pretty things, Gonko? No foolin', you just gotta tell me."

"You seen 'em before, ain't you?"

"Heck no. Gosh they're pretty. What is them things?" Rufshod looks equally confused.

"They call 'em sky-pretties," says Gonko. "All the real super duper clowns get a chariot ride across the sky to have a lick. Like ice cream, is what I hear."

"Gee, swell!" Doopy's voice is awed. "And them tall things?" he points at the buildings.

"You seen it all. Don't you remember outside jobs for Kurt?"

Rufshod laughs, embarrassed. "Bit scattered," he says, hitting his skull with the corner of a brick, presumably to work out the kinks. Each collision makes a sound like a dog's squeaky ball toy, causing Goshy to wildly spin around seeking whoever in the gloom around them shares his secret language.

"It's all spooky," Doopy whispers. A car horn blares. "Goshy's scared, Gonko. Don't leave us here why don't ya?"

A van drives slowly by, with MR. MUSCLE CLEANING SERVICE painted on its door and rear, with a small cartoon man resembling Popeye cocking a bicep. Rufshod stiffens. "I know that fuck!" he yells. "Hey, Mr. Muscle! Remember me?"

"Ruf, relax."

"He owes me. Owes me big!" And he's off, tearing across to the fence and over it in one bound before Gonko can collar him, sprinting after the van as it rounds the corner.

"Whatever," says Gonko. "All right, you two. Have a look around, a quick search of the city. See that club where JJ used to work before we clowned him. Stay in the dark, don't get seen. See if the sights jog your memories, looks like the MM turned your brains to custard. Meet you back here in four hours."

From his pocket Gonko pulls a compass with the letter J for JJ instead of N for North, and R, D, G for Rufshod, Doopy, Goshy instead of East, South, West. The compass point will keep track of any of the clowns when he twists the dial. He is nonetheless nervous about setting them loose up here. "Let's find this rat bastard," he says, grabbing another compass for each of the clowns. Though the dials do not always agree where the J ought to be pointed, they seem reliable enough to at least keep track of each other. "Here." He tosses them each a large poncho, pulled from his pockets. "Cover up. You ain't clowns for a little bit, just to be safe."

"Gee, Gonko. That's mighty confusing. Cause see I coulda sworn we was . . ." Doopy elaborates at length, but Gonko has already fled, following the J on his compass til it leads him to a bridge above a passing train. He drops onto its roof and clings tight as it carries him north.

Gonko arrives after midnight to stand before the brick two-story home, sniffs the air, and can somehow tell JJ has been here recently. But as he stands at the driveway the compass point twists about and points south, frantically extending its point to indicate JJ is a long way away. It means either his magic pants are damaged from their stint below, its trinkets damaged with them, or it is just some quirk of circus magic, whose mechanics often escape those who wield it; perhaps it is not merely leading him to where JJ is but also the best time *when* to find him. An older version of JJ, some trick relation, looks out a curtain and sees him. Gonko contemplates busting down the door and causing some possibly fatal damage to the trick, but decides against it, in case it puts JJ on notice that he's hunted.

He rides into town on the roof of a freight train, unseen in the dark except for the glint of garish color now and then catching the corner of someone's eye as the train sails by. Not far from the house he visited he eyes again the parkland by the river when the train rumbles over a bridge through it. It's a campsite, tucked nicely out of the way of the main roads with plenty of room to set up some circus acts. Maybe this place will make a decent first stop for his new traveling show. He kisses the little compass. Looks like it steered him well, after all.

It is near dawn when he tracks down Doopy and Goshy who stand exactly where he left them in the construction site. They have not moved so much as a footstep. The ponchos sit at their feet. Doopy's head is tilted back. "They taste like ice cream, Gonko, ain't that swell? Just like ice cream, and all the real super duper clowns, they get to—"

It is hard to stay mad at them since it feels good to have his crew back, so a quick round of slapping suffices. "Don't hurt him, Gonko, gee-whiz, it's not funny," Doopy reproaches him as he slaps a little sense into Goshy, who in turn peels back his lips, body heaving up sobs as clown tears fall at his feet and flop around like dying fish.

"Wise up you dick maggots," Gonko snarls. "Where's Ruf?"

"He, why, he beat up Mr. Muscles, Gonko, got him real good, and got back that tire Mr. Muscles owed him. Then he went chasing Mr. Whippy."

"He's got his own pass-out anyway. You sorry pukes need a little more time to adjust, it looks like. Daytime now. Time to hide."

45

"We gotta find JJ, Gonko, we just gotta, or Gonko's gonna be soooo mad . . ."

"Truer words never spoken, Doops." They take the porta-a-john elevator back down below.

When he returns, Gonko sees JJ's trick chum Steve slowly making his way from the elevator, with a withered old hag in his arms who looks vaguely familiar. She looks to be, say, three hundred years old, give or take a decade. Gonko mugs the guy for his pass-out (never hurts to have spares in case George gets shitty and confiscates them back) and thinks no more of it.

Steve, not too bothered by the mugging, watches the clown boss strut away, lashing his boot at various inanimate objects that seem to bother him. Feebly the hag whispers in Steve's ear. He sets her gently down. "I'll be right back," he assures her. "You're already looking better."

And she is. As the minutes pass, days of age fall away from her. Steve finds his way to George's trailer, breathing with relish the popcorn-scented air he has missed so badly, marveling at the newness and polish to everything. He clears his throat, knocks on the trailer door. "Excuse me, Mr. Pilo? I'd like my old job back, sir. And I've brought the fortuneteller."

A little later George stomps over to Shalice and laughs himself hoarse. She looks a sprightly hundred-and-fifty now, but it's comedy gold to George. "Don't dress too skimpy please," he warns. "This is a family circus. You want directions to the freak show?"

The crone regards him with ancient eyes. "I've missed you terribly," says Shalice. She produces a tear.

George falters—he's slightly touched. Conflicting emotions wrestle briefly across his face. He spits. "Eh. Get set up in your booth or whatever. And don't let the clowns know you're back. I send 'em up looking for you every night." George laughs at their shared joke, and she favors him with a smile. "Show day soon," he says happily. "I'll send your crystal ball and some instructions from below. You'll be busy, lots to do up there."

"Thank you, Mr. Pilo," says the now hundred-year-old crone, curtseying from a seated position while George bustles away. She too takes a deep whiff of the popcorn-scented air, but unlike Steve her face sours as if she has scented pure death.

It is five days before Rufshod returns triumphant, dragging with him a tire, an empty box of ice cream cones, a computer monitor, and all manner of other bits and pieces, most smashed beyond recognition. Gonko is too busy scheming to be pissed at him. While naturally someone has raided Gonko's main stash of velvet bags full of wish powder during his long absence, they haven't found the secret compartment holding his smaller emergency stash. Nineteen bags sit in a happy pile, probably more loot than George himself has got these days. He first wishes himself a quick S&M session with a virtual Marilyn Monroe, gets his rocks off, which keeps the George-rage at bay a little, then commences doling out bribes. As instructed, Doopy starts a war of words followed by a war of head-butts with the acrobats to distract George, who is soon popcorning his way through another "Reconciling Our Differences" therapy session (although judging by how little mirth George gets this time, it sounds like Doopy is just sitting there confused, agreeing to whatever is said to him and babbling about Mr. Bigbad.)

Gonko visits Curls. "How close does George watch your crew?" Gonko asks, none too subtly wiping his forehead with a velvet bag.

Curls watches its every move. "He don't care about us," he says. "We look busy and it's all right. We go to him if there's a problem. We're just carny rats; we don't matter none."

"Here's the deal, Curls. You're a ticket collector now." He tosses Curls the bag. "I'll go chat to the other collectors and tell 'em what's what. What's what is that you're their boss. And don't do nothing without seeing me first." Curls makes the velvet bag vanish into his pockets like magic. Gonko can feel the envious eyes beaming out from hidden places; powder has never been scarcer.

Which helps Gonko set things up nicely: instructions for smugglers, with maps pointing to the upstairs show site. Using Doopy's pass-out, they sneak up— slowly, and with great care—tent canvas, pegs, crates of costumes, and other supplies. It takes two full bags of powder to convince a gypsy who keeps the Ferris wheel working to knock on the Matter Manipulator's door and distract him—no fun job, admittedly—and also a promise that he can join Gonko's operation "up there." The Matter Manipulator clearly sniffs a rat by the way he looks around upon leaving his house to follow the gypsy.

Gonko dashes in, steals two tubs of clown face paint, a chair made of living human parts and from a back room swipes a head in a glass case, presumably an unfinished freak show creation in progress. It's a fifty-something-year-old professorial head with severe eyebrows, fat cheeks, and an impressive glower. "Buh, hm, what? What's all this? Preposterous!" it grumbles as Gonko covers it in a towel.

Not much of a freak show yet, he knows, but it's a start. When night falls, he takes it all up to the surface world with Doopy's help and checks in on the carny rats up there. The caravan has arrived and is assembled; all is in order. The carny rats each get another full bag of Gonko's stash, which ought to keep them sweet til it's just about show time.

A week has passed and it's time to head surface-wise for the JJ hunt. Gonko figures the clowns ought to stick tight since they're all still a little sludge-brained, which works fine til Rufshod spots a Super Geek PC repair van with a cartoon nerdish version of Superman painted on it, then he's off into the night with a war cry of "Not this time you don't, Super Geek." Thankfully, Gonko got a trench coat on him in the lift so the only clownish thing about him is the face and shoes. The other clowns are similarly obscured, but the trench coats sit uneasy on them, eager to slide off or tear and spill clown out into the cool evening.

A leash for Rufshod seems to be in order next time, Gonko decides. On the plus side, a check of the three compasses—Doopy's, Goshy's, and his own—shows the arrows agreeing on the direction of "J," give or take the odd flicker. Gonko leads them through the city. They thread through crowds of shoppers, students, commuters, and tourists, people who don't seem to really *see* them. The only ones who do are a few homeless men, presumably whacked out on some kind of perspective shifter, given how they cringe back and in one case run away at a fast hobble.

The compasses point them around the block a few times, indicating JJ is on the move. Goshy waddles along behind, bowling people over who don't quite see him and causing a grappling match between two young hotheads in the process. That aside, it's uneventful until they come to the corner of Adelaide and George Street, where Doopy grabs Gonko by the shoulder and says, "Gee-whiz, wow! Look, Gonko, George has got his own *street* up here, up here where tricks come from. Ain't it swell?"

When below, Gonko can emotionally prepare for interactions with George so this kind of thing doesn't happen. Right now his guard is down, and as he stares at the GEORGE ST sign, it turns into George Pilo's sneering face, laughing with popcorn spilling out its gob, before everything goes red with flashes of white lightning. Suddenly little Georges are all around him. "George," he says quietly. "George . . . GEORGE. GEORRRRRGE!"

Doopy and Goshy observe Gonko stampeding over the pedestrians to get at a couple of rather swish cars which evidently remind him of George, since he proceeds to stomp them. Expensive car alarms blare in panic. The passing people suddenly see Gonko crystal clear. "GEORGE! GEORGE!"

Doopy leans close to his brother. "Goshy, we gotta help the boss, we just gotta! Let's go find JJ, coz Gonko, he's just, he . . ."

Goshy makes a low whining whistle—a sad sound.

"I know, Goshy, I know. I don't wanna wear the not-clown clothes no more neither." So off come the ponchos and the two of them leave Gonko (now on the run from some police who'd cruised by) and head towards Queen Street, where JJ used to have his old job when he was just a trick they were stalking.

"Just wait here, Goshy," says Doopy, going to some length to shove his brother into the exact right spot, right in the middle of the mall. "I'm gonna climb that building and bring back JJ, so Gonko won't be so shouty-breaky. You remember JJ, don'tcha?"

Goshy's left eye narrows.

"Now, don't be mean! Aw c'mon, shucks, don't you be mean when I fetch him, you gotta promise! Gonko's gonna beat him up, beat him up real bad, so don't be mean, okay?"

Off goes Doopy, leaving his brother startled and confused, turning on the spot and forgetting to keep hidden in the shadows. It is not long before he acquires a crowd of drunk and tipsy Friday night revelers who stand in a ring about him. They laugh and point, all of them shouting things he doesn't understand. He tries to shut the sound out with his fists, spins about, looks for a way to escape, but there are just faces, faces, faces, laughing, laughing, laughing . . .

Doopy is up on a windowsill of the Wentworth Gentleman's Club when the scream rings out. His grand plan was to pry open the window, sheepishly call, "Hey, JJ?" then climb back down, but that will have to wait. His descent is a comet strike into alleyway garbage cans. He bounces over the fence. And there, a crowd of people are holding their ears, some writhing around after having been trampled. "Hey, you, you shouldn'ta ought not done did it," Doopy yells, barreling into them and laying several people flat in a human traffic pile up. His fists windmill about, his boots thud down, his buttocks are swung like a club. It's a weird but effective way to pound a lot of people, but someone manages to brain him with a rock or brick, which snaps him out of attack mode. There ahead Goshy waddles fast, fists firm at his sides, kettle noise steaming "mmm, hmmm, hmmm," and beyond him at the top of the mall the redheaded JJ makes a running escape.

Gonko appears at the top of the street in a snazzy fake beard, glasses, a new trench coat, and has no cops on his trail. Doopy jogs on the spot for a moment, nervous and undecided. Being alive is hard without the boss to think for him. He waves until he has Gonko's attention then points to JJ, who ducks around a corner.

Gonko herds the other clowns together, absentmindedly swats them both, but their target is close: the compass is working properly and has them on his tail. Fifteen minutes later the clowns have found Jamie's building. "The nerve of this guy, living it up like a normal trick," Gonko says as they stare up the rows of windows. There, that place: a light goes on right as they watch, and a redhead stands at the window with binoculars briefly trained on the opposite building.

"We goin' up there, Gonko? We just gotta get JJ back."

"Tomorrow, after we find Rufshod. Then JJ will get his beat down."

3. ABOVE

The front door burst in and footsteps scuffed on the carpet. Doctors, nurses, police. Dean frowned, probably wondering for a fleeting moment why the hospital people didn't just knock, wondering why they would spook a mentally ill and violent patient with such an entrance. For he had indeed told them on the phone that the violent clown they were after was Jamie.

Meanwhile Jamie was still reeling with an unbelievable sense of betrayal, so shocked that the appearance of the clowns hardly surprised him. The thinnest clown was tethered to the fattest by what looked like a dog chain around both their necks. "How ya been, JJ?" said the clown with the wide pants, a tinkling-bell hat and a mean face.

Dean looked from them to Jamie with his jaw hung loose. Dean's look of shock was so sweet and intoxicating for Jamie, and so intense was his anger at that moment, that he felt not quite in control of himself. One more second to pause and assess the situation and he'd have done something entirely different. Instead he pointed at his roommate and said to the clowns, "Get him."

"Sure, we'll start there," said Gonko with a shrug.

The clowns rushed Dean. He swung the baseball bat, nailed the clown leashed to it with a flush strike. The tether snapped. Baseball stadium home run music briefly filled the room as Rufshod sailed across into the kitchen bench. After he'd swung, Dean was off balance and easy prey. The bat was plucked out of his hand. The other clowns laid on a fairly conventional beating aside from Goshy, who invented a kind of full-body head-butt without even bending at the waist, up and down like a ninepin in fast motion. Jamie felt a weird sense of inertia. He looked around the room, unsure if he was really seeing this or not. Next thing, his roommate's face was a sheen of blood. "Stop it," he said. "Don't kill him. Stop!"

"Make up your fucking mind!" Gonko screamed. In a moment of eerie quiet as Jamie and the clowns stared at each other, Dean's bedroom door's lock clicked. Jodi—apparently she'd heard enough to know something serious and uncool was going on in the living room. The clowns left Dean in a battered heap and turned to Jamie. Suddenly there were axes, crowbars and lead pipes in their hands.

"Why are you here?" Jamie said, backing away.

"What's with you, JJ?" said Gonko, actually confused. "You don't remember us?"

"I've never seen you before in my life." It was a lie of sorts; he did not know their names, but he knew he had seen them all before, and that they knew *him*.

Rufshod whispered in Gonko's ear, got a nod. A white tub of face paint appeared and they wrestled Jamie down, slopped it on, and held up a mirror so he could see his reflection. The weapons came again to hand and were raised over him. "Now what say you, JJ?" Gonko said. "Do I hear the beginnings of a 'Sorry, Gonko' for what you did in that trailer?"

"For the love of God," Jamie yelled, thrashing under their hands. "Would you tell me what the hell is going on? Who are you people?"

"He really doesn't remember, boss," said Rufshod.

"By George, that's weird," said Doopy, looking sidelong at Gonko.

Gonko pondered things for a moment, said "'Scuse us," and pulled the other clowns into a huddle. They whispered back and forth. Doopy cried out, "But that's telling fibs, boss! You shouldn't oughta—" till Gonko thwacked him, and more whispering ensued.

In that time Jamie lay on the tiles, gingerly touching his face and examining the white smear on his finger. There was something peculiar about the face paint they'd put on him. It had to be a drug of some kind, for rushing through him was a similar but far more intense sensation than the feeling the clown clothes had given him last night. The shoulder he'd tweaked doing push-ups on awakening suddenly didn't hurt. A giddiness came over him and he felt like cavorting around the room. He had to actually remind himself he was in some danger here. It helped when Dean moaned, rolled to his side and burst a blood bubble from his smashed nose. But even then Jamie marveled to note he was suddenly not all that *scared*. He said to the clowns, "Look, you obviously know me. And we've had some kind of disagreement by the look of things, what with all the weapons and violence. Maybe we could just talk things out peacefully then all go have a jam donut together, how about that?"

"Just a sec, we're getting our stories straight here," Rufshod snapped at him.

Gonko said, "All right, go. JJ—Jamie, whatever. This is gonna maybe be hard to believe, but we are superhero clowns who help people in need. We come from a superhero circus, and you are one of our special agents. Now we need your help because our circus has been overtaken by our archenemy, a total shitbag named George. Do you believe? Are you with us?"

Jamie let this ridiculous explanation sit in the air. *Is it even remotely possible this is true?* he thought. He thought back to the mall clown—yes, that solid flabby looking thing staring at him now with weird eyes—and the things it had done, how its belly had blown out, its shrieking noise. He knew at the time and knew now those were *not* special effects. More like magic. *Actual* magic.

"I think I'll need some convincing," he said at last. "But that would certainly explain a few things."

"You'll get all the proof you need and then some, sweet cheeks."

"You want to start by making sure my roommate lives through the night? You superhero clowns kind of beat the living shit out of him."

"Eh?" The clowns took a moment to remember Dean.

Rufshod crouched down, peeled an eyelid back with his thumb. "Look, he's probably gonna be dead in fifty, sixty years anyway right? So what's the big deal if it happens now?"

Gonko kicked Rufshod across the room. "Bad taste joke there, Ruf," he said. His voice caught with emotion. "Can't you see we're talking about a trick's life here? We need him to thrive and prosper and make baby tricks, and be all happy and to know joy and stuff."

Doopy applauded gustily. A tear was in his eye.

"Of course we'll save your trick buddy," said Gonko. "We beat him up only because you told us to, special agent Jamie. It seemed he musta felt you up or done some other perverse evil."

"It looked like you were going to beat me up too for a minute there. All those axes and lead pipes."

"Now see, that's an example of thinking too much. Ruf, help me here." The two of them carried Dean to Jamie's bedroom.

Gonko twitched, lashed out a fist at Jamie's stereo but held back his punch with visible strain. Veins throbbed in his forehead. He raised a boot to smash the bed but kicked an imaginary cat instead with a whoosh of air. "What gives?" he whispered. "Where's JJ? Why the face paint ain't worked?"

"It ain't JJ the clown, boss," said Rufshod. "But it's for sure the same chump trick we auditioned."

"He ain't lying neither. Don't remember us. Something weird musta happened that night when Kurt lost his shit."

"Or maybe this face paint's no good?"

Gonko snatched the tub, sniffed it. "Seems like the real deal. One way to find out."

They both looked at the unconscious figure at their feet. Rufshod shifted uneasily. "But boss, we didn't audition him! What if he ain't got any clown inside him?"

Gonko called through the doorway, "Say, Jamie, would you call this trick pal of yours a funny guy? He ever makes good with the giggles or what?"

"Dean? No offense, but what the hell does that have to do with anything? He needs an ambulance, and I need a really good explanation for them."

"We're gonna perform some circus medicine, works real tidy. Called a humorectomy. What say, he makes you laugh much or what?"

"Sometimes, I guess."

Gonko shrugged. "There," he said. "Emergency audition passed." He crouched down. "If he don't work out as a clown, we'll need grunt workers in the new show anyway."

As Gonko smeared white greasy face paint across Dean's face, the bleeding slowed, then ceased. The bruises seemed to deflate just a touch. Dean groaned.

"All right, so now this chump lives, and Jamie knows we're good guys. Ruf, there's a blubbering girly trick in the room next door. If she's pretty, it's night-night time and the whole abducted-by-clowns gag."

Rufshod darted out. There was the thud of a door kicked open followed by a brief scream.

Meanwhile in the living room Jamie was confirming for his own amazed eyes that magic was real. Something in that face paint made him feel nearly invincible. When he jumped, he floated up to the roof and gently landed back down, just like being in water. "Wow," he said.

Doopy and Goshy's eyes silently followed his motion up, down, up, down.

"Superheroes," Jamie said, tasting the words. "Just like a comic book. So what do we do? Stop robberies? Help old ladies cross the street? Battle archvillains with lame, shitty names?" Doopy and Goshy just watched him. "Guys?" said Jamie.

A hissing angry sound spurted out of Goshy. His lips peeled back from flat white teeth. His eyes doubled in size with an audible pop. One ear slipped loose, connected only by the thin thread of snotty gristle on which it swayed. He waddled at Jamie stiff-legged. Jamie could only stare as the fat clown stomach-butted him backward into the kitchen bench and breathed reeking swampy air over him. "Ungh, hnng, hnng, unghh!" came an urgent high-pitched whine. Jamie cringed down into a ball, more scared now than when they'd menaced him with axes and crowbars. He could not fathom what had brought on this attack. "Call him off, call him off!"

Doopy finally stirred to action. "Oh hey, gee." He took his brother's shoulder in hand. "Hey now, Goshy, don't be mean, just like I told ya. C'mon now, this ain't JJ, this is Jamie. It's different, Goshy, it's real different."

Being pulled away made Goshy more determined—he pushed in closer, his grunts turned to sharp chopping screams, shrill needle jabs at the ear. Yet it seemed Goshy was the frightened one, even more than Jamie crouched in his fetal ball, shivering. The flower in Goshy's top pocket squirted water at him.

Gonko rushed back out, grabbed the length of tether still around Goshy's throat and wrenched him back. He hauled Jamie to his feet. "Don't worry. That means he digs you. He got a case of the brain custards on our last mission. It ain't his fault. Superheroing is tough."

Goshy lay on his back, hyperventilating while Jamie calmed himself. Everything spun and swam in his head. The outburst was something he could have done without to be sure, but it almost seemed the poor retarded clown had been trying to tell him something. Then he remembered what Dean had done. "The cops— look, there's hospital people and maybe police on their way here. I don't know when, maybe tonight, maybe tomorrow. My roommate called them. They think I'm crazy and they're going to interview me."

"Then we gotta bail," Gonko said, "or else it could get real messy here. Doops, grab the new chump real gentle. And don't you worry, JJ, he's on the mend."

Doopy bustled off to fetch Dean, who he carried in a show of strength belying his stature. Rufshod emerged with Jodi slung over his shoulder, her face obscured by a curtain of auburn hair.

"What are you doing with her?" Jamie said, alarmed.

"No time, chumbo," said Gonko. "They're both in great danger."

"Say, that part's true, Gonko. Because—"

Gonko shut Doopy up with a look. "We gotta take your trick buddies to our secret superhero hideout. We'll explain later." Gonko grasped Jamie by the shoulders. "Trust me. You ain't got a choice in this. Grab that clown outfit in your bedroom, and put it on. A better life is ahead. Chuckles and hot dogs for all. Fight the good fight; ride the cackle train. Whatcha say, Jamie?"

With an apprehensive look at Goshy—who now rolled from side to side on the carpet, silently weeping—the words *ain't got a choice* echoed in his mind. They were taking Dean and Jodi anyway, and he knew he couldn't stop them. If he stayed, he'd be explaining impossible things and disappearances to authorities, which would not end well. The carpet was stained with Dean's blood.

Play along, something deep within him cautioned. *Play along, whatever else happens you'll get the answers as to what really happened to you. And you better at least* pretend *to believe what they say, until such time as you can actually truly believe it . . .*

So he fetched his clown outfit, and put it on quickly. Mingling with his doubts came a new burst of giddy humor, fun but slightly sickening, like a carnival ride. "Let's go then," he said.

4. BELOW

George had been too busy getting the ship in order to bother himself with the clowns' comings and goings. Pleasingly, new staff freak-outs and psychotic breaks (as their old selves rebelled one last time against what they were now a part of) had tapered off and the place was looking show-ready. Much as he detested them on a personal level, more coldly viewed, the clowns were useful tools for the business. They had been in the show longer than most, and should George need some heads busted, Gonko was at least smarter about it than the lumberjacks. They'd not be performing any time soon, not until George received some serious sucking up, but they were fun to torment.

Speaking of torment . . .

When the phone in George's trailer rang just yesterday, the icy voice said, "three days." Before the dial tone could cut in George had cried, "Wait! There's someone down there with you who I need for the show."

A long watchful silence followed. Slowly: "I am not . . . DOWN . . . THERE."

George broke out in goose bumps and shivers. He'd not expected a response, had at best hoped to be heard before he, she, it, hung up. Quickly he went on, "I need more performers. My brother Kurt. I wanna make him part of the act. Got it all figured out. I

59

know he was in some trouble with the high ups, but can I have him? I assure you he won't enjoy it."

Then the dial tone cut in. Not a *yes*, but not (as far as he knew) a refusal either.

Now he stood atop his goon, whose glassy eyes stared dead ahead while drool splashed off the goon's chin. They stood in the Funhouse basement with four strong lumberjacks, who had spent the past week building a carefully designed cage of iron and wood. It was welded into a cocoon of circular ribs, which could be tightened by twisting thick iron screws. Even on the night of his rampage Kurt would have been unable to break out of this contraption; now he'd be starved and weak, just as Gonko had been when he'd risen from the depths.

A long thick chain dangled down the tunnel below the Funhouse. Four strong lumberjacks stood holding the end, ready to pull. Like fishermen they waited for a tug on the line before they began. They had been waiting for two hours. George hopped down from the goon's saddle, and held a megaphone to his lips. "Kurt! Grab the chain. Can you hear me, Kurt? You're coming up. I'm rescuing you."

More tense minutes crawled by. Maybe Kurt hadn't been permitted to come up after all, or maybe they'd have to come back tomorrow and try again. But then the chain rattled a little, tensed. Frantically George waved his arms and barked orders. The cage was wheeled in place. The muscle men had been briefed on what to expect. At the first sign of trouble George would scream the pre-arranged code words—"DROP THE CHAIN"—at which point they'd drop the chain, sending Kurt back below.

The lumberjacks heaved, dragged. Gradually a figure—even smaller than George had envisioned—appeared against the tunnel's orange glow. Soon Kurt was so close they could see he looked relatively human from the collarbone up. The rest of him was more like a blackened skeleton of mismatched bones tangled together. The familiar thick lips curved up in a puzzled smile. George shivered, hatred and pleasure all mixed up. He spoke into the megaphone, "Welcome back, brother."

"George. What is all this? Rather a fine surprise."

"Oh, it gets better Kurt." More frantic arm waving. The muscle men got into position. Kurt passed through the tunnel's outer lip, the chain passed through the cage, and George screamed, "Go! Now!"

Struts were hit away; bolts snapped. Wood and metal fell in place. Kurt's smile crawled away and died somewhere. His eyes glared straight ahead. George cackled, danced, giggled, and capered. The lumberjacks tossed a black tarp over the cage, leaving only Kurt's head exposed. They wheeled him to the freak show tent, where Kurt's head was put inside a custom made glass case. In the darkness of the freak show, with some careful lighting, the bulk of him was hidden, leaving the illusion that only Kurt's head remained.

When he could at last rein in his laughter and wisecracks, George reached into the glass case and patted the head. "Welcome to your new job," he said. A sharp stick was leaned against the glass case; a sign hammered into the ground nearby said: POKE THE FREAK—SEE HIM CHANGE!

"Brother George, do you suppose some food—"

"Oh, sure," George said. "First we better test this out, don't you think? Before the tricks come through. Thousands and thousands of tricks, Kurt. Too many to count, as the years crawl by." George had first poke. Kurt still glowered straight ahead, his cheek and forehead dipping in with each sharp jab. Slowly, slowly the color rose in his cheeks until they flared crimson. George went till his arm got tired. "Who's next?" he said, passing the stick to the nearest lumberjack.

By the day's end nearly everyone had been through the freak show tent for their turn, with George making damned sure no one missed out. It took the fifteenth carny poking away before Kurt's face split open, elongated and shifted. The growl from his throat made the carny flee the tent. It was many hours after the last poke that his face resumed its more human appearance. In all, an effective freak show gimmick, George reckoned. He sprinkled some flakes of fish food into the tank, and drizzled in a little water. "You'll be a star, big brother," he said, having a few more jabs while Kurt silently licked up the food, eyes boring hard straight ahead, staring, staring until a black cloth fell over the tank.

5. ABOVE

Jamie could not help looking sidelong at Goshy every few seconds in fear of another outburst, but the clown seemed far receded behind his newborn boggle at the world they stole through. Dark streets and night traffic seemed somehow far away, though their oversized shoes slapped on it like applauding hands, though headlights like stage lights now and then caught them flush in their shameless blare of pink, red, white, and green. A balloon would now and then festively bubble forth from any of the clown's pockets, including Jamie's, and sail toward the moon. Dean's and Jodi's heads flopped around with the movement but neither woke.

And no one paused to stare, as Jamie would have done were he walking or driving by. One or two people glanced around, perhaps half-hearing something, their eyes confused by a flicker of candy cane pink and white, but never truly *seeing* them. The shadows swallowed them, seemed to wrap like blankets and coats about the clowns, and for all his reservations (and a growing suspicion that he was hearing—at the very least—*exaggerations* as Gonko regaled him with tales of the clowns' heroic deeds) Jamie felt drunk again on some alien intoxicating fizz which had burbled inside him since the face paint went on.

"So as I say, helping people out is our passion," Gonko went on as they zigzagged across a street thick with jammed traffic. "Only it might not look so pretty to someone who didn't know how it all works, dig? Same as a doctor who cuts someone open to pull out a bad heart. If you didn't know better, you'd say the doc was killing 'em, right? We got this place below, called the Pilo Circus. When you came to join us after we saved your bacon from a lot of bad juju, that's when an evil shit named George took over and started using the place for bad instead of good. He killed my whole crew, and I had to haul 'em out of the ground myself. You musta escaped. The deal now is, we make our own show up here in trick land, to compete, dig? We do it right and pretty soon, George will be gone."

Rufshod had stuffed a knuckle in his mouth to keep his giggling in check. Doopy's hand raised to ask a question, which Gonko ignored, though Doopy's confusion looked profound indeed. Now and then he whispered in his brother's ear, "You hear that, Goshy? We're the *good* guys now, you and me is the *good* guys. Ain't it swell?"

"So why can't I remember any of this?" said Jamie.

Gonko twitched, rubbed his palm over his face with irritation. "We dunno. Looks like George got at you, maybe hit you with the old suck-thought vacuum. You wouldn't be the first."

"Or maybe . . ." Doopy dropped to a whisper. "Maybe it was Mr. Bigbad."

"Who?" said Jamie.

"Gee, Mr. Bigbad. We *saw* him, back before Gonko dug us up, back where it's cold and bright and where they make you . . . they make you . . ." Doopy whimpered, fidgeted. Goshy emitted a puppy dog whine, and a flood of frightened tears poured out his eyes.

"No blubbering," Gonko yelled. "And no more about Mr. Bigbad. Jamie's gonna think we're nuts. Mr. Bigbad can't hurt you no more, Doops."

"Gee, Gonko, are you sure? 'Cause see, he can do stuff, weird stuff, and has a beard and sits in this great big chair and tells everyone what to do."

They crossed a footpath bridge over a railway line. A train clattered past down below, heading south. When one headed past the other way, Gonko motioned to follow him and leaped down onto its roof. The other clowns dropped with various degrees of grace

64

or clumsiness, Rufshod and Doopy managing to cushion their human cargo beneath themselves. Jamie stood on the edge of the bridge, hesitating a second or two before he followed the call of circus magic inside, threw himself out into the night air, whooped as he landed on the metal train roof as comfortably as a mattress. He lay on his back, watched the stars and marveled to be experiencing something different, something so freakish and weird that most people who'd ever lived would not think it possible.

The train began to slow as it neared Petrie Station, crossing the bridge over the Pine River. "Off!" Gonko called over his shoulder. Rufshod landed in the river's shallow and near motionless water, waking Jodi in the process. Her screams were drowned out by the train's noise until she was again good-nighted and carried up the riverbank. Goshy, naturally, plummeted head first to the dry ground and landed like a javelin, stuck fast from the shoulders down. Doopy and Gonko yanked his legs to pull him loose, but his distressed screams indicated he was happier like he was, so they left him. Jamie dropped down with catlike ease, again marveling at these new powers.

They were in Wiley Park, a small campsite just off a main road. No campervans were parked there tonight. "I know this place," Jamie said. "Hell, I grew up right around here. We used to fish in this river. And that paper mill across the road, we used to break its windows. Friend of mine tried to torch it one time. What are we doing *here*?"

Gonko spat in the direction of three tents, set up so the campsite's toilet block obscured them from the road. Large tents, with stripes like hard-boiled candy, and an antique looking caravan. In fact it was a marvel Jamie hadn't seen them until this moment. More circus magic? A few figures bustled around in between the tents, whispering to each other.

For superhero clowns concerned with the welfare of all, they were rather casual in dumping Dean's and Jodi's unconscious bodies in the nearest tent, and booting out the four strange people who'd been sleeping in there. Two were short—in fact they were dwarfs. One earned a kick when he grumbled at being woken. The other two looked Mediterranean, their necks and arms covered in brass and copper jewelry.

One of the dwarfs—in fact the one Gonko kicked—spotted Jamie and snarled, "You!" Fast as a rabbit he was on him, the little stubby kicks not so scary until one hand went behind his back and pulled free a dagger.

Gonko laughed at the initial attack but now jumped in, yanking the blade away and throwing it in the river. "I know you!" the dwarf screamed. "Let me cut him! My friends! You kilt Lucky and Banjo! You kilt em! You broke my record player too, dirty sumfabitch, I remember you!"

"Easy, this is a different clown," said Gonko, wrestling the dwarf to another tent. There came the murmur of conversation and the dwarf's angry weeping as Gonko explained things. The gypsies whispered to each other as they stared at Jamie. "What did I do?" he said.

"It was JJ," said Rufshod. "Don't sweat it. Ignore dwarfs, they get mad easy."

"Who or what is this JJ? Do I have an evil twin or something?"

Rufshod put his hands on Jamie's shoulders. "Look, JJ—I mean, Jamie. That is the craziest thing I ever heard."

When they were settled around a small fire, armed with marshmallows, Gonko continued his explanations. "So what we do is, we figure out what tricks have got bad stuff coming down the pipeline, see? Car crash or what have you. Then we get 'em in the show and do some circus magic, and we take away their bad luck. Some of 'em got a disease, but not after they been here with us. Some got evil in their hearts, they like to beat on puppies or swipe someone's oatmeal? Well after a show, they're all cotton candy and niceness sauce. Dig it?"

"Trying to dig it."

Gonko tensed up. The stick broke in his hand. "What's the problem?"

"For good guys, you seem to like laying on the violence, that's all. You may well be telling the truth, don't get me wrong . . ."

"A bit of slapstick, so what? Can't really hurt a carny, can it?"

"Dean isn't a carny. Nor is Jodi."

"They're carnies now. Don't you get it? There was gonna be a big train crash next week; they were both toast. We saved 'em. So now they can repay us by helping the circus out a little while. Then they go back to their normal trick lives."

"But Gonko," said Doopy.

"How long will you keep them here?" said Jamie.

"They're free to leave whenever they like."

"But GONKO!" Doopy wailed.

"Shut your shit pie," Gonko snarled. "One more word, Doops, and I write a letter to Mr. Bigbad." Doopy went quiet and bit his knuckles. Gonko said, "So I figure they owe us a couple of weeks. Month, tops. Clown's honor. Who knows, maybe they'll like it here and want to stay, like you did."

Jamie sensed he shouldn't say it, but he did. "Does that apply to me too? Am I free to go right now?"

A tense silence. "Why, sure you are, Jamie," Gonko said slowly. "But it would be a mistake."

"Because?"

"Let's just say it would put you in grave physical danger."

Jamie nodded. "I expected as much."

So then Gonko was bullshitting him to some extent—he was maybe seventy-five percent sure of that, though not completely. It was also clear he had a history with them, that they wanted him around for some reason, and that there was a fair chance if he played ball, for now at least, he'd come to no harm. And yet none of these apparently familiar names and faces had jogged hidden memories.

When the "explanations" had ended, he went into Dean and Jodi's tent to check on them, beyond the pulse check he'd done earlier to verify Dean, in fact, still lived. Someone had been into the tent to put a clown outfit on Dean—striped pants of nearly fluorescent green and red, a stupidly frilly shirt, a red rubber nose, and something like a sailor's hat with rainbows vomited over it. Not only was Dean still breathing, it was now hard to tell he'd been severely beaten only hours ago. There was minor swelling in one cheek, a dried crust of blood here and there, but that was all.

Quick as a snake strike Dean sat up, the shock of it setting Jamie back on his butt. "Hi," said Dean in a flat voice. Then, just as quickly, he lay back again, snoring. His leg kicked out to the side once, twice.

Jodi snapped forward at least as quickly as Dean had. Her hand was around his throat, two long fingernails pinching his Adam's apple. She hissed, "What the fuck have you gotten us into?"

He gently pried her hand away. "You aren't going to like this answer . . . but I don't quite know. We'll talk later, okay? I'm not sure it's safe right now."

"You're not sure? They beat him half to death and now he's crazy. What the fuck am I doing here? I've known him one week, and this is the first time I've even spoken to you. I heard about you running around in your clown suit. What kind of freak serial killer are you?"

"Look . . . this is not a normal situation—" Her hand went for his throat again, and he dodged. "What I mean is, this isn't a case of drug dealers or some criminal gang. They're not going to kill us." He thought this was *probably* true, but either way she'd need to hear it said. "Look, you are going to see some very weird shit pretty soon, okay? You'd better brace yourself. Play along, as much as you can. They say they want us to help them out for a couple of weeks, tops."

"What kind of weird shit do you mean that's weirder than what I already—"

"I mean *magic*, real actual magic." He saw the contemptuous disbelief in her face—she was a skeptic. That did not bode well for her sanity in the short term. "I'm serious, Jodi, they call it circus magic, it's real." She'd turned away from him, laying down again as if to sleep. He said, "They say they're the good guys, that they saved you and Dean from danger. I don't know if that's true, but there's enough weird stuff going on that it just *might* be true, in part anyway."

"They beat him half to death to save him from danger? Do you even know what you're saying?"

"That was a misunderstanding. He was standing there with a baseball bat like he was about to jump me. But you're right, they beat him half to death and look at him now. Hardly a mark or bruise on him. His nose was smashed, Jodi. He was probably in a coma. Look at him now." She had stopped listening. He could think of nothing better to say than: "Brace yourself, play along."

A hand yanked him out of the tent. It was Rufshod. "You're sleeping with us," he said. "You're a real clown, you passed your audition, just like I had to. Him? No audition." Rufshod's face bunched up in distaste.

"Well, you know, he didn't get much choice in it."

"Neither did y—I mean, yeah, good point."

"I'm not sleeping tonight, I don't think. Too much to think about. And this face paint's got me revved up."

"Take it off if ya want."

"No way!" Jamie jumped up to exaggerated heights then slowly floated down. "Had dreams where I do this all the time, off roof-tops and buildings."

Rufshod shrugged. "Want to go break stuff?"

Jamie laughed. Random vandalism, not an uncommon teenage hobby in these parts. Why not? "Sure. Let's go get that paper mill."

Meanwhile in the clown tent, Gonko threw himself across the mattress, muttering curses.

"Wh—whatsa matter, Gonko?" said Doopy.

"This whole fibbing-to-Jamie gag. For starters, where's JJ? Say what you will about that slimy chickenshit, he could accept a little moral creativity when it came to running a circus. But now I gotta create a train wreck in a few days just to prove these two tricks woulda died if we didn't take 'em."

"Hey, boss, but at least you don't gots to pay the new JJ, he don't even know nothing boss, not even about powder."

"I ain't gonna stiff a clown out of his pay. I'll save Jamie's cut, assuming he earns it when we bring some tricks through. George's first show is tomorrow. I'll head down to keep an eye on it."

"What about the new clown, Gonko? Did you hear, we got us a brand new clown and we done beat him up real bad, and Rufshod's blue coz of no audition."

"Glad you reminded me. Let's go see what this new clown's made of."

It was just after dawn when Rufshod and Jamie returned to the campsite. Teenage Jamie and friends would have saluted, had they seen what became of that paper mill. Howling fire trucks were just now starting to arrive and pull into the place. A plume of smoke billowed up in a thick pillar. The pair of them had also "decorated" the nearby train station and police station. They broke into a nearby Woolworths to swipe some supplies—chocolate, candy, as well as balloons and streamers.

Rufshod had said the boss would be pleased with this loot, but when they returned Gonko got Jamie in a headlock. "I thought you said this guy was funny," he said.

Dean was awake. Also, Dean was in perfect health; any lingering trace of the beating was gone. His new clown clothes hung loose and clung tight in places they shouldn't. He blinked around calmly at the others, with not the least sign of fear or alarm on his face. Doopy, Goshy, Rufshod, and Gonko closed in a ring around him. "Joke," Gonko demanded.

"Why did the chicken cross the road?" said Dean, peering through casually lidded eyes as though all this was rather beneath him.

"You go on and tell us why," said Gonko.

"I really don't know. That's why I asked."

"Tell us another," Gonko snarled. "Go on."

"You'll like this one," said Dean. "Knock knock."

"Who's there?" said Jamie when no one else would.

"Nokia."

"Nokia who?"

"Nokia mobile phone."

In the thick silence following Gonko shuddered, twitched. "What the fuck is that supposed to be?" he screamed.

"It's a kind of anti-joke joke," said Dean serenely. "Trust me, bro, the crowd will love it."

"Oh, no," said Gonko. "I am not jolly old Saint Theresa, I admit. But there's no way in hell I would inflict *you* on an audience."

"Just try and stop me, bro," said Dean.

Quickly Rufshod ran to Gonko (whose face was literally red by now) and whispered in his ear. Gonko looked at Jamie, somehow restrained himself, and staggered away, his whole body shivering.

"Gee-whiz," said Doopy.

"Dean?" said Jamie. "Are you okay?"

"Fine," said Dean. He lay flat and did ten pushups, then twenty, then just kept on going.

"We call him Deeby now," Doopy whispered in Jamie's ear. "Deeby the clown. But . . ." he squirmed, "But Jamie, he's not *funny!*"

"GEORGE!" came Gonko's scream from some distance away. Something broke. Something quite large, by the crash it made, maybe a tree. "GEORRRGE!"

While that went on, Jamie poked his head into Jodi's tent to see how she was holding up. She wasn't there. A quick stroll later he found her sitting at a table with a gypsy woman who, like someone coaxing an animal, looked like she was trying to get Jodi to accept a makeover. Lipstick and a small box of makeup lay before them on the table. Jodi was saying ". . . just want to go home. You people are insane."

"This first, yes, honey?" said the gypsy woman sweetly. "Just make you up a little first? Five minute? Then can go."

"Can go right now," Jodi said. "What will you do if I just get up and walk away? There's a cop shop five minutes away and

71

you've already got assault and abduction. What else you want to try for?"

The gypsy waved this away with long-nailed fingers and a rustling laugh. "I no keep you! You free! But Mr. Gonko, he instruct. Just a little color for you. Such pretty girl! Little color, then you have your 'cop shop.' Yes?"

It did not look to Jamie that what he'd told her had sunk in. She happened to look up at that moment and their eyes met. *Play along*, he mouthed at her. She scowled like she'd gladly bite him.

A rough hand pulled Jamie away. It was Doopy, frantically asking if he'd seen his brother—Goshy had gone missing. So he helped Doopy on a half-assed clown hunt through the campsite for a while then went back to Jodi. She sat before a hand mirror while the smiling gypsy braided her hair. "Wow," Jodi kept saying in a dreamy voice. It was the voice of someone deeply in love. The hand mirror obscured her face, but Jamie guessed she'd had her "little color." "Oh wow," Jodi said.

"We call you Emerald now, hm?" said the gypsy. "Emerald, yes? Call you something pretty, Mr. Gonko say. Then you get your own booth in show. Is nice? They all buy your kiss, yes?"

"Pretty," Jodi whispered dreamily.

"Hey, shoo clown," the gypsy snapped at Jamie. She swatted the air, made a spitting noise at him. He shoo'd, went and sat by the river. "Circus magic," he muttered to himself. A remarkable change of heart. Jodi would not be in such a rush to leave anymore, he sensed.

Nor was he, for that matter. He did not quite understand much yet, but he had to admit he was having fun here and experiencing something the normal world would never be able to match. One hell of a mess may well have been accumulating right now back in his old life, just like last time. Maybe he needn't go back and face it at all.

Goshy returned to the campsite several hours later, much to everyone's relief, since Doopy's entreaties for help finding him were growing truly insufferable. An emotional reunion took place, ignored by all who could get out of earshot as clown tears of all kinds flew out of three eyeballs (two of Doopy's, one of Goshy's): bouncing tears, colored tears resembling skittles, great fire-hose blasts which half knocked over one of the tents, curled paper streamers and more, until Doopy himself seemed to forget what the fuss was about.

In Goshy's hand was a red clay flowerpot filled with black soil. He set it down outside the tent the clowns slept in, and sickened everyone with his eerily triumphant smile. None bothered to ask questions about it, but over the coming hours the whole melodrama replayed itself exactly: Goshy would vanish, Doopy would panic, Goshy would return with another clay flowerpot, setting it carefully next to the others, and spent much of his time guarding this private treasure.

During the day, the carny folk showed much more concern about being seen by passing cars and those which occasionally pulled into the campsite to set their children loose on the swing set and slide, a long stone's throw from the circus encampment. Circus magic hid them far better in the night. Jamie sometimes watched people stop to stare in their direction, seemingly right at them, but not quite seeming to *see*. The children in particular seemed to linger their gazes longer in this direction before returning to their games, playing not quite as loud or cheerfully as before. Did they see a group of regular RV caravans? A traveling family taking a break from the road? Just a hint of color perhaps, leaving the afterimage on their closed eyes in light-drawn outlines of what was actually there? They would see it all, Jamie knew, if any of the clowns went to them and called out, in the process inviting them within the illusion. They did not do so, of course, not even to sell a hot dog or some cotton candy, nor—as Gonko might have claimed—to save them from some miserable awaiting fate.

Jodi—whom everyone now called Emerald, who answered only to Emerald (if even then)—spent a lot of time behind her mirror, being braided and pampered by the two gypsy women in preparation for tomorrow, when this small traveling show would put on their first performance. The shift in her attitude, and in Dean's for that matter, disquieted Jamie. Apparently at Gonko's own orders Jodi/Emerald wore a veil now, and would show her face to no one.

Gonko and Rufshod had vanished earlier in the day to "check on things" below, leaving Doopy in charge, a duty he took seriously for the twenty minutes he remembered it. At last the long day took its toll on Jamie and weariness overcame the face paint's buzz. He watched Dean/Deeby trying to teach Goshy how to do a push-up, then slept in the clowns' tent for the rest of the day to troubled and confused dreams.

6. BELOW

The lift lurched and rocked as it headed down. "So, boss, it's show day down there," said Rufshod.

"And?" said Gonko.

"And so, are we, um, gonna mess with George's show or what?"

"Next time. I gotta scout out how they do so, we know what acts we're gonna steal for our own show."

"Kind of dangerous, boss. Ain't it? Like, the big bosses will be way pissed if they find out."

"If we get Kurt back in charge of this whole shebang, it will be the most ultimate suck up job in Pilo history, Ruf. Life will be all soda pops and shoulder slaps and round the clock chuckles for us, you wait and see. And you'll have Uncle Gonko to thank. Just wish I knew what to do about the new guy."

"Jamie?"

"Deeby." Thinking of him, Gonko had to fight not to vomit across his shoes. "'Knock knock?' I'll knock knock his fucking teeth out."

"Sure! Why don't ya?"

"Jamie and this whole clowns-are-good-Samaritans gag. Dunno how long I can keep this up, this whole don't-lash-out-at-the-deserving thing. Bad enough I gotta play nice to George. But the kissing booth might just make up for all. You get a look under that veil? The MM's lipstick is golden pancakes with butter on top. We gotta steal some more while we're down there. I even felt a little pluck or two at my own heartstrings, Ruf, when Emerald got dolled up and made kissy faces at me. She's gonna be a hit, our star draw. You'll see."

"So where's JJ? Me and Jamie went out breaking stuff—was great and all, but it's not the same. JJ woulda helped me burn that house down or at least set that dog on fire, but Jamie didn't want no one to get hurt! Not even a dog. Weird."

"I don't get it neither," said Gonko. "Maybe the real JJ will just pop out of him like old times, but we know there's nothing wrong with the face paint."

"You sure? Deeby ain't much of a clown."

"He wasn't any part clown to start with. That's why we audition 'em, see if there's something for the face paint to work with. No sweat, we'll keep him around for now, but when we come back down he joins the lumberjacks for all I care."

The lift bumped to a halt and filled with the scent of buttered popcorn, hot dogs and, most of all, swarms of fresh tricks now shuffling dazedly across the grass and dirt. The circus music jingled, jangled, and moaned for the first time since Kurt had lost his temper nearly a year ago. Gonko grabbed Rufshod. "Now remember. If we see George, reverse psychology time. We hate it upstairs. Make your hat droop and get some cry streaks down that face. Bitch to any carny rats you see about how it's not fair we can't put on a show here. Tell 'em Gonko's losing his shit he's so sad about it."

They did see George, and only a minute or so after threading through the crowds of sleepwalking tricks. Already they left behind them a thin sprinkling of soul dust and they'd barely seen any acts yet. George was on his way from Mugabo's tent, where his ride-on goon had been left as a warning that the magician should do his list of humble magic stunts and nothing more. As a result, George was short on security detail and shriller than usual. "Gonko!" he screamed, assuming the position with his nose pushed to the clown boss's navel, eyes glaring up.

76

Gonko twitched but held in the rage for later. "We got a few good leads on the fortuneteller, boss, and we found JJ. But can't we just do us a quick little act down here today? Just some juggling and maybe the whole pants on fire gag? We clowns are so sick of being up there, away from the action. Which is the total truth."

George's laugh clattered angrily until he was gasping for breath. "Hate it up there, don't you? Well guess where you're going when the show's done? Right back up, until you bring me Shalice and everyone else on that list. And I'm working on a new list for you too. We had ten more staff abscond. You're going to find 'em."

Gonko sighed heavily. "But George, please George . . ."

"Shut it! Now listen up. Keep an eye on the dust collectors. There's thieving all over. They haven't been paid a good wage in a long time, so I want you checking pockets and give any thieves a good kicking. Report names to the lumberjacks, and I'll deal with 'em after the show. Got it?"

"I obey with great reluctance, even heartbreak, feeling the sad twang of yearning within for what may never be."

"Perfect! And stop by the freak show, Gonko, to check out my surprise new exhibit. You'll love it. Help yourself to a poke or two while you're at it. That's an order. All must poke the new exhibit." George stomped away. They heard him shrilly berating someone in Sideshow Alley.

Curiosity aroused, Gonko headed to the freak show, stopping first at the acrobat tent where their act had just begun. *Ohhs* and *ahhs* from the crowd, the works. Poking his head in, there was a healthy sprinkling of soul dust already poured across the floor—the circus was hungry. Onstage, under bright spotlights, three lithe bodies sailed between swinging rings, flipped, spun, soared a dazzling dance with gravity. Their first show, and he hated to admit they were at least as good as old Sven and his crew had been.

He checked in on a surly Mugabo who was now on his second magic show for the day, with red lash marks cut through the back of his shirt. Same old bunny trick, same old doves flying from handkerchiefs, with nervous looks over his shoulder at George's goon, waiting backstage. The crowd laughed and made their sleepwalking trick sounds of delight as the powder spilled out of them, to be picked up by dwarfs scuttling down around their feet. Gonko checked the nearest one's pockets, found a little dust had indeed been pilfered, and applied a moderately gentle kicking by his standards. He didn't want these carny rats rich and satisfied either, for that matter—it would make them harder to bribe if needed. The other gatherers got the message, sullenly emptying their pockets under his gaze.

The revamped freak show was curated by Dr. Gloom, whom many suspected possessed no physical body beneath the black leather overcoat, gloves, hood, pants, and boots, wrapped about an imposing nine-foot frame. Dr. Gloom was ever hunched over to a mere seven feet. The hood covered all but a thin slit for eyes, though they could not be seen. "Welcome," a rustling hiss occasionally seeped out. "Enjoy . . . the exhibitsss." Sooner or later Gonko would need to lay a smackdown on Dr. Gloom to confirm which of them wore the pants, as with all these new acts and performers, but now was not the time.

The circus was quieter here in the freak show dimness, the air colder. Gonko's lip curled in distaste at Wallace the Walrus, the sluggishly fat human-walrus hybrid staring stupidly at the tricks who stared stupidly at him. Now and then someone tossed a fish in for him, which he'd eat, then spray against the wall of his glass cage in a stream of projectile vomit.

"Stop that, stop that!" yelled the mermaid across from him in her harpy voice. "I won't have fish treated this way. I'm ready to sing now, you haven't heard real singing yet. Who wants to hear me sing? Ha! Who doesn't, honey." Gonko turned about to find the dirty bastard who'd shoved a screwdriver deep in each of his ears, to discover it was in fact the mermaid belting out some forgotten pop hit about how hard it was to have everything you wanted except enough attention from your man.

The next display was something Gonko could truly have done without seeing, which was the point of a freak show, he supposed. Fatso was doing his special act: eating himself. Fatso vaguely resembled a man-sized baby with rolls of soft wrinkled flesh piled in rings, a pig-like snout and large eyes, no neck, a G-string hidden by overhanging fat which quivered as he reached a shoulder to his mouth, squeezed a mound of doughy meat into a ball. His mouth had no teeth but had what seemed to be jagged pink gums, razor sharp. They sucked and sliced off a bite with the sound of slurping soup. Blood pooled in the gap he'd bitten away, dripped down in rivulets to join the streams of red his other bites had spilled. He chewed fast, swallowed, his expression somehow endearing for its innocent enjoyment. "Remember, folks, you are what you eat!" he said cheerfully. "At least, I know I am!" He went back to the same shoulder for more, then for a taste of bicep. The tricks stood disgusted and enthralled, Gonko feeling the same. But as the soul dust poured to the grass he suddenly knew what act he'd be swiping for his own freak show. This guy, at least, seemed to enjoy his work.

Moving on, Gonko came to George's surprise new exhibit. Gonko was surprised all right, to find the still living head of Kurt Pilo in a glass case, being prodded that very moment by a beer-gutted, bearded, trucker-looking trick.

Kurt's lips did not hold their normal serene smile. His eyes glared fiery hate at the trick, whom Gonko quickly tossed across the room, bowling over a handful of other tricks and maybe risking rousing them from the circus sleepwalking spell. Kurt glowered up, recognized him, and some of the fire went out of his glare. "Gonko! This is unexpected. I suppose you've been ordered here to . . . have a poke?"

"Boss. What gives?"

"Oh, I'm better than I look. My body is obscured by sheets and lighting, but I'm still attached to it. George has . . . decided to keep me confined in a rather well-designed cage, which can withstand all manner of thrashing and flexing. You know, in some ways it's nicer than being below. In other ways . . ." Gonko saw where he was coming from: being mauled and tortured below had a certain rightness about it, if it was the big bosses doing it. Being poked by every shit-kicking carny rat and trick while George laughed? That was something else, even if it was physically less painful. Kurt's voice regained some of its joviality. "Further, it is an opportunity to practice the virtues of patience and tolerance. The fish flakes I am fed have helped my flesh to regrow. It's down to my chest now, isn't that nice? And I'm growing more adept at maintaining my . . . composure." By which, Gonko knew, he meant holding on to his human form despite the sizzling hot rage that must be boiling inside him almost constantly.

"Boss, I'll get you out. I just need some more time. Hang in there."

"Oh, no hurry," said Kurt. "I'll need to regain my strength to . . . handle various managerial tasks, once I am liberated. But I eagerly await the chance to stretch my legs. Among other things."

"I get the picture, boss. Anything I can do in the meantime?"

"Be the best clown you can be, Gonko! Strive for excellence, that's my motto." Kurt looked to the entrance, lowered his voice. "You would need to ensure that Dr. Gloom is not nearby, if you wished to assist me in some way outside of the stricter regulations. He keeps a close eye on all visitors."

Indeed Dr. Gloom had entered, his hunched-forward head slowly swinging about to find the source of the disturbance Gonko caused by bowling over those tricks. Dr. Gloom's head swung their way, and he began to amble over. "I'm out, boss. Back as soon as I can."

"No rush, no rush," said Kurt serenely. "Oh, but Gonko? Hurry."

Gonko ran from the freak show and barreled into Rufshod. Both went flying in a tangle of arms and legs. A group of tricks laughed at them dreamily. "Fortuneteller's here," Rufshod said, springing to his feet.

"She what?" Rufshod led him to her hut where, sure enough, Shalice (young and beautiful again) sat before the white glow of her crystal ball, doing her whole hypnotize-the-tricks-and-get-them-to-do-seemingly-pointless-stuff-in-the-real-world-which-has-secret-long-term-ramifications-for-influencing-the-turn-of-wider-events gag. She glanced up, locked eyes with Gonko, and was knocked back in her chair in an apparent mix of anger, surprise, and fear.

Gonko bowed low, not sure where things sat with the fortune-teller. "Need to talk," he mouthed.

She nodded to the trick before her, so Gonko waited out front, eyes peeled for George. This whole go-look-for-someone-who-ain't-actually-up-there gag was fine with him just now, and would buy useful time. The trick came out; Gonko went in. He happened to have in his hand a bag of bribery soul dust, and sure enough the fortuneteller's eyes lingered on it for a good while. He tossed it to her side of the table. "Little present to say welcome back," he said.

"How generous." She made the bag disappear. "I'm very busy today, Gonko. What is it?"

"Just a friendly little chinwag."

"Friendly would make a nice change, considering two of your troupe tried to kill me."

"First I heard of it."

"Is that so?"

"You can spot lies, right? Check it out, I got all kinds of honesty happening here."

"You clowns are not so easily read, sometimes." But he sensed a slight easing in her.

"Sabotage, that's all it was. Someone was messing with everyone, Shal—Fishboy and his crew. Never would have guessed it. Nor would you, eh? What say we let bygones be? Who knows, we could even be useful to each other, should some things need to change around here."

Now he had her attention, though she smiled in a way he found ambiguous. "Useful. Are you offering to watch my back in a more general sense, or do you have something specific in mind?"

Gonko hesitated. He'd been thinking of smuggling Shalice out to his upstairs show, but suddenly it seemed a risky thing to mention—this wasn't some dwarf like Curls he could just stomp to meat paste if squealing looked likely. For all he knew, if things were going to pan out that way, she'd already be wise to it and taking some kind of fancy action to change it before he'd even know what hit him. In fact, he wished he'd not come in here at all. "So George is in charge now," he said.

"Yes," she nodded. Silence stretched out. Gonko waited. "For the moment," she added at last.

Gonko smiled, reached into his pocket for another bag of powder—he had only three left, but tossed one of them her way. "I'd guess we're on a similar page here. One thing I'll ask of you. If George gives you the whole *where's Gonko?* thing, do me a favor? Where Gonko is, is he's up there looking under every rock and shrub for the fortuneteller, and the other escaped carnies, and he's real shitty about the whole no-clown-show deal. Got it?"

"I remain a loyal servant to the circus," she replied, but he could tell—or hoped so—that she was on board, or at least wouldn't mess with him.

"Me too, lady. And if any of these new chumps gives you the lip, you let me know. Glorious days ahead, when the little storm clouds clear."

She chewed on her lower lip, debating something. "Gonko, there's a spare music box in the shed. More than one, in fact."

Ah, so she knew—knew the whole works, and he'd thought he was being careful as all get out. It so happened he was going to check for a music box before he headed up, and if there wasn't a spare, to steal the one they had. Of course she'd heard of the missing carnies, maybe even of the Funhouse break-in and the stolen head. Good thing he'd come, then—maybe she'd have worked it out regardless, with the idea still in her head that the clowns were out to get her. "That's damned sensible of management," he said, poker facing. "Never know when your music box will break or go missing or something."

He left her to it as another trick wandered in. So, she was now on the payroll. Nervous business, but it couldn't be helped.

Off to the shed, where a one-armed dwarf (impressive arm, though) snored into his chest, hand turning the handle that made the carny music sprinkle through the air. He didn't wake while Gonko grabbed the spare box and hauled it to the clown tent draped in a blanket.

Show day was nearly over. The crowd was a small one, compared to how things were humming along under Kurt, but as the night wound down, the floors were littered thoroughly with sparkling dust. The new carnies and performers did their jobs well enough to please even George, though he expressed this only by reducing lashings. Shalice had cleared a long backlog of Earthly disasters, having today set in motion fated threads like little rivers of misfortune one day to coalesce and flood the bejesus out of thousands, maybe millions of people. Below, the bosses were content when their cut was dropped down the chute. But their appetites were not quite sated. When the phone in George's trailer rang that night, the voice at the earpiece was less cold than usual when it said, "Another show . . . tomorrow."

"Two days straight? You nuts?" George whined to the dial tone, his complaint unheard. *Well, they'd gone without shows for a long time,* he supposed. So had nearly everyone else. Now the velvet bags were being passed about, a full one for each performer, a half to each carny rat. Lousy pay by old standards; a fortune to what they'd received in the long hiatus. Those caught stealing got a thrashing and nothing more, and wept into their pillows. All about the show, wishes began, in the quiet hours and places, to come temporarily true.

Gonko sent Rufshod up with the music box when all was quiet, then went himself to Sideshow Alley, seeking Curls and his crew of ticket collectors. Those were always the last to turn in after a show, having to ensure all the tricks got safely out. He found them disassembling their fancy gate pieces, which looked just like ornate garden gates with an arch on top made of black iron lattice. They were telling dirty jokes to one another, but none laughed; over the long, long years there hadn't been a foul joke they hadn't heard, and they could only hope for a reminder of when a particular joke had been funny. All fell silent as Gonko approached them.

"We ain't been stealing, Mr. Gonko, sir," said one of Curls's friends. Word had got around with typical exaggeration that Gonko had stomped four carny rats to death in Mugabo's show.

"Never mind that," said Gonko. "Curls. Tomorrow is the special day. You in?"

Curls looked at his feet. Not leaping for the chance, was Curls; a little pay from George and suddenly the risk was not quite as enticing, given what may happen if they were all sprung. Gonko crouched down, an arm around his shoulder. "Half a bag, is that all he paid you? Half a measly bag to an old-time carny?"

"Almost half. Was really more a third of a bag."

"It ain't right, Curls, ain't right at all."

"Yeah. Yeah no, you're right. Was different in Kurt's day."

"That it was. That it shall be again, and soon, if you wise up and help out Uncle Gonko. Of course, if you don't feel like it no more, that's just swell and dandy too, cause Uncle Gonko knows he can trust you forever." He said it so sweet and condescending that Curls whipped his head up, sensing a death threat (which indeed it was.)

"Oh no, Gonko. We're in, all of us. Ain't we, lads?"

The lads glanced at each other and nodded. None looked happy, but the short folk seldom were. Gonko gave them a map and some directions, walked them to the elevator, and saw them out. That done, there was just one more thing to see to. He grabbed a shovel.

Back in the dung pit, the turf gave easily to Gonko's gouging, a good thing since the first half hour's dig brought nothing but bones too old to be a recent corpse. Life and death played by different rules here in the showgrounds; so did the rules of decomposition, it seemed. He finally struck a lump, found Fishboy's head and let it drop back into the muck, muttering "Little bastard."

Next he found Winston, whom Gonko hadn't had the pleasure of killing for his sabotage while wearing clown colors. He didn't actually expect to find what he'd come for, and was about to call it a night when, with half a dozen more spades of dirt, there it was after all.

"JJ," Gonko said. "What the hell are you doing here?"

Now this was a puzzle he didn't get at all. He brought the rest of the body up—someone made a mess of it all right, no doubt Kurt himself—then tossed the shovel away. Some carny rat tomorrow would refill all these holes. He dragged the two main parts of JJ by an arm and leg across the dirt behind him, tossed them on the ground at the Funhouse door. A light was still on in there. He withheld his knock when the quiet hiss of Dr. Gloom's voice rustled out through the door. ". . . performancssse was exquisssit."

The Matter Manipulator: "Ah but I knew it would be a success! He loved to eat in his old life too. Any news about the break-in?"

"Sssussspicion and rumor, that is all. Ssome ssay thiss, ssome ssay that. Many ssay the clown iss behind it, never proof."

"The fortuneteller, they say she has returned, yes?"

"I did not ssee her today. She perhapss will assisst you better than I. You have your own inklingss?"

"Inklings come easy. Not proof. But only one performer I know has the required iron casing about his testes, to break into *this* house and steal from *me*. Oh, it has been too long since Gonko was brought before me in supplication! Not since he was a fresh new recruit was I even able to chastise him and savor a little fear. How I've yearned, yearned to make some . . . improvements to his form, a few twists here and there. His is such fine skin."

Gonko felt nauseated (and slightly flattered) to hear all this, but he couldn't stay longer—with Dr. Gloom away from his post, it was time to strike. He ran to the freak show, dug through his pockets for disguises, and ended up with a nun's habit and fake beard. His pockets gave him a second habit, much larger, for Fatso. He stalked past sleeping exhibits, including Kurt, whose eyes were rolled back to show their whites. Just to be sure, Gonko draped the cloth over his case.

Only Fatso was awake, spooning protein powder from a tub to his mouth. He was so absorbed in this he didn't notice Gonko til he stood before the glass tank. "Real sorry, lady, but show time's not til tomorrow," Fatso whispered so as not to wake the others. "But come back, you'll see a swell show!"

"George needs to see you now. Put this on, no time to explain."

"Aw, but Dr. Gloom, he told me to watch—"

Night night, said Gonko's fist. He had to think of George to summon rage-fuelled strength in order to drag the heavy lump out of the freak show, then maneuver him into his nun habit in

7. ABOVE

The trains roaring across the little bridge, spitting distance from the tent closest to the riverbank, fast became a familiar and welcome sound, helping cover with their clatter and rumble something which did not want to be heard or seen. Jamie marveled at the way the faces aboard those trains gazed out without so much as a second look down at the array of tents and stalls, all of them a bustle of activity as the carnies and clowns prepared for their first show. The camping spot seemed to be fast losing its popularity, given the number of drivers who pulled in, looked around and left almost immediately, as if sensing something amiss. Rare now were any who stayed longer than a few minutes to use the brick toilet block, and always they were in a greater hurry to leave than they'd arrived.

Dean/Deeby, when he wasn't doing push-ups or giving annoying lectures to others about what comedy was really all about, spent time showing off exaggerated clown biceps to any female in sight, most certainly including Jodi/Emerald, the shirt inflating like a balloon to absurd degrees. Experimentally, Doopy snuck up behind him on one such occasion with a pin, but rather than popping the inflated bicep a thin jet of blood squirted out. Deeby informed the world it hadn't hurt at all then stomped Doopy pretty badly before rolling him down the riverbank, provoking a Goshy attack soon after, despite Jamie's attempts to calm things down. Goshy got up on the train bridge, waited til Deeby passed below, then landed on him like an anvil. Something went crunch, but Deeby ended up bench pressing his confused attacker for the next half hour or so, which Goshy seemed not to mind at all, judging by the satisfied chirping and whistling he made. Doopy danced around this display nervously, promising to tattle to Gonko and maybe even to Mr. Bigbad.

Deeby then went fishing with a spear he'd made, pulling from the river all manner of exotic things, none of which actually existed in the river before. In Jamie's day it didn't yield much more than occasional catfish, but Deeby's haul included a shark and an octopus, which the gypsy women gladly cooked. Soon Deeby was their favorite clown, and Jamie hardly had to tell him anymore to play along. Dean was clearly having the time of his life, and it did just a little to swing Jamie's opinion back from the sinister conclusions he'd been drawing about this circus and its people.

And okay, yes, it was weird here, ugly at times too . . . and these were weird people, if they could even be called people. Did that make it necessarily sinister or evil? Usually evil disguised itself as normal, even seemed pleasing to the eye and blended in. These beings and their ways hid from sight mainly because the world would not fathom them, even if they were good beneath the visible ugliness.

Emerald/Jodi too seemed right at home. She loved being fussed over, groomed, dressed by the gypsies, and adorned with their strange jewelry. She paid Jamie no mind when he went to check on her well-being, in fact disdainfully dismissed him with a regal flick of her fingernails, prompting the gypsy women to chase him off with knives bared. He just once got a peek under her veil when she adjusted it and could hardly believe his eyes. He'd thought of her as merely "cute" before—still a level of attractiveness for which Jamie would traditionally have undergone all manner of insane male questing, should he have a chance with such a girl. Now though, she was something else altogether, a drop dead knockout in some odd unearthly way, and it wasn't even clear what exactly had changed—the same face, same not-quite hourglass body and auburn hair. The eye was just drawn to her and did not want to look away. It was a good thing (for her sake) she wore that veil; he, and maybe everyone else, would otherwise spend most of the day staring at her, and some of these clowns seemed not so great at impulse control.

He was still no closer to answers about what happened "last time," other than what peculiar (even miraculous) things he'd seen with his own eyes. The only info he got was from a dwarf named Knuckles on his cigar break. It was not the dwarf who'd tried to kill him yesterday (that dwarf still glowered when he came near.) A stout bearded thing fresh from Tolkien's pages, Knuckles pulled from his pocket some paper and hesitantly read a prepared answer: "What we do at the shom—I mean show—is to extract the bad luck and stick—sickness? What man if fests? In the form of this crystal stuff what falls to the grond. Ground. Like what were in that bag you have. We then collect the bad stuff and so it can be destroyed and . . ." The answer (or the effort reading it) was enough to put the dwarf to sleep, until the cigar burned down to his fingers.

A prepared answer to a question rather different than the one Jamie had asked? Suspect, yes, but hardly the strangest thing that had happened lately. Maybe the dwarf was none too bright and needed to keep a written reminder of his own life's purpose. Or of course that pesky other possibility, like an itch that wouldn't quite go away: they were all pulling his leg, maybe pulling the rest of him too, down into places where he did not want to go.

And as always when that itch arose, he soothed it by thinking of the family who no longer trusted him, of phone calls calling him a murderer, and of workmates who felt he was suspect. Not to mention the more usual pains in the ass of everyday life: traffic fines and phone bills, a culture yearly more depraved and perverse (morning music video shows alone a good indicator of the sickness), waking early to play the role of a slave, caught in traffic, ageing, dying, all for no real point unless you could become emotionally invested in the outcome of a football game. If he was going somewhere bad, how much worse could it be than where he'd come from?

When Gonko finally returned—preceded by the arrival of several new dwarfs, for whom an extra tent had to be raised—the clown boss had with him a large being draped in a nun's habit. The rest of them got a glimpse of knees and ankles like huge marshmallows of milky flesh, and feet whose skin jiggled liquidly with each step. "Say, I'm going to be able to perform here soon, right?" said a frightened voice before Gonko ushered him into the one tent Jamie (and the other new recruits) had been forbidden to enter.

That done, Gonko gathered the other clowns together (excluding Deeby and Jamie) for a whispered conversation that involved much pointing and staring in Jamie's direction. He saw shrugs, baffled expressions, and was given the distinct impression he'd done something wrong. When the huddle parted, however, nothing was said to him about it.

Gonko approached. "Rest up. Show day tomorrow. We'll knock 'em dead."

Jamie said, "Cool. So aren't you going to put signs up to draw a crowd? How you plan to get people in here? We're kind of hidden away."

"Fret not, my sweet." Gonko pointed to the train now clattering over the bridge loaded with commuters. "Every one of those tricks is going to be here tomorrow. Ticket collectors will set up the gates between seven and eight, over at the train station."

This meant little to Jamie. "Not very selective, then, the process of who needs their bad luck and illness removed?"

"Eh? What the f—oh, right. Selective as all get out, my young caperer. Each one of them tricks has been thoroughly vetted by the research department. Now, we ain't had time to rehearse an act, so we're doing old material, unless you can think up some new gags by tomorrow. If not, your mission will be to keep Deeby the hell off my stage. He messes up my act, I mess up his physical structure. Got it?"

"Sure. But yeah I have a couple of skit ideas, like this one where—"

"Later, later. Gonko has had a busy few days and is gonna kick back a little with Marilyn. Oh, and what the hell is Goshy doing with all those flower pots?"

"Looks like he's just collecting them." Now a dozen of the red clay flowerpots sat in neat rows of four beside the clown tent. "Seems harmless enough, unless I'm missing something?"

"Yeah, well. He's got a history with that kind of deal. Advice: stay away from the pots." Gonko stomped over to the clown tent, kicked out Doopy and Rufshod, and then hung a DO NOT DISTURB sign on the front. Some minutes later they heard him say, "I'll make you a star all right, toots. But it's gonna cost you."

Doopy, adjusting his hat, said, "Did you hear, guys? The boss found JJ! Gonko done gone and went and found himself JJ! And he's gonna bring him back, just like us was bringed back."

"Shh!" said Rufshod, wincing.

"Oops. Oh gosh, it's a secret, ain't it?

Jamie looked from one to the other. "Who or what is this JJ?"

"It's nothing," said Rufshod.

"Yeah, there's no such thing as no JJ," said Doopy. "Besides, JJ is dead. Just like we was, hey, Ruf? JJ's all dead."

Jamie's sleep was not deep that night, with the face paint's stimulating effect, the odd train's racket, and his own subconscious murmuring unsettling things. The other clowns snored on air mattresses beside him. It was still dark when Doopy's hour-long fart woke him and forced him to bite a knuckle to keep from waking the others with his laughter at the variety of sound, some of it in fact rather melodic, but the rancid stench that soon filled the tent sent him staggering out into the night. Thick clouds veiled a nearly full moon, and it was graveyard quiet in the carny camp. Muffled giggling and Deeby's voice from a tent across the way indicated he and Emerald were still an item, albeit a quieter one than before. Again, their obvious comfort here took the edge off some of his doubts.

He'd noticed without noticing that Goshy hadn't been on his mattress with the rest of them. A rustling sound came from the other side of the tent, where the flowerpots were. He crept round behind it and went still at what he saw.

Goshy's pants were down; his back was turned to Jamie. Two bulbous wrinkled flesh pads glowed white as twin moons. He stood among the flowerpots, each filled with lush black soil. Now and then Goshy's hips gyrated, causing ripples and shudders through the flabby whiteness of thigh and backside. His arms as always were locked stiff at his sides, fists bunched in white gloves. Slowly, with apparent difficulty, he bent at the waist, opening with horrible inevitability the golf ball sized chasm between the buttocks as he lowered himself down upon the flowerpot at his feet.

The movements had been so slow and careful til now that Jamie was nauseated by the sudden speed with which Goshy jerked his pelvis back and forth, pressing waves of exposed flesh together like kneaded dough. Faintly his whining breath squeezed out with interjections of surprise wedged in: "Nggh, nggh, oo! Ngh . . . oo!"

Jamie was transfixed, hardly able to guess what he watched. It may have been some odd form of masturbation, or it may have been defecation into the pot, but it seemed too removed from such normal earthly behaviors. Maybe the clown enjoyed the feel of dark moist soil on that one region of his skin, and for some reason did not think to apply it by hand.

Suddenly Goshy stood. In the motion of standing Jamie had the briefest glimpse—it was less than a second, so he could not be sure—of a thin tube-like appendage, not genitalia but something more like an aardvark's snout, sliding up from the dirt to vanish into the flabby wrinkled mass. Pants still down, the clown turned. Its flat teeth were bared, the flesh about its face pulled tight in pink rings, its eyes wide, moist, and insane. They locked onto Jamie's.

He couldn't move. In that moment all the half-hearted explanations fell away like the nonsense it all was, revealing *this* thing, shameless and insane and evil. This was his family now, said a gleeful cackling demon dancing victorious inside him, mocking him and rubbing in his loss. This is what stole your life and is now to use you, for a while, as its plaything.

Goshy's teeth clattered together, loud as typewriter keys. His eyes bored in, unreachable and foreign. A train rumbled across the bridge, its cars loaded with cattle. Jamie screamed and ran.

Crouching by the river til the sun came up, it was some while before he could rationalize what he'd seen, but more to the point what he'd *felt* in those seconds. Soon—not convincingly, but well enough—he found again the comfort of the lies, and managed in a small, half-hearted way to believe in them.

It was show day. The rage Gonko flew into was minor by his measure when he saw no stage had been built yet (Doopy had been ordered to see to it) nor any seating arranged. The dwarfs hurriedly got busy stealing wood from the campsite's fence and barbecue tables, then wandered across the river to the other park for more. Seats were pulled or sawed off their concrete bases and stacked in rows in the largest tent, the result being a tight squeeze for maybe fifty or sixty spectators, and standing room at the back for half as many again. Over the following hours, with much yelling, hammering, sawing, and weeping, a platform was built. It was only a meter and a half high since wood and time were scarce, with nowhere near enough stage room for Gonko's liking.

Done with his latest outburst, he grabbed Jamie by the collar and snarled, "Skits! You said you had ideas. Lay 'em on me."

"Well, okay, so Goshy gets up in a high place, maybe on a stepladder? And the crowd is told he's going to dive into a glass of water below. And they're maybe expecting some magic trick or stunt, since it's obviously impossible. But he dives and lands flat on it, crushing the glass of water with a big noise and all that. Just a kind of slapstick thing, only you'd want to use a plastic cup so as not to cut—"

"It ain't slapstick without actual blood," Gonko said. "Meh, we'll use it. Real glass, though. What else you got?"

Jamie was halfway through telling an idea about a restaurant sketch involving food that caught fire when something akin to a baby's cry turned both their heads toward Goshy's flowerpot collection.

Throughout the day Jamie had forced himself to hang around with the other clowns and put last night into the neat and tidy overreaction/misunderstanding he now almost believed it was. He'd gone out of his way to be polite to Goshy, examining the clown's strange face for any sign of malice or anger at his having witnessed . . . whatever exactly it was. There was no clue given—the boggling eyes peered at him, ever bewildered, now and then the left eye narrowing to a slit, the only indication of any displeasure. But that same look was given to Dean/Deeby, and to the gypsy women who shooed the clowns away from Emerald.

Goshy now stood among the flower pots, a smile pulling his face taut and bunching skin in flabby rings about his neck, forehead, and up under his hat. Goshy peered, bulging eyes glowing with proud delight as Gonko, Jamie, and Rufshod came over. Doopy, already there, was too worked up for words—he could only hop from foot to foot making excited attempts at speech. "Oh, gee, guh, mmbh."

In one of the pots—in fact, in three of them—were tiny clowns. Doopy reverently picked up one pot with a trembling hand and showed them. A miniature Goshy—the exact image of him, even down to its clothes—stood and swayed in the pot, knee deep in soil. Its mouth opened and made tiny wailing sounds, baby cries.

Jamie bent over and retched up the stolen Woolworths chocolate he'd had for breakfast.

"Ain't it super?" Doopy managed at last to say. Gonko poked the tiny Goshy with his finger; it attempted to suckle the end of it. Doopy promised, "I'm gonna feed 'em milk, and, and learn 'em to talk real swell. Can't we keep 'em, Gonko? You just gotta say yes—you just gotta!"

Gonko himself was struggling for words. "Freak show," he said. "Keep 'em there. Maybe we'll use one in the act."

"He's gonna make *more*, Gonko. Ain't it super?"

Goshy emitted a proud noise, "Gahhh." His mouth hung loose.

"How big they gonna get?" said Gonko, eyes roaming to the river more than once.

"Well, gee, we dunno Gonko, cause this ain't never, it's the first time we, we didn't never have to—"

"All right, goddammit, keep them. Don't make too many more. I don't even wanna know how or why. It's that MM, I'll bet, that scumfuck. But both of you owe me a bang-up show tonight; I wanna see some first rate clowning. You got that?"

"Sure, boss, you name it!" Doopy pawed Jamie's shirt, pushed his face so close the beads of sweat on his nose touched Jamie's skin and dripped down. "Ain't it the bestest thing in the whole wide world?" he whispered.

"They're . . . they're cute. Real, really cute," Jamie said. Doopy's wide white eyes were suddenly bigger than the whole world to him, his fingers still pawing and paddling Jamie's shirt. God alone knew what he may have done with a different kind of answer.

"Help, help!" one of the baby Goshys on the ground cried. "Help!" The other two joined in. "Help, help!"

"What the fuck?" Gonko screamed, jumping away from the flowerpots.

"It's the first word I learned 'em," said Doopy. "Ain't they clever? They can talk so neat."

Gonko staggered away and frantically looked for something else to think about. Jamie did likewise.

Night came. Gonko studied his pocket watch very carefully, waiting, waiting . . . at last he gave word to Curls and the other ticket collectors, who seemed to realize by now that all of this was far beyond anything George had ordered despite what Curls had told them, and that by now they were just as doomed as Gonko, should word get back below. They were very nervous as they trudged at last over to the train station, a short walk made longer by the gate pieces they carried. Their location was supposed to be a country fair halfway across the planet, but they set up the gates almost entirely unnoticed even as trains pulled in and spewed out hundreds of commuters. When these tricks got below, after Gonko's circus had milked them, it may be noticed: very few children and babies, rather more suits, briefcases, and newspapers folded under arms than the usual crowd. And of course, much less soul dust.

Emerald was unveiled. The gypsy women made no secret of the knives tucked into their belts. They had a busy time shooing clowns and others away from her wooden booth, where KISSING BOOTH was painted across the front with no mention of a price. Emerald stood radiating her unearthly beauty and regular earthly boredom as she, with the rest of them, waited for the tricks to come through the lattice gates.

"Music!" Gonko screamed. The dwarf assigned the task began to spin the music box's handle. A calliope moaned, xylophone notes tinkled down like rain, brass wind wheezed good cheer, and cymbals crashed.

"You ready, Goshy?" Doopy said into the ear of his statue-still brother. "We gots to make the people *laugh* soon. We gotta make 'em laugh for reals."

And the freak show tent was opened just as the tricks began to come through, with only a few seconds of confusion at the sudden change in their surroundings from train station car park to *here*. By then the music was in them, as was the scent of cotton candy, filling them with giddy good cheer. A small carnival, but a happy one. A dwarf with a dice game, his velvet case filled with glittering rubies and sapphires for prizes; another who made a coin vanish under paper cups, with more pirate treasure on offer if you could guess the right one. And, further around in between the two small "streets" of tents, a woman of exceeding beauty, smiling, waiting for the gypsy lady to bring forth, one by one, her customers. Nervously they were led to her; and now there was no such thing as a girlfriend, wife, fiancée, or even a woman. Emerald was the first they'd ever seen; the first to plant cool, long fingers on each cheek and for three, four sweet seconds of bliss, the first explore their mouths with hers, leaving them in a giddy happy daze. Emerald was a hit, even with some female customers, though not one person was allowed back in line for a second kiss. None guessed as to the reason why she crouched down in her booth, after each customer—as the gypsies had coached her—and spat into a bucket little glittering shards like crushed precious gems. The buckets filled fast. The gypsy women smiled secretly at each other and carried filled buckets away.

In less impressive amounts, the powder littered the floors of the small makeshift Sideshow Alley. In the freak show tent, one of the baby Goshies thrashed about in its flowerpot, frightened of all the people who stepped in to stare. Nearby, the head in a case grumbled, "Preposterous! Blocks the view . . . never seen such rot. Medical science. Pish posh!"

Fatso ripped huge chunks from his other side, letting yesterday's wounds heal, and was a sheen of blood which he could hardly wait to lick clean, or scoop to drink with a desert spoon. His one-liners were delivered with cheer: "I make sure to get plenty of the three major food groups—me, myself, and I!" and "They say putting your foot in your mouth is a bad thing. Not me! Watch!" and out came a bite sized morsel from the marshmallow flesh. The Matter Manipulator's living chair watched on sadly, and it watched the powder raining across the floor. "Anyone want a taste?" said Fatso, pointing to those parts of himself he couldn't reach, but there were no takers.

Of course the freak show was not everyone's cup of tea, but few wanted to pass on the clown show. Their tent was packed, with Jamie backstage watching from close quarters, as he'd be performing on the next show day, or so he'd been told. Deeby was nowhere to be seen—Gonko had made it murderously clear to all that Deeby was allowed to meet and greet the tricks, and twist a few balloons into shapes, but no more than that.

Doopy and Goshy had been told they owed some bang-up clowning, and they delivered. Laughter filled the tent as the pair of them played husband and wife in the delivery room with Gonko in the role of the clumsy doctor. Goshy, the expectant mother, staring about in bewilderment as Gonko produced a hatchet and made all manner of chopping, sawing noises beneath the sheet between Goshy's legs. Rufshod the nurse played a relatively straight role, though he set the sheet on fire right before Gonko emerged with a flowerpot. The baby Goshy thrashed around in actual fright, squealing "Help, help!" Though he was the father, Doopy breastfed it from his bicep which somehow squirted milk all over the place.

Following that, Gonko did some corny hat-falls-off-and-can't-be-put-back-on gags (with all manner of objects falling from the hat) while he pretended to run for president, miming a speech to the others, his constituents. Each of them responded to misinterpreted commands in Gonko's wild gestures. The eventual result was a riot among the clowns, with Rufshod trampled half to death . . . to be revived by Gonko the clumsy surgeon, who whipped back on his white coat and stethoscope but (comically) could not bring himself to do mouth-to-mouth. Doopy did it instead, and there followed a parody of a movie romance scene: the lights dimming, sexy saxophone music playing, lunging and thrusting under a sheet, and the same baby Goshy was pushed shyly out, crying again "Help, help!"

The crowd loved it. They loved the Goshy-diving-into-a-glass grand finale, the realistic way he plummeted down from a three foot step ladder to crack the glass with his sternum, the way the blood gushed out, and the clown's kettle noises of distress. "Hmmm! Mmmm!" beseeching the front row for help.

And Gonko the clumsy surgeon reappeared, ready to operate . . . but he froze, growled, anger standing the cords out in his neck. To his, and Jamie's consternation, Deeby picked that moment to make his way through the crowd and up onto the stage.

"Get out," Gonko hissed at him.

The other clowns peered, perplexed as Deeby cleared his throat. "Your attention please. We're all enjoying tonight's antics. But there's one thing no one should laugh at: pollution."

"Oh my God," Gonko said. He went to Rufshod, whispered an order, and Rufshod dashed out of the tent.

"Did you know that discarded cigarette butts end up in our waterways and are mistaken by fish and even dolphins as food?" Deeby went on earnestly. "Did you know that plastic six-pack rings can choke turtles and inhibit their growth? While these clowns may recycle their jokes, you can bet they also recycle their plastic. You do the same! And please, please don't litter."

The timing of this worked out pretty well, in the end. Rufshod came back with a large aluminium garbage can from just outside, handed it to Gonko, who now tipped the lot over Deeby's head, spilling uncounted weeks' worth of filth, food wrappers, old fish bones, and reeking garbage water. He jammed the can down in one brutal motion, splitting the bottom so Deeby's head burst through it. The crowd—who'd not known at all what to make of the pollution speech—laughed like it was all a planned gag, and some of the murder went out of Gonko's eyes.

Some, but not all. He rolled the garbage can off the stage and outside, gesturing for the other clowns to clear the tricks out of the show tent to make way for the next batch; judging by the thick carpet of sparkling dust over the floor, this crowd had been harvested for all they were worth. He rolled Deeby towards the river. Jamie ran out after them.

"I don't appreciate this," Deeby said. "Just because we have different ideas about the true purpose of comedy. Emerald is totally going to hate this garbage smell."

"If that's the worst thing happens to you today, you be grateful, chumbo," said Gonko as they reached the riverbank.

"Real comedy makes people think," Deeby said. "Your act was superficial and needed some social commentary. I gave it much needed depth."

"Uh huh, you just keep right on talking, pal."

"When my hands get free, bro, it's on. You and me."

"Oh, it's on all right," said Gonko. The garbage can rolled into the river. Gonko stood on its side, balancing like a surfer as Deeby thrashed beneath the surface. "What say now, professor?" said Gonko. "Glug glug glug?"

"Gonko, come on, get off him," Jamie said nervously.

"Sure, pal, just give me a quarter hour, and I'll be right off."

"I mean it, Gonko, you're going to kill him."

"That's the plan."

"Come on, maybe he shouldn't have gone onstage but they laughed when you threw the trash on him. It worked out all right."

"You liked that improv, eh? Watch and learn, young Jamie. This gag is called *Drowning Some Fucker*."

"Gonko, get off him."

Air bubbles popped on the water's surface. Deeby thrashed hard for a little while then went still. Jamie ran forward and threw himself at Gonko, knocking him deeper into the river. The bin tilted. Deeby's head broke the surface, and he gasped hard. The face paint had begun to run off his face.

Gonko burst through the water's surface with an axe in hand. "There are some things you need to learn vis-à-vis the whole interfering-with-clown-chain-of-command thing," he said, raising the axe.

"Hey, boss," Rufshod called from the riverbank. "Jamie's okay. Don't you remember?" He mouthed the words, *good guys*.

Gonko paused, considered. "I dunno, Ruf. That's getting to be a bit of a hassle, that whole deal. Frankly, this Jamie ain't exactly clowning the house down neither."

"You need to give me a chance," Jamie said, backing away. "You didn't even let me on stage tonight."

Gonko dropped the axe over his shoulder. "Well, now's your chance. Get up there and caper some, sport. *This* pile of puke is never again wearing the clown uniform. You got that?" He pointed to Dean, who had, in rubbing mud from the river from his face, cleared away most of the face paint by now. He coughed up river water then sat bewildered like someone who has woken up in an expected place.

"Anything you say boss," Jamie said quickly. "Just give me one minute with Dean?" Gonko wasn't listening. He strode out of the water, back toward the stage tent.

"Dean! You okay?" Jamie said. Rufshod watched them for a moment more then followed Gonko up the riverbank as a train thundered across the bridge overhead.

"Jamie," Dean said, coughing. "What the hell is going on?"

"You pissed him off, that's what. He was going to kill you. Why the hell . . . man, I *told* you not to go onstage! Why the hell did you get onstage? I just saved your life, do you realize that?"

"I . . ." Dean tried to think. "I wasn't myself. Something changed."

"What do you mean? Are you drunk? High?"

"I'm getting out of here, Jamie. I haven't been *me* these last couple of days. It's like someone else took over, and he's not afraid of these people at all. He thinks he can take any one of them on. Why? What the hell changed me?"

"I don't know. The clothes? The face paint? They make me feel a little different too, but not like what you're saying. There's magic here, Dean, some kind of magic. I don't understand it . . . but look, you can't run away. They'll find you, just like they found me. And maybe kill you. You know about them now, you see? They won't like that."

"So we're in deep shit, huh?"

"Maybe. . . I mean, they told me they're the good guys, but they don't act like it. There's something weird going on, weirder even than the crazy stuff we can see. Stay cool, okay? The clowns aren't dangerous if you don't make them angry. Stay cool, lay low, play along. At least until we know what we're really dealing with."

Dean looked at him—his face showed fear, but not only fear. Jamie also saw that he was thoroughly, righteously pissed off. He said, "And when we know what we're dealing with?"

"I don't know, Dean."

"Well, I do know. We take them out, Jamie."

So Jamie the clown got onstage and had his moment. He capered and clowned like his life depended on it, with a potent mix of adrenaline, fear, and face paint magic coursing through him. He shrieked like a hysterical woman when chased by Rufshod the Romantic, armed with roses and a heart-shaped chocolate box. He copped a cream pie followed by a brick pie to the face and hardly felt it. He threw, when prompted, a rolling pin at Goshy's belly, which bounced back at him and knocked him stupid. The crowd of tricks hooted, jeered, laughed. The sounds were like an ocean far away. When they cleared out, he still lay flat on his back breathing hard. The other clowns' faces popped into his field of vision above.

"He's . . . why, he's a clown, Gonko," Doopy said breathlessly. It was high praise.

Gonko's lip curled. "Then he's very lucky. You did okay, I guess." The four heads withdrew. Jamie heard in Gonko's words the unsaid: *Forgiven, for now. You live to fight another day*. And in Jamie's mind, it was said reluctantly.

When Gonko's pocket watch alarm went off, he sent word out to the ticket collectors, who'd brought their gate pieces back from the train station. "Send 'em down," Gonko told them. "Show time below."

Curls and his friends had set other gate pieces up further down the way, beneath the train bridge. Gonko and the others herded the tricks like border collies herding sheep, with just as much barking and growling. Jamie watched them go through the gate and vanish to God knew where. When the last of them was through, the dwarfs disassembled the gates.

"What's eating you, Curls?" said Gonko.

"The lice on my nuts," Curls snapped.

"You'll cheer up real pretty when we see the pay packet coming your way tonight."

In fact Curls cheered up right then and there, but was still troubled. "It's this thing with train stations," he said. "You got people in car parks, waiting to see their friend tricks come through after a train pulls in. But their friend trick is late. And he don't show up at all. And there's heaps of friend tricks maybe still there waiting and getting scared."

"So?"

"So they report 'em missing to their cop tricks, and then their friend tricks show up in the car park, few hours later, when the two shows get done with 'em. They'll know somethin' happened."

"Don't worry your curly little head. The cop tricks will look for 'em and not find squat. They'll be home late is all, and have to explain it to wife and husband tricks. Which ain't my problem nor yours. Any of these tricks notice you?"

"Didn't look like it. We know how to hide."

Jamie left them to it and observed the feverish new activity all through the tents and the grass around them. On their hands and knees, carnies crawled over every inch, picking up little glimmering shards with pinching fingers and tweezers, digging around at times for particles that had been stepped on. It was the look in their eye he found troubling . . . this stuff, according to Gonko, was a manifestation of illness, bad luck, bad karma, and whatever other problems infest a person. Those who collected it, their faces shone with hunger and greed. Buckets were filling up with the stuff. They were carried to the clown tent, each bucket's passage followed by eager eyes. In the clown tent, Rufshod scooped the stuff with a soup ladle into velvet bags, just like the one Jamie had found in his pocket "that night."

This alone didn't strike him as any more suspicious than, say, Gonko's eagerness to use violence or Goshy's creepiness. But later, when the exhausted carnies slept—and while Jamie naturally couldn't—he crept among the tents, watching, listening.

Gonko had distributed the velvet bags—three for each carny, more for certain favored individuals like Curls. All of it received with simpering gratitude, many bows of thanks. It was like a boss delivering pay—exactly like that, in fact, only more so. So why would the bad luck, bad karma, et cetera of "tricks" be the carnies' *pay?*

Curls himself helped answer some of this, though everyone had clearly been told not to answer any of Jamie's questions. The dwarf took a bag and a little glass beaker with him and snuck off into the park, til he was over by the gazebo, now robbed of most of its wood. There was a swing set there attached to a slide. Curls climbed to the top of the slide, looking over his shoulder many times, but seemed unable to see Jamie the clown, with the night's darkness pulled about him.

Curls tipped the powder—it wasn't clear just how much—into the beaker, lit a match with trembling hands and held the flame to the glass. The firelight lit up his twitching face, the lips smacking and licking. "I wish," he said, and mumbled the rest.

Half a minute passed and nothing seemed to happen. Then Curls seemed to see someone Jamie could not see. The dwarf stared at the empty space beside him on the platform, reached out a hand and seemed to touch someone invisible. "No, taller," Curls said. "And fatter. So fat she'd break this slide." He spread his arms wide as he could. "And she's got to have a shock of black hair on half her head. And a little red dress."

The strangest thing then happened. Curls's face lit up in a moonlit leer. Down came his pants. He threw himself horizontal and began thrusting over something invisible. What made it strange was that Curls seemed to be hovering just above the surface of the platform. Jamie squinted, going closer. For just a second— and then another—he glimpsed the outline of an obese woman with her red dress rucked up around her belly, looking down the length of her torso at the vigorously moving dwarf, whose head was level with her sternum. She patted his head, then vanished, reappeared . . .

Jamie backed away from there, replaying all of it in his mind. "Superhero clowns," he whispered. "Superhero circus. Circus magic."

"Help, help!" a thin cry came from the direction of the freak show tent. "Help help help help help!"

A chill shuddered through Jamie. Something about the baby Goshy's cry was different from the way the things normally parroted the only word Doopy had taught them. Slowly and heavily his feet carried him to the freak show door.

The head in the case watched, scowling, now and then with a mutter of "Pish posh . . . nonsense. Medical science." Fatso lay on the ground inside his makeshift cage of monkey bar parts and wood, hands over his head, face to the floor. Sobs shook his jiggling flesh. The "living chair" watched on in horror as Goshy sat on a little stool. Blood covered his face. An empty flowerpot lay strewn at his feet, the soil spilled out, as were two tiny clown shoes with glistening stumps of mangled gristle poking through.

"Help, help, help . . ." wailed the little Goshy on the small round table. Goshy's eyes were unblinking. His small square teeth looked now larger than normal as he leaned slowly closer. *Clackity-clackity-clack* the teeth beat together. His shoulders shuddered. "Help, help . . ." Crotch first, he bit, bit, ate. "HELP HELP!" Goshy chewed, made a contented gurgle. A gaping bleeding mess was left in the thing's crotch. Goshy began on its thrashing arms, small fast bites. Tiny bones popped and broke in his teeth. The head he ate next, ending at last the horrible pleas, then worked through the torso til all was gone but two knobs of gristle above the soil.

Goshy stayed still, shivering. The solid slab of his head dripped sweat through the blood. A confused little whistle seeped out of him, asking a question of nobody and getting no answer. With a sudden jerk of his arm he knocked the flowerpot off the table, made a whining sound as clown tears fell through the blood caking his cheeks. Then he reached to his left, picked up the last flowerpot with the last baby Goshy inside it, placed it with stiff arms on the table, leaned back and battered his teeth together.

"Help!" it began, and Jamie had to leave. He knew all he could ever have wanted now about this circus of benevolent clowns. He'd stood frozen in horror and fear, a small part of him raging and screaming to stop the obscenity, but he couldn't, couldn't set a foot closer, couldn't even look for one second more, just couldn't. He therefore could not fathom why or how he ran in there, grabbed the flowerpot from the table and sprinted away. "Help. Help?" the tiny clown said.

From back in the tent came a blistering fire alarm scream: "EEEEEE! *EEEEEE!* EEEEEEE!"

Tent doors opened, shouts rang out, feet scuffed across the turf. Someone somehow mollified Goshy, guided him out of the freak show and back to his bed—Jamie heard it all from down by the river's edge, holding the flowerpot to his chest like a newborn's mother. "Help," it said, though its tone had changed—no fear now, and a smile on its little face. *Help* now meant thanks, Jamie supposed, and it said it over and over.

Off by the swing set and slide, Curls's little body kept on moving; his wish was not yet complete and the noise hadn't fazed him. Jamie eyed the gate pieces, now in parts, to be reassembled by Curls and his crew in a couple of hours, back at the train station. When finally the commotion died down, Jamie hid the flowerpot among some tall weeds by the river, crept silently to the gate pieces and, wincing at every chime of metal on metal, assembled the parts just as the dwarfs had done. At any moment, Gonko's hand would grab his shoulder, spin him around and lay down some "slapstick" . . . but that didn't happen. Not sure whether the task was done properly or not, or whether it mattered, he stepped through the arch . . .

And was no longer in Wiley Park.

Curls, sweating and somewhat worn out, but most assuredly satisfied, jumped down from the slippery slide's platform, marking the end of his "rest break." A dwarf just has to take the edge off sometimes. His pocket watch told him it was time to amble back to the train station with the gate pieces, and he felt so good he wouldn't even rouse the crew to come help him. They needed their rest; he'd had them chewing his ears off all day about the danger they were in. If George below worked out something was wrong with this batch of tricks, and put the word on the ticket collectors, they had a useful though not bulletproof excuse: Gonko forced 'em. If all remained roses up here, the extra pay was worth a little danger. The crew would come around, he knew—they sure didn't complain so loud when the velvet bags came their way.

The plan: set up station gates, get below, set up exit gates, herd out tricks, sneak back up here. Except now he saw someone else had set up the gate pieces here in the campsite. Nervously he checked the formation—if it were off by much, whoever had passed through could have ended up in the Funhouse basement, or even further afield. Hell, if they went down *there*, wound up in the big boss's laps, the truth would be out in quick time and they were all screwed. The settings looked okay enough—the knobs and dials were on the same setting as before.

Still, Gonko probably ought to know about this . . .

Nervously he went into the clown tent and shook Gonko's shoulder.

Gonko listened to Curls without a word. His fists shook, veins throbbed, skin reddened. He tore through the campsite to work out who was missing. Only Jamie. The bastard had gone to the showgrounds. If Jamie's gums didn't remain stapled shut while he was down there, if he blurted out so much as a hint about the secret show in the wrong company, the shit was neck deep and rising.

Sheer curiosity on Gonko's part had helped keep Jamie alive till now. Where the hell was JJ? Why was JJ's corpse buried in the showgrounds? Why did Jamie not remember them and why did the face paint not change his personality to something else? Also now in Jamie's favor was his more than decent performance onstage tonight . . . but the guy didn't quite fit in with the crew like JJ had, what with his whole *Please don't kill Deeby nonsense*, and Gonko scented possible trouble there. If Jamie went below and made a mess for him, it was axe time. Keep his yap shut, and maybe a loyalty test was passed. Time to find out.

Gonko rushed through the gates and back into George's show.

8. BELOW

The tricks were right on time. The music played, and another smallish crowd walked in a daze across the showgrounds like floating bubbles on a river, going this way and that on little ripples of current. Only . . . very few children, almost no babies. Few in the show gave this even a first thought, let alone a second. Tricks were tricks, strange and contemptuous whatever size and shape. From the window of her hut, the fortuneteller observed the tricks with interest. She sat thoughtfully before her crystal ball, sucking her lip, flicking the view here and there with a long hand, looking firstly for a sign of the clowns (there was none) and then for George.

The proprietor was in a foul mood indeed. Never a fan of consecutive show days, was George, and normally the rest of the circus felt the same. Now though, poorly paid and half crazy with wishdust withdrawals, the carnies and performers were more chipper than yesterday. They brought to their work a fevered, desperate energy. On the back of his goon, George lurched through the acts and games, screamed at slackers, and sent whip lashes in all directions, now and then tagging a stray trick. Mugabo was behaving himself, doing his paltry stunts with minimal scowls and sarcasm. Sideshow Alley was busy with tricks enjoying the games, shooting ducks, knocking bottles down, tossing balls too big to fit off the rim of baskets. The acrobats did their swooping soaring act again with the same grace. The lion tamer made his clever animals act like people. All *seemed* to be normal. Yet something was . . . off.

She panned back to George in Sideshow Alley. His arms flailed around, and he was screaming, reaching that level of agitation he sometimes got to, where all he could do was holler gibberish. Five baffled carnies stood with pockets out-turned, flinching back from the goon's raised lash. More thieves? Hardly surprising, given the state of things, but these ones looked honestly confused and certainly had no stolen dust in their pockets. More carnies were called over, Steve among them—the foolish boy who had minded her when age had fallen hard upon her, who had talked the whole time of returning here to his magical secret life. In spite of his help, she felt no overriding affection for the boy . . . yet she didn't like watching the lash whip down four times, once across his face, when clearly—by his facial expression alone—he'd not stolen anything.

That George. What had gotten into him? He'd been unusually venomous since this morning. She remembered him storming out of the Funhouse, where the Matter Manipulator had called him for a meeting with the new freak show curator. Something he'd heard in there had gotten his mood rotten indeed . . .

At last Shalice saw what was missing in this picture: dust! She quickly covered territory with waves of her hand across the glowing glass. Mugabo's show and the acrobat tent both had a meager pattering of sparkling grains, but not nearly as much as yesterday. Sideshow Alley's takings were pitiful, even this early into the day. The freak show was bare, totally bare. A very confused Dr. Gloom was craning his long body forward at the bare grass. The lion tamer, whose monkey was now serving the tigers tea, had the merest sprinkle. Even in those places making a minimal profit, the sparkling crushed-glass stuff was spattered with grey and black, like powdered coal.

Shalice sat back, pulling thoughtfully at her lip. Suddenly she knew: Gonko! The carnies who'd supposedly fled—Gonko had taken them upstairs, Gonko had his own enterprise! He was starving out the circus, all to get at George. Would George figure it out? Maybe not without her help.

Still no sign of the clowns as her hand flicked across the crystal ball. Not until nearly halfway through the night's show, when the new one came in, JJ or Jamie, whichever he was called. She remembered his first day, her own part in "conditioning" him to accept his new life. Right now he gazed around with the confusion, fear, and wonder of someone who had never seen the carnival before.

But he had seen it before, and Jamie knew it without remembering it. It was like walking through a recurring dream. The music poured down its cheerful notes; the air smelled sickly sweet, promising candy, popcorn, fun, rides, and prizes. The "tricks" all around the place moved in slow motion while Jamie threaded through them, barely seen by their glassy eyes. Many young women were among them, which made his Sir Lancelot instincts tingle in frustration: this wasn't right, these people had no idea they were even *here*. Dean's words and Dean's anger reverberated through him: "We take them out, Jamie." And now Jamie knew why he was really here: to find a way.

Instinct prickled his neck hairs, told him to get out of sight of the small furious man screaming and raging from his perch atop a lumbering giant, its whip lashing down spastically at anyone near. He hid behind a hot dog stand, and whispered "shh," to the startled vendor.

"Where's Gonko? Where's Gonko?" the little man screamed. "Which of you knows? Who's covering for him? Find him! Find the clowns! Any clowns!"

The screaming finally faded from earshot. The smiling hot dog vendor had his hand extended—apparently it was bribe time. "Later," Jamie said, knowing a bag of powder was what the gypsy wanted. "None on me. Later, okay? After we're paid." He ducked out from hiding and crouch-walked, staying as hidden as he could among the crowds. This decided his course—they thinned out to his right but made a fairly steady stream into Sideshow Alley.

Rides and games. A small roller coaster course, only a short walk in length but spiraling up high in the vague shape of a huge curled snake. This platform gizmo with seats which rose slow then dropped very fast. And not an electric cable in sight to power any of it.

Voices to his right, arguing and complaining. One of them was familiar, though now it seemed to come from several lifetimes ago. He came out from hiding among the herd of people, looked at the group of carnies—two dwarfs, a gypsy, and two other men. One of them looked his way and said, "Jamie! Where the hell have you been all this time?"

It took him a moment—the red lash mark across the man's face didn't help. He was shorter than Jamie, with a solid build and a round, somewhat child-like face. Many lifetimes ago, they had been roommates in a share house. "Steve?"

"Hell, yes it's me. Dude, you'd better get out of sight. George is looking for Gonko and any of his crew and he's not happy."

"I noticed. How long til the ticket collectors set up the exits?"

"Not long now. But George is pissed. He thinks someone's stealing all the powder. And maybe somebody is. But if you look closely you never see any of it actually dropping out of the tricks. So maybe he'll extend the show. Things aren't working right. There's been hardly any powder at all."

"I'm not surprised." The others had watched this exchange with indifference until that remark—suddenly all eyes were sharply on Jamie, and he quickly shut his yap.

Steve frowned. "Why aren't you surprised? We're all surprised. We're damned surprised. Yesterday there was no problem."

Think and think fast . . . "Well, you got no clown show, do you? How can you expect a decent profit without the clowns?"

The faces relaxed a little but still looked at him warily. Steve said, "Nah, that's not it. All we can think of is, this is the second show in two days. But the old carnies here—there's still a few left—they don't think that should make any difference."

"Hey Steve, is there somewhere we can talk alone?"

"I'm supposed to be working, but . . ."

One of the others said, "He go with you, eh? But clowns owe us a favor. Hear me? Us here at the duck game. Clowns watch our back, right?"

"You got it," Jamie said. "I'll do all I can."

They made their way to the clowns' home tent, Steve going ahead to keep an eye peeled for George. They sat on an old bed stiff with dirt and sweat—it may have once been Jamie's own bed, for all he knew. Jamie learned what little Steve could tell him about the circus. He told the tale of their being brought here, something Jamie struggled to entirely believe. The way Steve told it, Jamie had been forced to join, forced to become a clown and had never liked it here. "You were such a sniveling coward," Steve said. "You were the clown the carnies hated most. Some remember you too, so you better watch your back." The powder was indeed pay; according to Steve, it made small wishes come true, or at least gave the appearance of doing so. Wish for small things and you could keep them—cigars, a chess set, so on. Wish for more intricate things like a lover and she'd be there for a while before vanishing. The dust came from the people brought here. "Like milking cows," Steve said, though he seemed to know not much more than that. Most of what was milked got sent below to the big bosses whom no one ever saw, and who rumor held could not actually come up here without getting sick.

"That's where George gets his orders," said Steve, falling gladly into the role of lecturer. "George acts like he runs it all, but he's just a manager, like Kurt was." Steve laughed. "That Kurt, he used to creep everyone out, but the place was a lot more fun then. George in charge? Those lumberjacks are treating it like their playground. They beat up who they want or steal anything, and will just say you did wrong if you make a stink about it. They're getting paid when no one else is, so they like George all right. Tell you what, I kind of wish I hadn't come back sometimes." His hand went to the lash mark on his face. "Why don't you know any of this stuff? You worked here."

"I don't know. Can you think of what might have happened to stop me remembering? No one seems to know."

"Sure, one thing. The dust. Maybe you wished your memories away cause you got freaked out by some stuff."

A chill went through Jamie. Somehow he knew that could be it. "I wished it all away."

"Yep, so what? Just wish the memories back. I'd help you out but I used most of my stash already."

"So do you think they'd just let you walk out, Steve? If you got tired of being whipped, or worse? Back to your mother who is convinced I murdered you?" Jamie didn't realize til then that he was pissed at this guy, who'd come back *voluntarily* for God's sake, and left him last time to deal with the "real world" alone.

"I really don't know how they handle resignations," Steve said guardedly. "Most carnies don't try to leave. Guess I got off without punishment because of what Kurt did. And because I came back."

"So what if we found a way to make it so it doesn't matter how they handle it?"

"Oh, come on, Jamie, they got all kinds of magic and shit."

"I'm just saying, what if?"

Steve hesitated, lowered his voice. "Maybe I'd go back to my old life. Don't know what I'd tell them up there . . . but yeah. Guess I'd go back, if it was easy to do it."

"Listen. Keep your eyes and ears open for me, okay? Any info you learn from these carnies about the show, where it's vulnerable—"

"Whoa, I'm not agreeing to anything, not signing up for anything."

"And I'm not suggesting anything, okay? Just . . . keep me posted, if you learn anything potentially useful. That's all."

"BEAN SPILLER!" Gonko's roar ripped through the room, made both of them jump. Gonko flew vertically from the doorway, landed on Jamie and began choking. "Who'd you tell?" he said.

"Tell . . . what?" Jamie gasped. The thumbs on his windpipe eased off a little.

"Go on," said Gonko.

"Tell what, boss? There's nothing to tell. Oh, you mean how you swiped that bottle of barbecue sauce from the acrobats?"

"Good one," said Gonko. He gave Steve an appraising look. "Don't tell no one about that sauce bottle."

"Sure thing. Laters," said Steve, running from the room.

"Not a word of it?" Gonko said, shaking the collar of Jamie's shirt. "Not a word about my show?"

"Of course not, boss. I've only been here what, half an hour?"

"And you came down here because . . . ?"

"Goshy. Look, those baby things he made. He was eating them. I freaked out. I rescued one, and it pissed him off, so I ran in here to hide. But boss, listen. George is really angry at you."

This brightened Gonko's mood a touch. He patted Jamie's shirt back in place and helped him sit up. "What's his beef?"

"I dunno. They got no dust down here. Maybe he knows something."

"I doubt that. All right, you stay put. Don't move til I come get you. Know what they say about loose lips?"

"They sink ships?"

"Nope, they make Gonko stomp Jamie into a pile of slush. Here, keep yourself busy." He tossed Jamie a small velvet bag, perhaps forgetting that as yet, Jamie didn't officially know what the powder was for.

There was nothing else for it but to march right up to George wearing a pained expression of exhaustion, and to say, "George, boss, fortuneteller's not up there. We followed every lead we had and got no sign of her."

George's goon wheeled about, drool spraying from its mouth. Its eyes were dead as the lash whipped down. Gonko dodged three slashing cuts until George pressed a control panel button to stay its arm. He was shivering with anger, a sight Gonko drank up like fine wine, not to mention the first hints of panic, so sweet to taste. And it was just the beginning. George hadn't yet spoken because he couldn't—rage had locked his jaw tight. Gonko pleaded, "Boss, you got to give us our show back. We clowns are desperate and suffering and all that caper."

"My . . . trailer . . . now!" George spat out at last. Gonko bowed low and most respectfully, then went into what had once been Kurt's trailer, waiting on a rickety chair by the desk. The place stank of George and bad coffee.

Gonko's bright triumphant mood vanished as George entered flanked by the Matter Manipulator and the fortuneteller. That alone meant this was, at the very least, delicate. Then just before George slammed the door shut behind them, he had a glimpse of six musclebound lumberjacks gathering outside.

It was game on for real. Just perhaps Jamie had said too much after all . . .

Gonko feigned surprise and outrage at the sight of Shalice. "Boss, what gives? Has she been in the circus the whole time? Has our questing and searching been for naught?"

George had composed himself a little and indulged in a big shit-eating George-type grin. "She just returned. So you can start looking for the other runaways. Maybe. First you got some explaining to do."

"Like what?"

"Why is my show not turning a profit today?"

"How the hell would I—"

"Where's Fatso?"

"Who the hell is—"

"The Matter Manipulator tells me you left a clown corpse outside his door the same night Fatso disappeared. Coincidence?"

"Whoa, am I answering for the freak show now? I hardly even been on the showgrounds, now when stuff goes wrong here, I get the blame? Boss, this is madness!"

George looked at Shalice but spoke to Gonko. "Did you have anything to do with Fatso's disappearance from the showgrounds? Do you know anything about the other carnies who have fled?"

Gonko said, "Boss, that's all news to me. I wasn't a traitor last time the show had troubles, and I ain't one now. Me and my crew, we're following your orders to the letter, looking for people. But if I find out who's messing with the show, let me at 'em."

The MM leaned forward, rubbing his hands together eagerly, already appearing to measure Gonko's body parts. No doubt he was certain the fortuneteller would tell George Gonko was lying.

Shalice's eyes, cold and distant, bored into Gonko's. Her look said she wasn't playing his game, and he was right now at the mercy of two words. She had only to say *he lies* and he was back below. His hand went into his pocket and closed upon a fat hand grenade. His thumb poked through the pin. Eagerly George watched Shalice, waiting.

Shalice sat back, met George's gaze, and said, "He is telling the truth."

A stillness fell. Three heavy seconds ticked by. "Out!" George screamed. "OUT! OUT!" And he kept on screaming it long after the three of them passed through the group of waiting lumberjacks (ropes and chains in their hands) and went their separate ways.

Just to be safe, Gonko gave it a little while before appearing at Shalice's door. Wearily, she waved him inside. *This* was certainly awkward. He dropped two fat velvet bags on her table, figuring there'd be a haggle for more pretty quickly.

She made the bags vanish sure enough, sat back in her chair and said, "I hope you don't think we are now even."

"Gonko's busy. How much you want?"

She extended the palm of her hand, slightly cupping it. "You tell me, how much are these worth?" It took him a second to figure out she was referring to his balls, which were indeed sitting neatly on that long tanned palm.

Unusually short-sighted of her, was his first thought; if all went to plan, within a few more shows the big bosses would summon George below and put him through the meat grinder for years or maybe forever (far tastier payback than merely beating George to sticky paste, though Gonko still thirsted to do it). Kurt would be back at the helm, and Gonko, his pet performer, would review a mental list of who played hardball or otherwise fucked with him when stuff was risky. Shalice was now penciled in on that list. "What are they worth?" he mused. "Buyer's market, ain't it? You tell me."

Her hand bunched into a fist, withdrew. She stood and paced. "I weary of all this, Gonko," she said quietly. "Down here you lose track of years, of decades. The way normal people lose hours in a day. When I lived above just recently, it took six months before the mirror told me the truth and the years fell on me. I saw a hag."

"Looking good now, if you'll pardon my—"

"And I watched the news up there in their sad, sick world. They are nearly as depraved as we are; they prey on each other the same way we prey on them, and just like when they come here, they seldom know it. I read through their histories—much of which I created and steered from here, in this little hut, seated in that little chair. I saw things in a new light and began to hate myself and everything else. Yet when I realized the circus would return to me my youth . . . back I came. The most powerful woman in the world, known by no one, up there. And of course, replaceable the minute it suits George, or whoever else should run this circus. Perhaps you, one day."

Gonko fidgeted. "Where's this going, lady? I don't want nothing more than a bunch of cackle magnets to boss around. What I'm doing up there is a quick fix to a little problem we got named George, and that's it. I ain't ever gonna be in charge down here."

She shrugged. "Maybe so."

"Trying to grab your drift here. Almost sounds like you're sick of your job and you want out."

"Do you never get tired?"

"Nothing the dust can't fix."

"Maybe I've said too much." She sighed. "I'll tell you what I want in return for my help. One day, maybe soon, maybe years from now. I will call in a favor. It may be something small or something big. When I name it, whatever else is happening, on the day I call that favor you will drop everything else and do as I ask. Are we agreed?"

Gonko did not get her vibe at all—this was the weirdest black-mail scheme he'd heard of. "Within reason, I guess we got a deal. And here." He tossed her another velvet bag, happily in fact; had their roles been reversed, he'd have made it cost fifty times as much, at least.

The tricks were being herded out by a nervous Curls with his nervous crew. George had been by to scream at them, and though Curls played dumb in a rather ham-fisted way, panic and constant rage had taken their toll: George hardly even know where to point his questions and dust thievery was all he could scream about. The ticket collectors disassembled their gates and waited in the clown tent, as Gonko had ordered.

Jamie was still there, now and then fondling the bag of powder, listening to what he could outside. If it was true he'd wished away the memories, it had been done for a pretty good reason, and getting them back may be most unwise. But then, he'd erased them thinking he was headed back to a normal life, and look where he was now. In those memories could be key clues as to how this place may be—as Dean had put it—taken out. And if he got the memories back and found himself too traumatized to go on, he could wish them away again, right? But then, what hidden effects did all this wish-brainwashing have? How did he know he'd not end up a vegetable or stuck with total amnesia? And round and round this personal carousel he'd gone since Gonko had departed.

"How are we getting back up there?" he asked Curls, who looked tired and irritable.

"Lift," he grunted.

"That lift can take us pretty much anywhere in the world, right?"

"We're going back where we were, damn you. What you want, holiday in Jamaica? Want to see the ocean, eh? You'll have to wait. Just like I have to." Which Jamie took to mean *yes, the lift could go pretty much anywhere.* That might be something useful to know, but he had no idea why, just yet . . .

Meanwhile Gonko, done at Shalice's, went right to the funhouse and pounded at the door. With coffin lid creaks it swung inward. The Matter Manipulator's pale sweating face thrust out the gap.

"What's the big idea getting me in George's bad books?" said Gonko. "And where's JJ? Why you ain't brought him back?"

"I wasn't asked," the Matter Manipulator said, hunching his shoulders around as if convulsing with laughter, though he did not laugh. "The clown body at my doorstep, sans request, I took to be a gift from who knows who. It will be useful for parts."

"Oh, no. I owe that clown a beating and he owes me a very simpering apology. Bring him back!"

"The ah, payment has not yet been—"

"What, you want me to dip into the last of my private stash? You notice I ain't been paid today? I got two bags left to my name, you greasy fuck. How much you want from me?"

"Two bags will suffice."

Gonko wailed and moaned up a storm, the whole not-letting-this-guy-know-two-bags-was-hardly-a-dent-in-the-fortune-amassed-in-just-one-show-above gag—what with so few carnies to pay and no tribute to send below. He flung the bags down, feigning disgust. The Matter Manipulator smiled, victorious. "And while you're bringing him back, if this one has extra dicks or starts laying eggs or whatever you did to Goshy—"

"No threats please, Mr. 'the Clown'. They distract the mind and lead to . . . errors."

In George's trailer, the phone rang. It rang and rang, the loudest and worst sound in the world. George cringed away from it, wanting to let it to ring out, but he knew *they* knew he was here.

There was no choice. He lifted the receiver with a shaking hand. "Hello?"

"YOU. FAILED."

"Hey now, wait just a minute."

"TRIBUTE. INSUFFICIENT."

"Look, it's not my fault. Something fishy's going on here."

"SHOW. TOMORROW."

"What?! Three days straight? You're nuts. Give it a day to rest; they ain't been paid. They ain't—"

"SHOW. TOMORROW." The line went dead. George buried his face in his hands.

Electric light flickered, flashed through the upper Funhouse windows. A bolt of lightning had been captured and was now being tortured to death, or so it looked to Steve and the others who walked by that evening, out on secret errands in the private network of loyalties, factions, betrayals, and paybacks among the circus's lowest rung staff.

Indeed something had been captured in that sick, sickening room. Many eyes embedded here and there in the walls, paintings, furniture, and from inside of jars, watched in mute horror. Talking to himself excitedly, just like someone pretending in his kitchen to host a cooking show while he made dinner, the Matter Manipulator lurched between jars of liquid, the electric chair, and the dials and panels of what looked like radio equipment: its purpose to find, in the etheric plane or beyond, the essence of JJ the clown.

"And with just a twist of this lever," he said, examining the panel's flickering dashes and lights, listening carefully to its beeps, "Aha! Yes, we have found the essence! 'Tis easier on the more recently dead, still all lost in limbo seeking new homes. One year past, there is no guarantee, but tonight we have found the essence! And we have the particular frequency, the unique energy frequency derived from readings taken of the flesh. The unique energy signature, the fingerprint of the soul, my darling darlings." He snickered. "And we match that on this chair with a careful twist of this dial, til the frequency is identical, creating resonance which can reach above, beyond the physical! And we activate the magnet trap, for when it's just close enough, just close enough . . ."

The chair spat sparks and shook JJ's carefully remade body, whose organs squeezed and clutched the fluids of life about the body, though no conscious life was yet there. It was a doll of flesh, vacant and waiting. Wet stuff flew from its lips. "And the law of attraction summons the essence home! It dons its suit once more—it has life! Breathe!" he shouted, hoarse. "Breathe again, clown; the circus calls you! She is your mother and your jail cell and your only only!"

JJ breathed. Slowly his brain switched on, and his eyes peeled open to look about the room, uncomprehending at first. As memory dawned, sadness and fear formed like a cloud above him. "Why?" he whispered. "Why did you bring me back?"

The Matter Manipulator's shoulders hunched with mirth. "Happy, where you were before? Ah, but that place can wait. What of this, the physical realm, the heaven of pleasure, the spice of pain? Yours again! Have a time to recover your wits, your . . ." his fluttering hands quested for the word ". . . your *motivations*. Later we shall discuss the why, the what, the who. There is a task I have for you. And there shall be rewards for compliance, the punishment for failure. Do you hear me, clown?"

"Yessir," JJ whispered.

"Tricky business afoot. I suspect, and George suspects. The clowns do ill to the show, we know not how, just hunch and guesses, fleeting thoughts. Rebellion! And the fortuneteller . . . well, we do not know, but we *watch*—watch her now, very close. And that is your task: watch. Learn. Report. Discover what goes on." The Matter Manipulator dropped one of the velvet bags Gonko had given him onto JJ's lap. "You remember this little vice, the joys it brings, itches scratched? More awaits you, clown, if you do this well for me. More than that: your heart's desire, the friendship of the carnival overseers. Maybe it will be JJ the Clown who leads the rest!"

121

The Matter Manipulator produced a glass case. Inside it was a still living head, with nails driven through every inch of flesh. The lips were stitched shut. Only the eyes were unharmed. They peered, pleading at JJ through the glass. "Shall we discuss the price of refusal, or of failure?" the Matter Manipulator said. "For now you know, even swift death is no escape, should you displease me. I call you back as I see fit. This head has been alive for a hundred years. I refresh the nails, oh, every so often."

JJ shook his head. "I'll rat them out, sir. I'll snitch."

"Good boy. Then you keep your head, and next time you rest, I shall not wake you."

9. ABOVE

The campsite was a bustle of activity, waking Jamie from a few hours of fitful sleep not easily come by in the clown tent. All night the weird noises and sleep-talking utterances of Doopy and Goshy had colored his dreams with sickly pink, red, and blue monsters rising from the depths of garish rainbow lakes to lunge at him with clattering teeth.

He rose and went to find Dean, who'd been helping dismantle tents and trying to act as naturally and fearlessly as he could. Jamie took him over near the gazebo, where they crouched from the carnies' sight behind a waist-high wall of hedge. Jamie said, "There's a circus down there, bigger than this one. I went through those gate things and saw it."

"Down where?" said Dean.

"I'm not sure. But it can be reached with the gates and with those elevators. The lifts can take you anywhere in the world. We'd just need to learn the number code of each location and to take one of those card gizmos they call pass-outs." Jamie related all he'd seen yesterday, including the run in with Steve and the apparent plan of Gonko's show: to starve out the show beneath and get George removed as boss.

"So how do we use this?" said Dean.

"See that's the thing. Gonko was terrified that I'd blabbed down there about what he's doing up here."

"Terrified?" Dean said skeptically.

"He expressed it with homicidal anger, but yes. So he has a weakness there, but it does us no real good. If they learn down there what he's doing, they'll punish him, maybe kill him, maybe kill us for helping him, then just put someone else in charge of the clowns. We'll be just as trapped beneath as we are up here. And having been down there, I can tell you, we're better off up here. At least we're not getting whipped all day like they are."

Dean scoffed. "Just the odd drowning up here, right?"

"You can't make Gonko mad like that. Obey him and you're fine. You shouldn't have gone up onstage."

"Wasn't me, like I told you. It has to be the face paint—it changed me. I came back to myself when it washed off."

"So here's what you do. Tell Gonko you don't want to be a clown, that you'll do some other job. Say sorry for yesterday, suck up to him, then ask if you can be a ticket collector."

"Why?"

"I just have a feeling it might be useful if you learn how those gates work."

"All right. But get me a tub of that face paint."

"Why, Dean?"

"Because I remember how I felt wearing it. Bulletproof. Hell, I even beat up a couple of those other clowns. And it felt like I could have taken on Gonko and won."

"Bad idea, Dean."

"Just telling you how it felt. Get me some of that face paint. I'll hide it until I need to use it. Okay?"

"Fine. How's Jodi?"

Dean's smile was grim. "You hear her screaming when they took the makeup off her? She freaked out, fought like a wildcat. Five of them had to hold her down. Now she's Emerald again, Queen of the Park. And I'm her Romeo, but she keeps asking what happened to my big muscles." He laughed. "This is some ride you got us on, bro."

Jamie sighed. "Maybe you can blame me for it all some other time? I'm trying to keep myself together here and that really doesn't help."

"All right, I'll blame you later. Let's get this out of the way."

They went back to the others, where Gonko watched, smiling, as Rufshod and Doopy squabbled and wrestled over whose job it was to tidy up the mattresses. Dean said, "Gonko, sir?"

"Well hi hi hi, Deeby. Wanna go for a swim?"

"It's Dean, sir, with all due respect, not Deeby. Just wanted to tell you I don't want to be a clown. You remember when I invited you into my apartment then begged and pleaded to join the clown show?"

Jamie winced at this boldness but Gonko just said, "Yeah, yeah. So spit it out, chump. I got word that George is having another show today so we've gotta hustle and get this show to a new location."

"Why are we moving, Gonko?" said Jamie.

"Curls was right," said Gonko. "The trick authorities smell a rat around here. You seen all the cop cars coming through? All last night and this morning. Not just cops either, some of those fancy intel cars, what with the men in dark sunglasses and all that fun. Normal tricks won't see us too clear, but you never know what gizmos those fancy dark sunglasses tricks might have. So we're shifting to a spot north of here, half an hour away. Plus we used up a good chunk of local tricks already. No point milking 'em again."

"Well, obviously I need to make myself useful, sir," said Dean. "How about I help the ticket collectors? I admit I'm not much of a clown."

Gonko shrugged. "Talk to Curls. But in the meantime you can drive the truck."

"What truck?"

On cue, Rufshod pulled into the car park in jerking lurches with a large semi-trailer. The truck clipped a tree, looked ready to veer right through the tents.

"Brakes!" someone screamed at him.

"I already broke it," Rufshod called, then figured out the brakes and brought the truck to a lurching stop. He jumped down, hauled from the passenger side the hog tied driver and dumped him in the toilet block.

"Load up!" Gonko screamed. In little more than an hour the box trailer had been filled with tent parts, the seats, and the disassembled stage. The caravan (to its owners' chagrin) had to be broken to parts again to fit. Dean drove with Gonko in the passenger seat, who said nothing but the occasional "Turn here." They dropped the load off at the new campsite—this one further from civilization than was Wiley Park. In three trips, all performers and apparatus had been moved, leaving no trace of themselves at the campsite beyond marks in the ground, and the truck driver, slowly regaining consciousness.

At the new site, the tents were soon up, the stage was reassembled, and the kissing booth was put in place. The freaks settled uneasily in their new home. Light was beginning to fade, and the ticket collectors (Dean among them) had a longer walk to the nearest train station to set up their gates. Curls had grunted his indifference to Dean joining their ranks; it was no secret Curls wanted an easier job than this, running a card game in the alley rather than being the guy in George's likely firing line at the end of each failed show day below.

Rufshod took the truck a short drive away and ditched it, in case it had been reported stolen by now. "So how many shows we gonna have to do up here?" he asked as the clowns sat relaxing in the brief interval before tricks arrived.

"Dunno, Ruf," Gonko said, poking a freshly made baby Goshy with a stem of grass, making it wriggle around crying "Help!" playfully. Goshy and Doopy watched, the latter fascinated, the former indecipherable. "See, this three-days-straight thing? Weird, and it tells us it's working. They're getting edgy, the bosses below."

"So why'd they wait so long to give George the go-ahead?"

"No one knows how they think. They see things we don't and are blind to some of what we see. But they had plenty of dust down there to last 'em, I saw piles of it myself. Managed to swipe a little, once or twice. See, they don't use it like we do neither. They just keep it around in little mounds and it keeps 'em fed til it slowly fades away. I seen 'em down there take a single grain of it, and just by looking at it they can see the whole life of the trick it come from. They could eat the trick's pain or taste the trick's pleasure, all that stuff. And they could look out through the trick's eyes and see what it could see . . . if the trick's still alive, that is. It's not just their food, it's their entertainment. And they get bored easy. I'd guess George could count on one hand the number of failed shows he's allowed to put on before they lose patience and send for him."

"And put Kurt in charge?" said Rufshod.

"Good old Kurt, who will owe us all kinds of payback, payback of the *Thanks, clowns* kind. Oh, and by the way. If the MM did as I asked, a JJ beat down is on tonight. So, come with me below when we're done here. Jamie, you too. You're in for a little surprise. But all of you, keep your mouths shut and don't go near the fortune-teller. Our situation's dicey til George is gone."

Doopy's lips were on Jamie's ears and the loudness of his voice made Jamie jump and scream. "A little surprise," said Doopy. "Golly, ain't that swell?"

Goshy hissed like a snake.

"Don't be mean, Goshy. It's time to make the people laugh again, just like a *clown*, Goshy. You gots to put on your funnies, you just gotta!"

And they did. As with last night, the tricks arrived fresh off the commuter train, weary from work, needing showers and bathrooms, but all that was forgotten as the music box handle twisted, sprinkling its notes and inviting them all into a cheerful waking dream. The sideshow games did a better trade tonight, despite the declining mood of unrested carnies who insulted and snapped at the tricks.

The clown show was a replica of yesterday's, with Jamie finding (to his own disquiet) that he enjoyed himself, loved the crowd's laughter even though he knew it was not real, that they were caught up in this as much as him. Onstage, there was no room or time to think about it, there were rolling pins and brick pies to dodge, and that was a blessing.

Emerald did another whopping trade, despite a prima donna threat not to host her booth tonight. In fact, she pulled in more powder than the rest of the show combined while the gypsy women cooed their approval at her shoulders.

The freaks did well, courtesy of Fatso, though the move had upset him and he was not as cheerful as usual. Nor had his special protein powder had time to heal the previous two shows' bite gouges. His one-liners ("The boss says to me, what's eating you Fatso . . . I says, well, I am,") were delivered deadpan flat. "Nonsense," the head-in-a-jar rebutted. "Healthy discourse. Pish posh!"

Exhausted, the carnies nonetheless collected the day's takings with the same greedy eagerness. It took well into the night for the lot of it to be bagged and stashed. Gonko paid everyone double yesterday's wages with plenty left over, this time including Jamie and Dean.

The ticket collectors got back just in time to coincide with George's show below. Once the tricks were herded through the gates, Dean took Jamie aside. "Come for a walk," he said. "Got something to show you." They went out of earshot of the rest of the carnies. Dean pulled from his pocket a folded piece of paper. "Map," he said. "See? I think this is the kind of thing you were after, right?"

It was a large map of the world, old and battered with small digits on many parts of each country and continent (only Antarctica was missing.) Some of the numbers were too small to read without a magnifying glass. Jamie pointed to them. "Are those numbers what I think they are?"

"Lift codes. Curls gave this to me. He hates his job; he's happy to have a new guy keen to do it, so he's telling me everything. I already know how the gates work. Well, not *how* they work but how to use them. The numbers, you put those in the lift somehow, on the lever or whatever. Can take you almost anywhere, except you see those gaps, where there's deserts or bodies of water. Ticketers need to know all this, since they're meant to be going to other circuses all over the place to set up gates."

"Can you get another copy of this?" said Jamie. "Maybe it'll be useful to have."

"I'll ask. And I'll show you how to do the gates later, when we won't be seen. As for this powder, don't use it."

"Hadn't planned to, but why do you say so?"

"Bad feeling, that's all. Keep it for trading or bribing, but don't melt it and drink it like the others do."

"Jamie!" Gonko's voice called across the dark. "Cometh hither, my sweet. We go below."

"A big surprise!" Doopy called. "It's gonna be soooo great."

Jamie sighed heavily. "Here goes."

Dean clapped him on the shoulder. "Good luck, stay cool."

10. BELOW

Through the gates went the clowns, into more strains of circus music—now up-tempo and desperate. The panic in the air was something one could feel, stifling as humidity—most of it stemming from George himself. But it was also evident in the other performers and carnies, all overworked and nervous. For it was happening again: there was very little dust, and what had fallen was polluted with black and grey ash, which would need to be picked out later, grain by grain.

Quickly, Gonko ushered the clowns to their own tent, where a bunch of hiding Sideshow Alley carnies huddled with lash marks all over them. "Aw, ain't this sweet," said Gonko. "Looks like some orphans escaped a Dickens book. Get out."

"You gonna hurt us worse than Mr. Pilo?" said one of them sullenly. In reply Gonko took from his pockets a small chainsaw that spat fire from its teeth. The carnies ran.

"So where's this surprise?" Jamie said guardedly, for Doopy was hopping from foot to foot, talking about it breathlessly. Gonko led them on a quick search of the partitioned bedrooms, until they found a human looking shape under a blanket. They waited in the doorway as gradually a redheaded clown peeked out from beneath it, the exact and identical image of Jamie. "What the actual fuck?" he said. He felt dizzy, stepped back, and had to be held up by Doopy and Rufshod.

"Well, hello there, JJ," said Gonko brightly. "I trust the MM gave you a gentle rebirth?"

JJ slowly got up, took a step towards Jamie—JJ's eyes were wide with wary surprise. Some little scratches on Jamie's neck and hands were not visible on JJ's, and JJ's face paint was layered on thicker; other than that, it was a perfect reflection. They stared at each other for what seemed a long time, til JJ threw himself at Jamie's feet. "I'm sorry. I didn't mean any of it. I just wanted my own body. Can't you see that? I just wanted my own body."

Jamie had no idea what this doppelganger was talking about. Then something clicked into place: Deeby, Dean. Jamie, JJ. It did not quite make sense to him; Deeby and Dean existed within one body, after all. But he sensed that this copy of himself had a place somehow within the circus's logic. "Look, don't worry about it, it's okay," Jamie said, not knowing at all whether it was okay or not. "Let's be friends. We're both clowns, aren't we?"

"Oh, thank you . . . thank you." JJ kissed Jamie's boots, then got to his feet.

"JJ," said Gonko. "Isn't there someone else you might oughta be groveling to?"

"Not that I can think of," said JJ. Wrong answer. For a moment the headlock Gonko held him in seemed almost tender and gentle, then he turned it into a wrestler's takedown. JJ was face down in the dirt as Gonko's white-gloved fist threw a few warm up punches into his neck and ribs, then gestured for the other clowns to join in. Jamie winced and turned away but the shrieking, begging and the *pop-pop-crack* were impossible not to hear, made worse by the comic noises sprinkled throughout (car horns, bicycle bells, splats.) When it was finally done, Jamie knew a normal person would not have survived it. Even with the face paint's protection, a blood-covered mess was strewn unconscious across the floor.

Until that day, Gonko had assumed he'd seen the maximum range of George's temper. Everyone and everything in range of his goon's clumsy lash arm got a taste. Games were broken. Some tricks were even roused from their sleepwalk and stood about in terror until they were led away, calmed down, and soothed back under the circus spell. All the clowns watched George from a safe distance, certainly including Jamie, who felt the beginnings of an idea forming when he saw the trick awoken . . . just parts and pieces lying separate in his mind, with the certainty that there *was* a way, somehow, to connect them. As yet, it eluded him.

Meanwhile George lost the power to articulate his grievances. What came out of him resembled: "Aya, who did, flamma joo, ree, arrrk," and so on, spittle showering, face red, the overworked goon groaning beneath him as the lash arm wore out but kept on lashing. The lumberjacks had their own version of "looking busy," which meant beating the crap out of whoever was unlucky enough to be near them when George came by. Phony "thief" culprits were reported as old scores and vengeances were settled among the short folk and gypsies. Some of these accused the lumberjacks carried away to the Funhouse where they were strapped to tables and benches before a salivating Matter Manipulator, rubbing his hands together with relish.

"One more show might just do it," Gonko mused. "This is not your typical George eruption. They've put the hard word on him. If he was Kurt, most everyone would be dead by now."

"We got two Jamies now," said Doopy, still struggling with the concept. "Gosh, that's nearly double what we normally got."

"Oh, no we don't," said Gonko. "They're different clowns altogether, you got that? Don't say a word to JJ about our upstairs shenanigans. Not til the plan's done. Jamie is your typical overawed getting-used-to-things-trick-come-clown. He can be trusted. Don't trust JJ with nothing important yet, especially after we just pounded on him. He'll spill the beans. Dig?"

They dug. When George seemed safely out of the way, Jamie excused himself and ducked off to Sideshow Alley. He'd not yet gotten over the shock of seeing his twin, nor the beating for that matter, but absorbing mental shock was becoming easier with practice—he'd had plenty of that. The dust and a wish would answer many questions . . . but no, not yet. He found Steve, who had fresh lash marks across his back and on his forearms, as did the carnies he worked with. Their eyes smoldered with anger. George seemed to be going the right way about starting a revolt with his lash alone. "Hey, Steve . . ."

Hands gripped Jamie's shoulders, and a knife was suddenly held up to his face. "Spill it," a voice hissed in his ear. To his amazement Steve just watched, waiting like all the others for an answer. He seemed just as angry.

"Spill what?" said Jamie.

The hands shook him. "Who wrecks the shows? We no paid, we whip all day, no rest, no pay. Just clean, work, show, clean, work, show, show, show. People ready to *kill* here, you get that? They kill who behind it all, they not care who. And *some* say, it the clown, he know! They seen Gonko talk to Curls, seen Curls have bag of powder he no share, then Curls no here! Ticket collector now? Pah! Something funny, that's what spill. Now you spill, or I spill you."

"All right, all right, put the knife down. Let me go, and I'll tell you what I know, okay?"

Slowly the knife withdrew, and the hands released him. The angry carnies waited in a close ring around him. "I don't know anything," Jamie said. "Honest." He leaped high as they grabbed for him again—one of those big floating jumps. The carnies took off after him til a lumberjack happened by, keeping a careful eye out for anything suspicious. They went back to their game stalls, still grumbling to each other, while Jamie leaped and floated for the safety of the clown tent.

The other clowns weren't there—presumably they were watching more of George's theatrics as his meltdown worsened. Jamie headed for the room where his double had been beaten, to check he was in fact still living. "JJ?" he called.

He'd no sooner walked in before something clubbed the back of his head, knocking him to the floor. For a moment—it seemed no more than a second—he blacked out, but when he came to his hands were tied together in chains, the chain's length wrapped around the steel bed frame. "Hey, I know you said let's be friends," said JJ, "and I know this looks bad. But let's put the friendship on hold for just a twenty-four-hour period, and then we can pretend this didn't happen, after I find out a few things."

"Why don't we pretend it's not happening now, and you can untie me?"

He watched the bruised, battered face he shared with this stranger consider this carefully. "See, though, if I was you, I'd say that. If I was you, get it?" JJ guffawed. "But then, I'd be squealing to Gonko, and then I'd be getting stomped again. Which really, *really* hurts, by the way. So look, a little switcheroo, just for one day. Promise! Then we can be chums again."

"We can switch, all right? I agree, we swap places. You don't need to tie me up for that. You could have just asked."

"Don't worry. Here's two buckets for the business, and I left you some water under the bed. Plus a hot dog. And you got all the air you need. See? I'm not so bad."

"Really kind of you. But have you noticed my face isn't all beat up? How's he going to fall for us being switched, when . . ." Jamie cut off the words the instant he realized it was the dumbest thing he'd ever said. Too late.

"Good thinking! Thanks, pal," said JJ, and with many apologies he corrected the problem. Jamie was half aware of the clothes being pulled off him and then JJ's being put on. Through a red mist of pain he heard Gonko and the others return to the clown tent. "JJ?" Gonko said.

"Nah, it's me, Jamie," said JJ.

"Then why is your face showing evidence of a well delivered stomping?"

"JJ attacked me. He was pissed that I just stood there idly, that's right, just stood there with my back turned, and let you guys beat on me. Him. I had to, like, chain him up and stuff, such was the ferocity of his onslaught."

Gonko nodded. "Guess I'd be pissed too. You shoulda joined in with us and let him know which of you is the top bunk clown. You want us to slapstick him real quick?"

Jamie whispered, "No, don't." Relief flooded through him when

JJ said, "Nah, no need."

"You sure? No one beats on my crew but me."

"I guess maybe just a few kicks?"

"You got it."

"Oh shit," Jamie groaned. Footsteps thumped closer til his vision filled with red clown shoes.

"You dirty dog," said Gonko, raising his boot.

"*I'm* Jamie!" Jamie screamed. "*I'm* Jamie. He swapped our clothes. He tied me up here—"

JJ sighed. "He said he'd try this: the ol' switcheroo."

"This warrants more kicks than I was originally going to impart!" Gonko cried, and several times his boot thundered down, til Jamie's world blacked out again.

Gonko and the others had planned like yesterday to sneak back out on the increasingly irrelevant pretext of finding the rogue carnies. To that end they watched the doubly drained tricks being herded back through the gates, but as the last ones went, George stood glaring with suspicion at Curls and his crew (not including Dean, who had remained above.) They disassembled the lattice gate pieces with the most strained attempt at looking casual Gonko had ever seen. There was no escape that way.

"Lifts it is then," Gonko told his crew, and they headed that way only to find a barricade had been put up around the lift with three heavily armed lumberjacks seated beside it. Gonko appraised them—the clowns could get past them without much trouble, but it would be reported and draw heat on them at a bad time. "All right something's going down here," he said to the others. "We'll get back later tonight, better find out what gives."

It didn't take long. George had taken the day's pitiful collection, a sum even less than yesterday's tribute and sent it to the Funhouse. As he'd expected the phone in his trailer rang soon after. He snatched the receiver, weeping openly as the cold voice said:

"YOU. FAIL."

"I know," George whimpered.

"YOU. FAILED."

George made mewling sounds.

"TRIBUTE. PITIFUL. *YOU*. PITIFUL."

"I couldn't have whipped 'em any harder, I swear it. They're gonna riot; they're gonna torch it all down. Help me, you got to tell me what's going on, what'm I doing wrong here."

"LAST. CHANCE."

"Oh what? Listen something's fishy here and I just need to find who's behind—"

"LAST. CHANCE. SHOW. TOMORROW."

"Impossible. Four days straight? That's nuts. Hey I need time to interrogate every single carny with the fortuneteller helping. It's the only way I'll find out who—"

"LAST. CHANCE." The line went dead. George stared at the receiver for a minute, and then trashed it against the desk, screaming. Parts of the phone broke off, but it would ring tomorrow, he knew. He grabbed a megaphone, mounted his exhausted goon, and fiddled the control panel levers. Two lumberjacks flanked him and his goon as he went through the showgrounds, hollering through the megaphone, "Emergency meeting. Acrobat tent, emergency meeting. All performers to attend. All game stall attendants to attend."

Hearing this, Gonko said, "Jamie: back to the clown tent. George don't even know you're back in the circus yet, and last time we had drama, you got blamed for some of the stuff Winston and Fishboy did. You sit this meeting out."

The clowns rushed to the acrobat tent and nabbed seats close to the exit. Gonko made hush-hush gestures to his crew as the other carnies filed in. A number of suspicious looks were shot Gonko's way. George bustled in last, stood at the top of a podium, and swept the room with a gaze of hot loathing. Into the megaphone he yelled, "I know someone in this room thinks they are pretty clever. Someone here is doing something to undermine my show, and to make sure no one is getting paid their share. The culprits will be caught. I have leads, I have ways to find out. Ways! You will not outsmart George Pilo. For now I have no choice. So we are doing another show tomorrow."

George allowed himself a moment to bask in the pleasure of the room's groans and angry murmurs. He glanced at the clowns and saw they were throwing their arms up in more distress than anyone, and that a couple of them were even weeping. "You heard me," George said. "A show tomorrow. And until we get good takings, the shows will go on nonstop. The tricks will just keep on coming until half of you drop dead with exhaustion and the rest wish you could."

"The clown!" Mugabo stood, yelling, pointing around the room. "My potions smash. The clown do! I remember now, is not the fortune witch—"

"Sit down," said George.

"Is Tuesday?" said Mugabo.

"Shut it!" George screamed, the megaphone squealing feedback. "What's more, no sleep for any of you tonight. You're going to rehearse your acts and test your games and rides all night. ALL NIGHT! The rest of you will clean, mop, polish, and scrub. Random inspections will go on all night. Anything less than perfection will incur WHIPLASH! Go! Go! Go! And you clowns?"

All heads turned their way.

"You have your show back. And you'd better be just as busy as everyone else . . . or else."

"Much obliged George," said Gonko through gritted teeth and the fakest smile ever faked.

"We'd better get some smashin' stuff ready, for the boss," Doopy whispered to Rufshod. "Cause, see, he's gonna smash stuff now, and if you and me is the only things to smash, we might be what he goes smash to. And it hurts reaaaaal bad, Ruf."

Rufshod nodded and scampered off, grabbing whatever furniture, glass and other breakables he could find before Gonko somehow un-paralyzed himself and staggered, shivering with rage, back to the clown tent.

"George. GEORGE. GEORRRRGE!"

It was a short sharp thunderstorm of violence, but merited applause from the other clowns when Gonko was done. The breakables were broken and made ankle-deep litter in one corner of the room. "Jamie!" Gonko snapped. "Listen. Get up top. Find Curls and tell him to sneak out with you. Put on the show just like yesterday. Can you do a one-man clown act?"

JJ's mouth hung open in astonishment. "I . . . see."

"What?" Gonko snarled.

"Nothing at all. Sure boss, I can do a one-man show," said JJ. "Jamie the clown, that's me."

"You're gonna have to. Hell, paint up Deeby if you have to and see if he can be funny by accident. Worst the tricks can do is not laugh. Emerald alone can probably suck most of 'em dry besides. Tell 'em up there: George is about to lose it. This'll be his last chance, just reading between the lines. We get it done tomorrow and it's bye bye George."

"And hello Kurt," said JJ. He went pale beneath the face paint. Like Gonko, his memories of "that night" were a bit of a jumbled mess, but one thing he'd never forget was begging for his life as the monster Kurt became shambled closer, closer, blood gushing from its mouth, dripping down its scales with a laughing growl from Hell's depths, *Ohh, ho ho . . .*

"Relax," said Gonko. "Kurt's just gonna love us. When you get up top, pay everyone four bags this time. The stash is buried behind our tent, ten paces back. Put the rest of the takings there and *get the timing right!* Two hours before George's show starts, have your tricks in. Two hours, send 'em down. Got it?" He tossed JJ a pocket watch after quickly setting its alarm. "The rest of you shit pukes, let's look busy." They filed out to the performance tent, leaving JJ open-mouthed where he stood and Jamie half conscious, chained to the bed frame.

Was it time yet to squeal? Not quite. JJ had to see with his own eyes exactly what he'd be squealing about.

He found Curls after a frantic search among the short folk—none were eager to help point him in Curls's direction. In fact every now and then he had to dodge a flung knife or hammer. They had not forgotten JJ the clown in these parts, and he didn't really blame them. He had, after all, indulged in something of a murder spree among these folks.

"Yeah, hey what?" Curls snapped when JJ finally found him. He'd been trying to sneak in a hot dog break in his hammock, hidden under a flea-ridden blanket.

JJ relayed Gonko's message and watched Curls carefully: was it as JJ suspected, that a second, secret show was afoot up there?

Sure enough, Curls gestured to follow him into a small hut's hidden room and locked the door. Spitting curses, the dwarf assembled one set of gate pieces. "Work never ends," Curls muttered. "Never rest time. He said I could see the ocean. All five, he said."

"Just do your job, you little turd," JJ said, raising his fist. Curls glared darkly at him but ceased complaining.

They stepped through the gates to the campground and into Gonko's secret traveling show.

11. ABOVE

JJ ambled through the tents, unable to clamp his jaw shut. He'd heard whispers, rumors, theories among the carnies that somewhere up here was a competitor—someone bleeding dry their tricks. It followed that they would have cohorts from the Pilo Circus. Some even claimed the clowns were in on it . . . but surely not, surely no one in all creation had the balls to even try it. Yet, here it was. The up-world show was sleeping now, snores and murmurs coming muffled through tent canvas. Curls grabbed a glass beaker, mumbled some excuse and went for a stroll, leaving JJ to explore the freak show tent on his own. And what do you know? There was Fatso asleep in his cage. JJ had never seen Fatso before, but he'd heard much talk today about the missing freak show exhibit; this had to be him. Fatso had hefty gouges over just about every part of him. Possibly meaning he'd just done a bunch of consecutive shows.

Which brought JJ to an uncomfy fork in the road: Gonko's plan looked like it was working, which meant JJ had to go down and squeal, unless he wanted the big monster back in charge. If JJ squealed, Gonko would kill him, which in itself was not so bad, but it wouldn't be a painless process (unless he somehow *secretly* squealed, but that would forgo any suck-up benefits with George.) If he *didn't* squeal and Gonko got caught, he, JJ, was now implicated in the conspiracy.

So he'd wind up a tortured head in the Funhouse for a long, long time. That could be insured against by only one course of action: get back down there and kill Jamie, right now, while he was chained up, then blame someone else for the death, maybe the stirred up suspicious carnies. The Matter Manipulator had threatened JJ, not Jamie . . . so if JJ took Jamie's place permanently, that might keep him safe from one nasty fate, at least . . .

A hand clapped JJ on the shoulder. He jumped and squealed. Some trick he'd never seen before stood before him—it was a trick all right, you could somehow spot true carnies from new arrivals. "What happened down there?" said the trick in a kind of conspiratorial whisper, looking around. The trick surveyed him. "What the hell happened to you? Looks like you got the crap kicked out of you."

"I was indeed brutally beaten," said JJ. "A rehearsal went wrong, I flubbed a line and they got me."

"Rehearsal? What the—why are you guys rehearsing down there?"

"Eh, long story."

The trick grabbed him roughly by the shirt. Curious! Some sort of macho trick. "So tell me the long story, dipshit. I need to know everything you know—there might be useful info."

JJ chewed on this for a moment, but could not quite get it. "Useful to what ends, sir?"

The trick looked stunned, looked like he wanted to punch JJ for this answer. "To take these fuckers *out*, remember? The map I gave you? Dude, don't you flake out on me now, not after what we've been through here."

"To take these fuckers out," JJ repeated, tasting the words experimentally. "Oh, right! To bring down the entire circus? Our . . . secret plan. Right?"

"It better be secret. That Steve guy have any new info?"

"Er, no. What about up here? Any news?"

"No. Emerald knows she's the big draw for these people, that's all, so she's making all kinds of threats not to cooperate. But she's as different with her makeup on as I am. It's not really Jodi, it's someone else."

"Deeby . . . Deeby, right? Listen." JJ related what had happened below, including Gonko's instructions for tomorrow, trying to mimic Jamie's mannerisms as best he could, all timid and trick-like, but this trick was looking at him strangely.

"You sure you're all right?" said the trick. "That beating you took, did it mess your head up a little?"

"You know I think it probably did."

"Keep it together. Come with me, I'll show you how the gates work." So the trick did just that, taking the gate pieces off to where no one sleeping would hear the metallic chime of their assembly. "Here, see? Now they're set up to go into the showgrounds."

"And how's this fit in with our secret plan to take out the circus?" said JJ.

Again the trick looked at him strangely. "It's like we said, we're just learning all we can for now. There *is* no plan yet, that'll come when we know . . ." The trick stopped talking and looked at JJ closely. "You're not Jamie," he said quietly. "You're not Jamie, are you?""

"I guess it depends. Philosophically speaking, we're all Jamie."

"What did you to do him? Where is he?" The trick went all macho again with the shirt grab and shoulder push. JJ considered laying down some slapstick but he ran instead, leading the trick on a long round chase through the darkness, til he rounded back through the gates and into the showgrounds again.

On the run he'd had time to come to a decision—for there was really only one valid course of action as far as JJ could see it. Eyes peeled for George, he stole through the night back toward the clowns' tent, where Jamie still lay helpless.

12. BELOW

Jamie had gotten some sleep, due to lack of other options. He was woken often enough by George's megaphone, berating performers about the show with shrill desperate rants, invariably followed by the whip crack and an occasional scream. This time, the sound of footsteps near his head and the feeling of being watched roused him. Two big red clown shoes filled his vision. A long way up stood JJ, peering down with Jamie's own eyes.

Yet there was something missing from those eyes, Jamie noticed that first; there was a flatness to them, like they were made of dull glass. The next thing he noticed was JJ's sad regretful expression as—very slowly—he pulled into view an object from behind his back. An axe. "I'm sorry I have to do this," JJ said.

Jamie sat up, pulled himself back, and ended up on his knees on the bed when the chain pulled taut. "But you don't have to do anything," he said. "Let's just talk it out, okay? There's no need for the axe."

JJ took a step closer. "There can only be one JJ."

"Fine, that's you. Chill out, and put the axe down. I want to be friends, like I told you."

"There can only be one Jamie."

"Oh, Christ."

"There may only be one. Only one of us." The axe raised high.

"You fucking bastard, kill me when I'm chained up like this? Look, stop, wait, wait!" He wrenched with all his strength at the chains, but he'd done that before, and again, they didn't snap or come loose. He writhed, squirmed, rolled side-to-side, afraid to look up at the axe he was trying to dodge. Time slowed to a crawl, and he heard the *whoosh* of the axe blade cutting the air. Jamie screamed, shut his eyes. He kept on screaming even after his eyes delivered the news: the axe blade came down on the chain, severing it.

Jamie got up, crazy with adrenaline. He started to sprint out, but JJ held him. "Wait, wait, I was joking. Sorry, just had to! I talked to your trick buddy up there. I'm in. I'll help you guys."

Jamie slowly calmed down. "What?" he gasped.

"I'll help you, okay? I don't want to be here anymore, but they'll keep bringing me back, even if I die. So I'm on your team. Whatcha say: we're buddies?"

"Buddies," Jamie repeated stupidly as his heartbeat slowly eased.

"Should've seen your face," JJ said. He laughed and laughed, and even tried to stop but a glance at Jamie set him off again, right up to when Jamie slugged him. JJ spun and fell into the wall.

"Good to have you aboard," said Jamie after an awkward few seconds. "But I'm on the top bunk. Got it?"

"Got it."

It took a while for Jamie to get his bearings back—facing off with death by axe will do that, it seemed. JJ waited patiently, distracting himself with a yo-yo. Over at the clown performance tent, a disturbance could be heard, with George's megaphone screaming, "You call that clowning? I'm supposed to laugh at this abortion?" The whip crack came, in turn followed by a piercing unearthly wail of rage that could only have come from Goshy. "Assault on management!" George's megaphone shrieked. "Code five, code five!" Footsteps thundered past as the lumberjacks rushed in to aid the boss. More squeals and shrieks from Goshy. The hubbub eventually died down as, presumably, Gonko smoothed things over.

"You guys ain't got much in the way of plans yet," JJ observed.

"Nope." And if they did, would Jamie divulge it to this clone of himself? He didn't think so, not yet. "We decided to let Gonko do his thing, not to interfere. We saw no point in getting Gonko booted out or killed, or whatever they'd do to him."

"It might mean you or me gets to be clown boss, if we did it. That might be handy."

"But we don't know just what they'd do. What if they just docked his pay for a year or two? Or if they confine him for a time but he eventually comes back? Then we'd be screwed. Look, we'd better get back up top. Steve looks like he's not going to be much help to us after all. Everyone but George himself seems to think the clowns are sabotaging the show."

JJ led them carefully back to Curls's hut and the gate he'd set up (though the lock had to be picked.) Back above, the camp was still asleep. Jamie woke Dean, led him out of earshot of the others. "Well, you've met JJ. He's my Deeby, you might say. JJ, this is Dean."

"So why is he apart from you?" said Dean.

"We don't know. No one seems to know. Something happened last time I was part of all this. But anyway, JJ's going to help us. He's on our side."

"I hope so," Dean said after a while.

"Hope no more, my friend!" JJ cried. "Together, we shall bring an end to—"

"Keep your voice down, idiot," Dean said, one hand at JJ's throat. "Talk again tomorrow," he said to Jamie before heading for his tent.

"He takes all this so seriously," JJ said admiringly. "Tricks, I tell you."

Jamie nodded. "Weird bunch, aren't they?"

Below, the hell night of rehearsals relentlessly went on. There was no sleep. Hours crawled slow. Doors to gypsy and dwarf huts were booted open, caravans were invaded. Those who'd passed out from exhaustion, or who hadn't found devious enough hiding spots for stealing sleep, were dragged before George. They were lashed, and if they mouthed off, sent to join those strapped to benches in the Funhouse. Even George's favorites, the acrobats, were not spared the lash; their cries of pain rang out as George happened to catch them sitting down to discuss a routine and deemed them shirking. Before every carny rat in the show there stretched an infinite hell of this treatment: all-night rehearsals, sleep a crime to be punished, the lash or worse, and beyond all this, no pay to take the edge off.

Eyes following George's movements about the place began to smolder with rage. A few private thoughts, unspeakable even a day ago under the gaze of GEORGE IS WATCHING posters began to whisper back and forth. Only a dozen lumberjacks stood between the carnies and a good night's rest; lumberjacks, the goon, and the heretofore sacrosanct understanding that one simply did not disobey the proprietor . . . for that meant trouble *below*.

But this proprietor was in trouble with the ones below. His shrillness and panic said as much. Some had been near George's trailer when the phone rang, had heard his whimpering. Rumor, exaggerating as it passed from mouth to mouth, spread quickly.

In the clown tent, rehearsals were over and the clowns lazed about on their stage. George would not be back to bother them after what had happened, Gonko was sure of that. Had he lashed Rufshod instead of Goshy, there'd have been little commotion. The moment the lash wrapped itself around Goshy's face, Doopy tackled the goon, spilling George in a backwards roll across the ground, Doopy's windmill fists busy pounding until Gonko wrenched him back. "Not fair Gonko, nuh uh, he shouldn'ta oughtn'ta done it, Goshy didn't do nothin,' was being the best super duper clown he could so's he can go lick the sky pretties one day, what taste like ice cream, Gonko, just like ice cream . . ."

"Ease off, George," said Gonko. "We ain't been part of this failing enterprise. Aren't there worse slackers than us you ought to go hassle?"

George had climbed back onto the goon's saddle and was frantically mashing buttons on its controls until the thing was on its feet again. Quickly George moved it to hide behind the lumberjacks who'd just arrived. "You'll hear about this later," said George. "All of you, after the show, see me in my trailer."

"Can't wait," said Gonko. "You're gonna be in such a sweetheart mood when you see how much dust we pull in, boss, I bet you'll just smother us in kisses."

Goshy's lips pursed, brow furrowed. Confused kissing sounds ensued. Doopy seemed already to have forgotten any cause for upset: "Why, yeah, that's gonna be swell. We're gonna kiss George tomorrow, Goshy, ain't that neat?" And that had been that. Now and then Goshy's hand felt along the lash mark across his face; his teeth would clatter or clown ears would spill out, sending Doops huffing and puffing about "mean old George," but on the whole Gonko was left to his thoughts: namely, what to do with his aboveground carnies when all this blew over. Would it be safe to let them back here, in Kurt's show, where they'd be paid a lot less than they'd lately got used to? What if one day they decided to pull the old competing show routine again? Certainly Fatso could not be allowed to return, lest the Matter Manipulator find out what had happened . . . but what of the others? Maybe they had to be permanently retired . . .

For the second time that night, a white bunny rabbit hopped past their tent's entrance. Two lumberjacks followed it, the big dumb bastards drunk with power and loving their new role as circus cops. One of them looked in, saw the clowns sitting idle, and with a cowboy strut, in he came. "What's this?" he cried, opening his muscled arms in outrage.

"What's what, pal?" said Gonko, eyes narrow.

"I see one, two, three, four slackers all sitting down for an unauthorized rest break. Did I hear Mr. Pilo say in tonight's meeting that we'd be resting and lounging? George warned us about you clowns."

The clowns looked to Gonko for a cue. He stared at the lumberjack for a moment, wondering which way to do this. Direct takedown? Nah, too obvious. Doopy sounded like he needed to blow off some steam anyway. Gonko stood. "Yeah, *about* that. A quiet word with you, sir?"

"I'm listening."

Gonko bowed low, took the chump aside, whispered: "You see that big sack of clay with the lash mark? He's the trouble. Been messing up the act all night. I was wondering. Maybe you could give him a hiding? Few little pops to the jaw should do it. Owe you a bag for your trouble."

The lumberjack scoffed. "Can't manage your own crew?" But at the promise of a bag, he rolled his sleeves over fat biceps, planted his feet before Goshy, shoulders squared. "Slacker!" he barked. "You don't like rehearsing? Don't like orders from George himself? You better answer me."

Goshy blinked with one eye, boggled around the room at the others, whimpered. He turned side-on. The lumberjack moved in front of him, so Goshy kept spinning. "Slacker!" the lumberjack yelled. "Tough guy! What, is this funny? This a joke to you? Stand still. Hey!" Two punches connected to the back of Goshy's head, causing an unseen bell to ring.

"Big meanie," Doopy whispered. "Big . . . meanie. BIG MEANIEEEEE!"

Gonko grabbed the lumberjack's arms and pinned them behind his back. Doopy did his thing. The big chump's head was already flopping around limp when Doopy got a good grip on it, wrenched, pulled, twisted. With the sound of meat being split, the pop of a vertebrae coming loose, the neck stump was encumbered no more and spat blood. Gonko dropped the body at his feet, pulled from his pocket a shovel. "Out back, Ruf," he said. "Dig quick." Gonko drop-kicked the head from their tent door, admiring the arc as it sailed high, to land in Sideshow Alley. More bunnies hopped past outside.

That was the first misfortune to befall George's muscle men. Maybe the head that fell among the exhausted and pissed off carny rats was taken as a heavenly signal to tolerate no more, or maybe it would have happened anyway. But it began to happen right then.

Certainly in Mugabo's tent, patience was already spread thin. The magician needed rest, a dose of powder, and maybe a kind word more than most in the show. On his stage he stood before an upturned top hat on a table. Every minute or so he jammed a gnarled fist inside it, pulled free a white bunny rabbit. "Oh, look, preety bunny," he'd say, tossing the creature to the ground before him. "Mugabo, great power. Big time wizard. But now he make the bunny. The bunny. THE BUNNY!" Interspersed with bouts of weeping, growling, and entreaties to the gods who continued to ignore him.

The bunnies now numbered in the hundreds, exploring their new world for food. It got the attention of George's henchmen. Two lumberjacks now stood at the front row of seats, arms folded, watching the culprit set more rabbits loose. "Hey, you," said one as they advanced on him. "Is this your idea of a joke? What you think you're doing?"

"Bunny treek," Mugabo said slowly for the benefit of these stupids. "I do *bunny treek*. Mugabo has the special magics." The magician spat.

"No more bunnies," said the second lumberjack. "Do different tricks. That's an order."

"Oh no. Mr. Pilo want rehearse? Then Mr. Pilo have the bunny. Lots bunny, more bunny. Here." He produced another and tossed it at them, striking the nearest in the chest.

"I'll give you bunny," the lumberjack said, raising a two-by-four.

"No, no, I geev *you* bunny," said Mugabo, tipping his hat and spilling a dozen more rabbits out. They fled in a blur of white and brown streaking in all directions.

The lumberjacks had bullied Mugabo before, even given the odd shove, but never had they manhandled him the way Gonko used to, with magic pockets to counter the magician's wrath. But the night's events had made them feel rather important and very self-confident, so the two-by-four swung. Mugabo shrieked, blocked the blow with his forearms, fell sprawling across his stage. Pain blasted through his arms. He examined the broken skin with hurt and surprise—in his scrambled brain, the two men and he had been having a friendly chat about the finer points of his magic act; the attack had come from nowhere.

Something happened and Mugabo passed out after, with no actual memory of sending sheets of winding red and orange flame through his fingers. The two piles of ash smoldering on his stage were a great surprise to him; he only knew he had grazed and bruised forearms and that a commotion was brewing out in the showgrounds. He even forgot the idea of rehearsing and wondered why the heck he was still awake. He stumbled to bed, prayed his usual sarcastic prayers of thanks to the gods, and then slept.

So it was that only nine lumberjacks now stood between George and many thoroughly disenchanted carnies. Soon it was eight lumberjacks—the flick of a knife as one blustered through Sideshow Alley saw to that, the killer lost among the crowds with no witnesses inclined to report him. Another lumberjack sipped delightedly at a cup of poisoned broth, handed him by a grand-motherly-looking gypsy woman, who had for many days been earning his trust reporting minor transgressions at every chance. The remaining six, one by one, did the rounds in search of their brothers, who'd not returned from patrols. So eager were the carny rats to do in wrongdoers of late, and so dimly did the lumberjacks perceive the hostility all around them, they were certain that word of any true foul play would have already reached them.

Gonko was not without concern for reprisals—having had one of the big fuckers decapitated—but he noticed that fewer and fewer lumberjacks were happening by on rabbit clean-up detail. He took a stroll through Sideshow Alley, wary of the murderous looks he got from those running rides and stalls. But he also spied with his little eye the occasional body left only partly concealed by old blankets. One of the few remaining muscle men loped through the stalls now, calling the names of his friends with profound confusion on his face.

A rather public demonstration was called for, it seemed to Gonko, one that expressed both solidarity with the murderous carnies to draw the heat off, and reminded them of an old circus tradition: don't fuck with Gonko the clown. From his pants came a baseball bat with jagged metal spikes. The carnies who'd been eyeing each other off to see who'd do the honors this time, saw some first rate clubbing-to-death, with the legs and arms pulverized to goo first, and some theatrical hollering Gonko assumed would hit the spot for these folk. "For too long has your lash fallen on the backs of these, my people! They may smell bad, but they are true carnies, and no longer shall blah, blah, blah!" Crunch, crunch, thump.

It went down well—too well. He had not meant for the gesture to be interpreted thus: *Hey guys, let's rush George and mob him, then get ourselves some shut-eye, and to hell with doing a show tomorrow.* But that's just how they took it. "To George!" the chant went up.

"Shit," said Gonko. Fast death by mob trampling was not the revenge he'd worked and risked for—the big bosses would dish it out far tastier, as he well knew. The carnies, old and young, dwarf, gypsy, and miscellaneous, rushed past him in all directions, knives and clubs raised.

Gonko launched springs from his heels, jumped across rooftops, and floated to the ground. The hubbub was sweeping through the whole place. "Where's George?" he asked what was probably the last lumberjack, who stood rather nervously a short distance away, trying to look important.

"Freak show," the lumberjack answered.

"Thanks," said Gonko. Then it was time for the ol' hatchet thrown into the noggin gag, and the lumberjacks became extinct.

George had hustled into the freak show only some minutes before, dismounting his goon and leaving it at the entrance. "Enjoy . . . the exhibitsssss," Dr. Gloom rustled.

Inside, George first hushed the mermaid, whose song was like red-hot matches in his brain. Poor Kurt would have heard rather a lot of her voice, and had George to thank for it, but George was entirely sure this exercise would have been futile even in kinder circumstances. But his options were few. He stood by Kurt's glass display, not quite knowing how to begin.

Slowly Kurt's eyes rose to meet his. The fat lips pulled up slowly to a grin. "Why, hello George," Kurt said. "Come to have a poke? Isn't it strange? One gets used to nearly anything, doesn't one?" Kurt considered this, then whispered, "*Nearly* anything."

"Yeah. Hey, Kurt, I could use some advice."

"Oh, ho ho."

"No, really. The show's gone to the dogs. No powder's coming out of the tricks. The phone's gonna ring again tomorrow, and I don't know what to tell the bosses. A show every day? It's nuts. I need to buy some time to work out who's messing up the shows."

"Hm."

"What do I tell 'em when they call, Kurt?"

"I fear I am only qualified to offer some general advice."

George leaned eagerly over the glass case. "Yes?"

"First, you must strive for excellence in all you do. Second, you must have a rapport with your staff. Cultivate a rapport, so that you may leaven authority with friendship! Third, if opportunity fails to knock, you must build a door."

George made a choking sound. "What kind of baloney—a door? You're full of it. What do I tell them, damn it? They're going to send me down there, you bastard. Help me!"

"Hm. Now, now, one mustn't name call."

George screamed, grabbed the sharp stick, and jabbed it in his brother's cheek. Kurt's smile slowly flatlined. "Jab, jab," George cried as he did it. "Tell me what to tell 'em. Tell me, tell me, tell—"

"Why, hello, Gonko," said Kurt.

"You want me to tell 'em that?" George screamed.

"Hope I'm not interrupting," said Gonko, strolling up behind George.

George wheeled about. "You should be rehearsing!"

"You got a little problem, boss," said Gonko. "Which is to say, you're fucked. Your goon outside's been messed up. The lumberjacks are all dead. And the carny rats are revolting."

"Now, now, one mustn't name call," said Kurt.

"Rioting, boss, is what I mean."

"I'm the boss here," said George.

"Uh?" said Gonko. "Right, sure you are. So the problem is, you set foot outside and you're gonna get trampled to death and set on fire. None of us wants that." Gonko glanced at Kurt. "Do we?"

"Oh my heavens, no," said Kurt.

"So here's the plan, I sneak you to your trailer, calm everyone down, and we do our show tomorrow like we planned. How 'bout it, boss?"

George whimpered, sat down, and put his head in his hands. Gonko draped a sheet on him with the eyeholes cut out, and without waiting for an answer, carried him like a baby through the stream of carny rats. Some of them spotted the now-deceased goon outside the freak show, and a stampede of them went in, giving Gonko a clear run to George's trailer. He kicked its door in, tossed George violently across the desk, grabbed the megaphone, and then began barricading the door. "What are you doing?" George said from within. "You're shutting me in so I can't run the show!"

"Nah, boss, just making sure you're safe," said Gonko, hammering on one last plank. "I'll come for ya when it cools down out here. Sit tight."

"Don't go, Gonko! Don't leave me here."

Gonko would have stayed to listen to that sweet music all night, but this riot jazz was getting a bit wild. He went to the busiest part and addressed the crowd with the megaphone: "Relax, you fucks. George has been dealt with. Repeat, George has been pounded into sludge. Go home and go to bed. You will be paid tomorrow from George's secret stash. Repeat, two bags each. And a partridge in a pear tree. Go to bed. Show tomorrow as planned."

For just a few seconds it looked dicey, like the lot of them were about to rush him and force him to pull something seriously heavy duty from his pockets. But they wanted rest and powder just a touch more than they wanted blood, so there were only a few among them who had to be individually stared down or threatened with a cleaver before they joined the others, slinking back to their homes.

13. ABOVE

As all this went on below, Jamie and JJ returned to the sleeping circus above, where JJ went digging to see the size of Gonko's stash (and likely to help himself to some of it, which gave Jamie a relieving break from his "new pal"). Jamie roused Dean, took him beyond earshot of the camp, over by the edge of a little stream. "This looks like the end for the show up here," said Jamie. "From what I overheard, George is finished down there after tomorrow. They'll have a new boss, and Gonko won't need all this up here."

"And what happens to us?" said Dean.

"I guess we'll be taken below, made part of their circus."

"You guess. That's the problem."

"What do you mean?"

"This up here is a big secret for them, right? And all of us know about it. Would the clowns like everyone running loose below with the chance to talk?"

"It shouldn't matter," Jamie said uneasily. "The only one who'd care down there is George, and if he's gone . . ."

Dean waved it away. "Yeah, maybe. We'd better hope that's how it is. From what you told me, the guy in charge isn't really the guy in charge. So, what's next for us? Can we do the same thing these guys did and starve out the circus?"

"Not right away. Like you say, too many people would know exactly what was happening. And there's really only three of us who'd do it, if you include JJ. Who I don't entirely trust just yet. So we'd have to bide our time, find people down there who aren't content, and recruit them. It might take years."

"No fucking way." Dean grabbed Jamie's arm and held it roughly. "I'm not giving a decade of my life or more to these cunts, this circus or whatever it really is. I want to get back to living my life or get taken out quickly. Don't you?"

Jamie sighed. "Your life won't be the same either way, believe me. And maybe some things can't be helped, and maybe we have a chance to do something more important than get a mortgage or get laid on the weekend. I'd wait it out for the ideal chance, even if it took years. But if you think of a better idea, I'm all ears ."

Dean released his grip. Some night creature cried eerily from the block of silhouetted trees around them, and they both jumped, looked at each other, and laughed. Dean said, "Anyway. There's four of us, if you include Jodi. I haven't been able to speak to her. Every day they take her makeup off as she sleeps and usually put it back on before she can wake up and freak out. We need to talk to her, and see if she can be any help."

"No better time than now," said Jamie. Dean nodded, rushed off, and returned some minutes later with one arm around Jodi's arms and a hand over her mouth. Her eyes were wide and she was wrenching herself around, fighting against his grip. Dean whispered soothing things into her ear until he was sure she wouldn't scream. "Me and Jamie are thinking of ways to get us out of here," he said. "Listen to me. *Stop* being scared, okay? Yeah, it's all weird, but don't be scared."

When his hand came off her mouth, she laughed without humor. "Oh, now why wouldn't I be scared? Aren't we all being held captive by a bunch of—"

"Yes," Jamie whispered fiercely. "So get *pissed off!* These freaks took you out of your life. What right did they have to do that? Get angry for fuck's sake." This struck a chord with her—she met his eyes and nodded.

"We can't just run away," Dean said. "We can't, I dunno, fist-fight our way out of this. We're going to take them out from the inside. Tell us about what happens to you when they put the makeup on."

Jodi shut her eyes and looked like someone trying to remember a dream. "She's . . . Emerald is just above it all. She loves herself so much she's hardly even aware of anything else, I've never felt anything like it. You heard of narcissism, but hers is off the charts. Thinks she's queen of the world. It's ridiculous. She kind of likes you, Dean, the same way a kid likes a toy, but she liked you better when you were a clown. She's getting bored with you now. She's getting a bit of a crush on the clown leader. So if you want Emerald to help in any way, I frankly don't see how you'll convince her."

They were quiet for a while, each thinking. "But we have you," Jamie said. "I don't think they'll be doing consecutive show days when we go to the main circus; that's only being done because we're starving them out. So they won't keep you in makeup all the time. Are you willing to help us, if we need you? Even if it involves risk?"

Distantly the thin wail of a baby Goshy reached them: "Help, help . . ."

"Not much choice, is there?" said Jodi, and her look told Jamie that the blame for all of this was still squarely on him. He guessed that didn't much matter.

He said, "Good. I guess we'll talk again when we have a better idea what we're going to do."

"One thing," said Dean. "Just a test. It may achieve nothing, but it might be worth a try."

"What?" said the other two together.

"The music box. Let's do an experiment tomorrow, when the show's on. Let's see what happens when the music stops playing, even for just a minute or two."

"Take out the dwarf who spins it, is that what you're saying?" said Jamie. "How do you think Gonko's going to like that? Which one of us gets that job?"

Dean smiled. "Let's see if JJ's really on the team or not."

JJ lay in some dreamy fantasy state next to the hole where he'd dug up Gonko's huge stash of powder. Jamie and Dean were lucky enough to find him before anyone else did. They refilled the hole, carried JJ into the tent and tossed him on a mattress, along with the clay bowl he'd used to make his wishes, whatever they were.

The show around them went about its business more relaxed than usual without Gonko's storm cloud temper hovering above. Dean and Curls went with their gates to the same train station as yesterday, unconcerned that some of the same tricks may come through their show again. It wouldn't matter if those tricks had been "harvested" already; sending them below, unable to be harvested again, was the whole point. The crop was a fresh one, however; when the show began, powder fell in its usual amounts. Jamie did a final patrol for Gonko, who did not come, but on his way back to try to finally rouse JJ, he came face-to-face with Emerald. Only her eyes showed above the veil, and she gave him a look he did not like at all.

Oh shit—he suddenly realized that she was privy to everything they'd said to Jodi. *Double shit* . . . He could not tell by her stare whether it was accusing, angry, or just her usual regard for the surrounding world—irrelevant unless it confirmed her beauty. To that end he blew her a kiss and bowed low; she faintly nodded before Jamie ceased to exist in her private universe. Or so he hoped.

"Shoo, clown, don't bother the real star in this dump," one of her minders said. He gladly obeyed.

JJ was at last stirring on his mattress. Jamie had tried cold water, slaps, and loud noises to no effect, but this time a few slaps did the job and earned him a kick across the tent in the bargain. "What the hell happened to you?" said Jamie. "We need you."

"Wished I was in a coma. Kind of like being dead, but it's nicer, with no one to bother you."

"We have a mission for you. As part of the grand plan. You have to steal the music box and keep it away from the dwarf for a little while, once the show has started."

JJ listened to the details, and shook his head. "But why?"

"We're just gathering intel for future plans. This will either give us something to build on or it'll rule it out and we can look elsewhere. And . . ." he'd debated whether or not to say it, "Dean isn't totally sure we can trust you yet. But this will prove to him that you're on our side."

JJ's face could hardly have better imitated a chastised puppy. "Aw. You trust me, don't you, Jamie? We're amigos, aren't we?"

"You seem okay to me."

"I *seem* . . . 'okay' . . . to you," JJ whispered.

"Don't take it personally! Look at it from my perspective, yesterday you tied me up, bashed me, then threatened to kill me with an axe. Come on, do you accept the mission or not? Gonko's not here to bust you. Just five minutes of your time."

"Eh, all right."

Jamie wasn't sure he'd do it. There was a new sullenness about JJ after that conversation, and he muttered one or two things about Dean. The tricks arrived, the music box began its song, and Jamie waited til Dean returned with Curls, before telling JJ, "Now. Go!"

JJ had acquired a thousand-stitch headband adorned with a rising sun. "Bonsai!" he yelled, and rather than sneak in to take the music box, he pretty much advertised the deed to all carnies in view, his shrieking war cry reminiscent of Goshy's finest. He held the music box aloft and ran, crying a number of slogans like, "Viva resistance!" and "You may chase the revolutionary, but you may not chase the revolution." Chase they did, four enraged dwarfs moving quick on stubby legs, yet with precisely no chance of catching JJ, who made a wide hollering circuit of the park.

Meanwhile, Dean and Jamie watched carefully. Those carnies by the games stood dumbfounded, utterly unsure what to do. They stopped trying to lure tricks to their games with their diamonds and gems. As for the tricks, they came to a standstill, but they didn't quite seem *woken* yet; it was more like everything had paused, tricks and carnies both.

Dean stood before one of them, a man in a business suit of middle age, whose white beard would have looked at home on a mall Santa. Dean snapped his fingers in the guy's ears. "Wake up," he said. "Wake up! Look around you. You shouldn't *be* here. Where are you?"

The man blinked, rubbed his face as he looked around. "Must've . . . fallen asleep on the train," he said thickly. But he was waking up now and staring about with growing alarm. As were one or two of the others.

"That's enough," Jamie told Dean. Now it came down to whether JJ remembered their prearranged signal, because no one was going to catch him. "Ouch! My foot," Jamie called on JJ's nearest orbit.

JJ remembered. He placed the music box down and kept sprinting, whooping like one of the Three Stooges, arms flapping like a chicken trying to fly. The dwarfs tripped over each other in their desperation to grab the music box and twist the handle. The calliope moaned, the music tinkled down in a thick mist of sound; gradually, the awoken tricks resumed their sleep. "What are you supposed to be, some kind of clown?" the bearded man said to Jamie with drunken good cheer. The traveling circus had missed a beat or two, but now resumed like nothing had happened. Glittering dust continued to fall to the grass.

The last phase of the plan was marching JJ visibly past the vengeful carnies, making a big show of his "arrest" so that ideally no one would report all this to Gonko. "Trying to ruin our show?" Jamie yelled. "You're a disgrace to all clowns."

"Come here and get what's coming to you," said Dean.

"But it was just an overly zealous prank," said JJ, "with no actual intent to undermine the show with any broader view to exploiting and or learning about its vulnerabilities! The shame I feel is surely punishment enough."

They took him into the clown tent, made some convincing sounds of a thrashing—thumping the mattresses with wood while JJ squealed and begged for mercy. Tomato sauce was liberally applied. Curls popped his head in to see Dean and Jamie standing over a shivering bundle beneath a blanket. "You kilt him?" said Curls.

"Not quite," said Jamie, "but he won't pull that stunt again."

"No, sir, I won't," JJ said, coughing. "I have learned via savage beating that there are limits to the ways in which one should express one's devil-may-care attitude, and music box theft is a big no-no."

Curls grunted. "Don't tell Gonko about it, all right? I'm in charge here; he'll have my nuts. And I need 'em!"

"You got it."

Dean and Jamie exchanged a look that served as a high-five. "Happy with how that went?" said Dean.

"Food for thought," said Jamie. "Talk to you later."

Without a clown show—Jamie didn't attempt a one-clown act, and JJ had to recover from his "thrashing"—there wasn't quite as much harvested as yesterday's show, but the other attractions made the difference negligible. Emerald filled several buckets herself as her gypsy minders crooned their approval (and handled her sulks.) The freak show outdid itself—in fact overdid itself: Fatso ate his way into retirement.

His depression had grown, since no one bothered to tell him why he was no longer with his friend Wallace the Walrus and could no longer hear the mermaid song he'd come to love. His act was not ever intended for several consecutive show days; he needed days off to munch protein powder and heal the bites. Well, after the last trick had been sent below, Fatso ate, and ate, and would not listen to a word anyone said. He twice bit at hands that reached in to stop him. His eyes were bright with hunger; blood flushed from his cage. His legs were soon gone, bones and all. His left arm was no more, his right remained in place only to help scoop the meat from his torso. Soon he'd consumed himself up to the waist. Panting, lunging forward with growing eagerness for one more bite, he gasped, "People always tell me I got bad taste." He ripped a chunk off his chest. "Now, I can prove 'em wrong." Fatso swallowed, sending the morsel plopping out the other end of his severed torso where it joined the pile of red chewed lumps and spilled-out organs. And those were his last words. Fatso shivered, fell back, and was no more. Those who were witness to the last bite staggered away, retching.

"Fiddlesticks," said the severed head.

14. BELOW

Below was no safe or easy time for anyone perceived as part of the circus hierarchy. Shalice and the Matter Manipulator wisely stayed in their dens, watching from windows, and waiting for order. Gonko warned the other clowns to avoid Sideshow Alley, though he himself strolled through on occasion to gauge the mood. It was simmering. His promise of payment alone probably kept the general hostility to glares and whispers. Some time later the bolder carny rats would need to be reminded of their place in the grand scheme, and Gonko took note of certain names and faces. Every time he went out of sight of George's trailer for more than a few minutes, a small crowd of carny rats gathered there, only to scatter when he reappeared. He considered letting Kurt out of his cage, but held off—it would need to be clear to the big bosses below exactly who was running the failed circus, or else they may just grab Kurt along with George if he were running around giving orders.

Gonko also itched to return to the surface and make sure the show up there did its job. If the tricks came down here and started making good with the dust . . . but then, odds were decent the carny rats would just help themselves to whatever they saw, with no one but Gonko to stop them. And of course, he'd let them help themselves.

His pocket watch alarm shook and bounced in his pants. The show above was almost done. *Fuck it,* he thought. He was going to risk a quick trip up there. He armed Doopy and Rufshod with axes, and set them at George's trailer. He hid Goshy under a tarp, and then waited til the tricks began to arrive. It looked like about half the carny rats were up for the job today; fewer calls than the usual "Step right up!" and so on. Only a couple of the rides had their flashing lights on and their mechanical growl of starting engines.

Curls and two others at last came through, the exit gate pieces in their arms. "Set 'em up now," said Gonko. "I'm going up. Oh, and Curls? Don't let anyone whose up there come down just yet, not til I debrief them. Got it?"

Curls searched Gonko's face, trying to see what this order portended, but he could read nothing in the hard lines and creases, in the black smile-shaped curve painted over the background of white.

15. ABOVE

onko found them picking through the grass for the night's takings with cigarette lighters and lanterns. He took JJ and Jamie aside and said, "You two, get below. No need to worry about George seeing you now."

"Kurt's back already?" said JJ with cheer so false it made Jamie cringe.

"Not yet, but today's the day. JJ, a private word?" Jamie watched the pair of them from a distance in quiet conversation and he could not say why it made him so uneasy. After, Gonko went around to every other carny and told each of them the same thing: "It ain't safe down there yet. You been marked down as runaways, and you know what that means. Don't you worry, I'll smooth it over real gentle. Stay put for a couple of days, then I'll send for you one by one."

With that, Gonko headed for the gates again. "Hey, Gonko," Jamie called as he jogged over. "Dean—Deeby—and Emerald. Is it okay if they come back with us? They're kind of friends of mine, and they've been eager to see the real circus."

"Is that so?" said Gonko. His eyes were thin slits, following Emerald as she breezed across the ground at that moment with her veil tossed back. As usual, heads turned to follow her; even now Jamie felt the pull of her enchantment. "Ain't she a pretty little number," said Gonko. "You know what, just those two, they can come down. But no one else. Keep her wearing that veil. You don't want Kurt or the MM to get too smitten with her. And *she* sure as hell don't want that." Gonko leaped through the gates without another word, and Jamie thought, *Why do I have the strange feeling I just saved Dean and Jodi's lives?*

A finger tapped him hard on the shoulder. JJ grinned from ear to ear. "Get this! Gonko's gonna kill everyone up here, except for you and me. Makes you feel pretty special, huh?" JJ laughed at a joke only he could see.

"So that's why," said Jamie.

"And he wants me to help him do it. He would've asked you but thinks you'd back out. Best part is, he's not even mad I came up here. He didn't want me to see any of this, he told me, but he says he knows he can trust me now."

"Why's he want *you* to help him kill everyone? Actually I'd feel better if you don't answer that. Dean and Jodi are coming with us below. When's he going to do it?"

"After he's sure George has gone for good and he doesn't need these carnies anymore. He's been paying 'em so well, he figures when they get back to normal wages below, they'll get the idea of setting up on their own again. That's what he says, anyway."

Jamie groaned. He looked around at the handful of gypsies and dwarfs finishing up the day's count with tired faces, but alight with greed as they pocketed their own helpings of the powder, more brazenly than before. Seeing them, they looked like utterly wretched creatures living wretched lives; he could not help thinking an end to their misery would be a mercy, not just for those they preyed on in the circus, but for themselves. It was a queasy thought that they would all soon be killed unless he said something, queasy only because it offended the sensibilities; he could not feel any love nor much compassion for these beings. Still . . . "Are we going to let him do it?"

JJ scoffed. "Carny rats? You want to blow your big grand plan to save a bunch of carny rats who'd gut you for a bag if they knew they'd get away with it? Look at these trash bags! See, here is a clown who never had to make tough choices. This one's not even tough. I'll kill 'em, no problem. You don't have to watch."

Jamie looked at his own face staring back scornfully. *These freaks took you out of your life*, what he'd told Jodi echoed through his mind. *What right did they have to do that?* And these guys were all willing parts of it; they'd chased after the music box, desperate to twist its handle again. If they weren't *willing* parts of it, they were little more than nuts and bolts of the circus machinery. "You're right," he said. "Let's get Dean and Jodi and get out of here."

But JJ was far too light-hearted about the business of murder. Jamie knew that he had to learn everything he could about this doppelganger, who could ruin them now with just a few words. Deeper than that, he had to see whether there was something connecting them beyond just physical similarity; did Jamie himself do these kinds of deeds, last time here? Was guilt the reason he'd blocked it all out? He could wait no more. He would recover his hidden memories and find out why he'd hidden them.

16. BELOW

Only the acrobats seemed to really give it their all down below, and of course even they could do little to bring in any takings from the pre-milked tricks. What little soul dust fell was very swiftly pinched up and stuffed into pockets, with now and then the odd squabble breaking out over it and turning nasty.

Gonko let it all unfold, enjoying every moment. He only had to contend with an arson attempt at George's trailer; since George hadn't been wise enough to keep from screaming, a few carny rats knew he'd not in fact been stomped to sludge. That small group, scheming for the mythical secret stash for themselves, thankfully kept their mouths shut about it or the whole lot of them would have stampeded to the trailer.

Jamie took Emerald to the fortuneteller, hoping if Shalice wouldn't take her in she could at least advise somewhere safe for her to live. The fortuneteller gave him a strange look when they arrived at her door. "Does anyone know you brought this girl here?" she said.

"No ma'am," said Jamie.

"You're quite sure?"

"Yes, ma'am. Why is it so important?"

Without an answer, Shalice glanced left and right outside, then quickly pulled Emerald within, slamming and locking the door behind them.

Jamie hid Dean in one of the clown bedrooms, unsure where to put him longer term. Maybe he could find Dean a home with the other ticket collectors soon, but that would mean getting embroiled in the deadly politics, etiquette, and factions—all of it a mystery to those locked outside of it.

Jamie paced nervously. "There had better be somewhere to hide you. Problem is, you stand out. No one down here knows you but the clowns, and you can't join us."

"Worst comes to worst, I'll risk making a run for it," Dean said, "whether they find me later or not."

"Trust me, they will find you. And whoever you're with at the time. And in the meantime, you'll have two missing people to explain. Remember when you reported me to the medical authorities? What do you think they're going to do when they turn up at our flat, find blood all over the floor, signs of a struggle, and three people missing?"

"Well, fuck it. I'll take the gates up, bring a whole bunch of cops down here—" Dean sat up so quickly it looked like a live wire had been pressed into him. "That's it! Man, it's so obvious. I know how we can beat these bastards."

"Shh!" Jamie said. He heard voices nearby; they weren't alone.

"You shouldn'ta said it, but, Ruf, it's downright no good to done said that," said Doopy.

"George said it, you big dummy. George, in his trailer, who we were guarding, remember?"

"But you didn't oughta have to call me a big dummy, Ruf! It was soooo mean."

"Go argue with JJ, I'm busy." There was a scuffle out in the living room area, the noise of a fist fight, with both clowns crying out in pain at random intervals filled with comic slapstick sounds. Jamie waited for it to end so he could hear Dean's idea, but it didn't end; the minutes ticked by slowly and still the two clowns battled.

Finally Jamie gave up waiting and took from his pocket the clay pot he'd seen JJ use up on the surface. "What the hell are you doing?" Dean whispered.

Jamie sprinkled some powder on the clay, with no idea how much to use. He lit it with a match (a box of them sat on the bedside table), watched as the grains melted with faint sounds like someone crying out. Did one wish before or after swallowing? He didn't know, so he did both, drinking down the tasteless warm liquid. "I wish for the return of memories I previously wished to be hidden."

Then he sat back, reeling as sights, sounds, feelings, fears, and experiences flashed and flooded into him, knocking him flat. He saw Goshy diving from a rooftop to land face-first into concrete. There was Winston, old, tired, and desperate for it all to end, sad eyes gazing blankly while his chest was jammed with hot coals. He saw Fishboy, the former freak show curator whose work had been futile in the end, his rebellion a mere disruption to the show's smooth running for a brief time, just a blink in its ancient history. He saw that what he had just melted down and drank was made of human souls—divine, pure things beyond this sad world, trapped here then ripped out of unknowing people like meat from their bodies. And he knew the moment of fear, weakness, and exhaustion that had made him blast all this from memory. There was Kurt—huge, howling, and inhuman—trampling down lives like fruit being squashed, biting, shivering the turf with his footfalls and his roar.

But most of all, he saw JJ. JJ, who was now his "pal" and comrade, drenching their shared body in murdered blood, killing for fun, for the rush of it. No wonder Gonko had brought JJ in on the task of killing those above; JJ would do it gladly. JJ who "just wanted his own body," whose idea of a joke was to stand above Jamie with an axe raised, murder on his face . . .

Dean was shaking his shoulder, had probably been doing so for many minutes. He looked worried. In the other room, Doopy and Rufshod still grappled and slapped each other. "What is it?" said Dean.

"We got a big problem." Jamie swallowed what felt like a brick sinking down his belly. "JJ. My God, I should have done this a lot sooner."

"What about him? He's doing okay so far. The music box, remember?"

"Oh, I remember all right." Jamie shook his head. Where to start? At least he remembered one useful thing: the place Fishboy and his rebellion used to go and meet. There was a fence down an alley with the board that came loose, a thin ledge behind it, and a platform stretched out over a long drop to nowhere. A hiding spot where none would see them. He gestured for Dean to follow.

Before they'd left the room, the tarp in the corner *moved*. It had been dead still til now, with not even the faintest rustle, but now Jamie lifted its bottom an inch or two and saw the red clown shoes beneath. He yanked the tarp off, and screamed. Goshy stared out with one wide bloodshot eye, the other slitted like a lizard's. His mouth peeled back into bunches of ringed flesh. A burbling whine spilled out: "Oo, ngh, eee." He spun toward the door, missed it by several meters, and walked face first into a crunched hole of plaster, screaming all the while.

Jamie and Dean sprinted away, past Doopy and Rufshod head-locking each other out in the main room. The circus music outside had stopped playing; the tricks had been sent home—the day's show was done. "He heard too much," Dean said when they came at last to a halt. "We're fucked."

"Maybe, but he can't *talk*. He can't tell the others what he heard."

"You sure about that?"

"Christ, Dean. No, I'm not, but let's hope it's right." They jogged through the showgrounds. It had changed its layout from what he remembered, but it wasn't long before Jamie found the alleyway with a popcorn vendor at one end. They walked casually into the alley's shadows, and no one seemed to see them. Jamie said, "Now look, this board here?" He wrenched it back. "Here's a place to hide. If you can't find a home in the showgrounds, stay out here. I can bring food and water, when no one's watching." Dean looked out at the abyss with wide eyes. "The path's only thin for a little while," Jamie said. "There's a wider platform out there. It's where the good guys used to meet when I was here last time."

"And how'd that work out for you?" Dean said, perhaps irritated because he had a bunch of new fears to contend with, including the drop to oblivion at his feet. "I'm going to try for a room first. This is—"

"JAYYY, MEEEEE!" a singsong voice called. "Wherefore art thou, most handsomest clown of all?"

"Fuck! It's JJ. Go, Dean, get out there. Don't let him know we're using this spot."

"Look, is he on our side or not?"

"I don't know. I'll be back as soon as I can. Hold onto the fence as you go around." Jamie sprinted from the alley before JJ could find him there, although maybe JJ would guess where he'd been anyway. A hand grabbed his shoulder; he jumped and screamed.

"So nervous," JJ observed. "That's quite a flinch. What shenanigans have got your nerve strings all aquiver?"

"Ah, you know, I'm just looking for some action."

"Look no further! Some action comes our way. Gonko sent me to find you, wants you to witness the proudest moment in clown history. That's what he said."

"Lead the way my man," said Jamie with forced cheer. JJ skipped off ahead and Jamie could think only of waking in their shared body, covered in blood, with shared memories of killing, murder, death . . .

On a patch of turf near the Funhouse there was a large bucket that spun on an axle. Below it was a steel cover, which opened when a pedal was stepped on. It was into this bucket that management—either one of the Pilo brothers or a trusted lackey—would drop the tribute for those below, sometimes several bucket loads, which then dropped down a chute, passed along a tunnel and fed the dust to the bosses beneath. Carny rats had an old tradition of coming by immediately after, to scavenge anything that may have spilled to the ground, the odds reckoned roughly a one perfect chance for any spillage at all, rarer still for a goodly amount (rare, but not unheard of.) Tonight's odds, of course, were substantially lower; for the first time in memory, a show had been put on with not a single grain of powder offered to those below.

Consequently, in George's boarded up trailer, the phone began to ring.

For an hour, it rang. In that time it became the sound of insanity itself. George knew he was fucked, whether he picked it up or ignored it. Taking it off the hook alone did not stop it ringing. So he ignored it, right up until it seemed the pain of its ring drilling in his skull was worse than anything *they* might dish out. He put the earpiece to his ear. The tense silence spread beyond his trailer; the din of expectant chatter outside quieted down to nothing.

Through the earpiece came what may have been breathing. George sucked in air to say "Hello," but at that moment came "YOU. ARE. DOOMED."

"Aw, c'mon!"

"COME. BELOW. NOW."

"I can't. I'm trapped in my trailer, see? Long story. And see, I'd love nothing more than to come explain to you all what happened, but we have a little trouble up here, and these employees are getting rowdy. It's Kurt's fault really. Kurt was interfering with the show. You gotta get rid of him, then it'll all go back to normal."

"COME. BELOW. NOW."

"Why wouldn't you ever help me when I asked?" George's voice went shrill. Outside, many listened with interest. "I told you something fishy was going on up here, but you didn't even—"

"COME. NOW."

"I can't!"

"THEN ONE SHALL. BE SENT. FOR YOU. AND YOUR. TORMENT. MADE WORSE." The line went dead.

"Say, George, everything okay in there?" Gonko called. "Just weep hysterically if there's anything Uncle Gonko can do for ya."

173

The quiet sobbing was not hysterical, but it was still a pretty sweet symphony. A fair crowd had gathered by now, mostly waiting for their promised cut of George's fabled private stash, but many who bore scars from the lash were, like Gonko, enjoying the show. JJ kicked and shoved a path through the crowd, earning hateful glares for he and Jamie, who followed him.

"Where's the cut you promised us?" someone in the crowd yelled at Gonko, provoking a chorus of "Yeah!" and "Where's the goods?"

Gonko looked out at the gathered faces for whoever had initiated this hassle, to make note of another carny rat to visit when all was normal again. In so doing he spotted Jamie and JJ, gestured for them to come near, whispered: "Go up top; get my stash. Divvy it into small bags—just a pinch in each. Any amount will be a feast to these turds. Hell, just get me twenty bags, then they can duke it out themselves. Hustle! I'm trying to enjoy the demise of George here, and now they bug me with this crap."

"Should we do that other thing, boss?" said JJ. Jamie looked at him sidelong and saw eagerness.

"Not yet. We ought to know George's future in the next hour or two. Then we'll talk."

17. ABOVE

It was quiet among the tents in the twilight above—in fact, so quiet Jamie felt the hairs on his neck stand up. There was no snoring, or murmuring in sleep that was the usual late-night soundtrack to the aboveground show at night. JJ seemed not to notice, happily whistling as he retrieved a shovel from under the caravan and went to the buried stash. "What's with you, Jamie?" he said, pausing mid dig and looking into Jamie's eyes with his own flat buttons.

"What do you mean?"

"You gone all quiet just lately. All quiet and thinky."

"Guess I'm just trying to think up a plan, as to what we can do about all this. It might be different for you, but I come from a place where all of this stuff is not normal. Freaks me out sometimes, you know? We're not taking on an easy job."

JJ resumed digging. "Job? Oh, all that stuff you wanna do. Guess I forgot about it."

Jamie tried not to make it obvious that he watched JJ closely. Could not a suicidal, homicidal loon be made valuable to almost any cause? Maybe tasks awaited that Jamie and Dean simply had no stomach for. But what he now remembered of JJ troubled him deeply; the clown may have agreed to help them on a moment's whim, which could change literally at any second, with JJ blabbing

175

what he knew to Gonko or Kurt. Suddenly Jamie and Dean were in one hell of a hurry or . . . a quiet voice suggested deep from his mind's recesses, *there were ways to ensure JJ wouldn't say a word of it to anyone, ever . . .*

"Help me bag this stuff," said JJ, yanking out one of the powder sacks from its hole. "Don't just stand there deep in contemplative thought."

They'd portioned out only three velvet bags with a meager pinch of dust in each (JJ pocketing a far greater amount for himself) when a strange voice warbled "Help, help." Strange because it was not too unlike the sound of a baby Goshy, but much deeper. JJ, Jamie, and the entire night—from the moon, stars, curtains of cloud, and silhouetted trees beyond the clearing—tensed and listened. Faint sounds of feet scuffing clumsy on the grass; a gargling noise. And "Help, help," again, deep and not quite human. The voice was filled with fear, seemed to say with its one word *Something preys on me . . .*

"Hurry," Jamie said. He crept through the dewy grass to the caravan. Dark drops and splashes spattered the cream-colored canvas at its rear. A small shape dropped out onto the grass when he parted the flap to look inside. The cry that came out of Jamie was as involuntary as his backward jump; really, he did not think by now that the sight of a severed hand should be this much of a shock, even when unexpected. There it was by his shoe, perfectly harmless, adorned with a cheap brass ring with crescent moon. *Shoo, clown,* he imagined he heard her say.

Gonko and JJ had done it already, was his first thought. But when? And there was no need to look in the caravan—he knew already what he'd see. He reached through the caravan entrance and fumbled around blindly, seeking the lantern the carnies hung on a hook. It took a very long time to find it. Longer to find the matches on their little shelf next to it. Finally the lantern was lit, and he was surprised to find his hands calm and unshaking.

"Help, help," came the call again. Drunken steps scuffed the ground, over at the tent where the dwarfs slept. Shadows reeled away from the lantern light. Jamie kept his footsteps silent. The dwarfs' tent front had been ripped away and left on the ground like shed or torn skin. "Help," came the fearful cry again from inside. Jamie leaned in, the lantern held high, its light thrown over the ruined mess of five bodies—their parts flung across the mattresses, the faces mostly chewed away. The gorge rose in his throat. The lantern nearly slipped from his hand when something in the mess moved, something covered in red on its front half. The back of it wore clown clothes identical to Goshy's, for this was one of his small replicas. Maybe it was the same one Jamie had rescued from the freak show tent just a couple of nights before . . . now it was the size of a large toddler. Its mouth opened again to say, "Help, help," in a voice mimicking helpless fright through jagged yellow teeth. Its eyes glowed white.

Jamie turned, ran. He heard it coming after him with steps unsteady but fast. Something tripped him—the thing had gotten under his feet. He rolled to a painful stop and lay still in one long, drawn-out second. The creature stood over him and breathed death over his face. Slime dripped from teeth that sprouted out in cruel shards. Jamie swung a fist up, landed on its jaw. It felt like concrete. Its teeth snapped at his wrist.

"Not to my best pal you don't," JJ yelled. There was a meaty crunch Jamie would not soon forget; JJ's shovel had swooped down and split the thing's head like a melon. From the wound spilled not blood or brain, but just a thick greenish sludge. It gave one final "Help, help," before it fell back into the grass.

Jamie panted up at his "best pal." Right then it was not a point to argue; JJ had probably just saved his life. And like nothing had happened at all, JJ said, "I got the dust all bagged, just like the boss asked. Let's head back. *Proudest moment in clown history*, Gonko called it. Guess I'm kind of indifferent, but you gotta suck up to the boss."

"Thanks," Jamie whispered, his heart refusing to slow down. He followed his dark reflection through the gates, back to the circus.

18. BELOW

Jamie wanted badly to get back to the loose fence post and check on Dean, but like JJ had said, it seemed important to watch the unfolding excitement by George's trailer. By now a sizeable crowd had come to witness and jostle for a better view—all but Mugabo and the Matter Manipulator seemed to be there. Gonko stood just outside the trailer door with a look of orgasmic serenity as he called the occasional word of encouragement in to George, or lashed out with a boot at someone in the press of bodies who got too close.

Again JJ beat a path through the crowd, winning few hearts and minds as he trampled and kicked. He tossed the sack to Gonko, who in turn spilled the velvet bags out into the grasping hands of the carnies. "Here's the hidden stash I told you about," he called. "Squabble amongst yourselves in an orderly fashion." Those lucky enough to catch their own bag or two darted off, followed by an enraged group who'd missed out. The crowd thinned.

A whiff of faint perfume, foreign and pleasant, trickled through the pushing bodies and reached Jamie moments before a hand closed on his wrist, pulled him close to a woman who'd come to stand behind him. Her lips were close to his ear. "It won't be long now," she said. The fortuneteller nodded to Gonko, who was having fun with JJ calling various "soothing" remarks in at George.

They were trying to outdo each other for saccharine sweetness, and were slapping their knees with laughter.

"You will soon see what you are really fighting," said Shalice. "Even now, it climbs the tunnel below the Funhouse."

Jamie tensed. She knew; she knew everything. He looked at her, tried to read her face, but saw nothing other than weariness. "Not sure what you're talking about," he said. "And if I knew what you were talking about, maybe I wouldn't discuss it here near so many people."

She looked about, and he'd have sworn it was the first time she'd noticed the jostling crowd around them, still numbering in the dozens. She said, "Why don't we retire back a way? But not too far. You will profit from seeing what comes."

They sat on small wooden chairs behind a hot dog booth, but not before Jamie looked into every hidden nook nearby for someone who might overhear. They had a vantage point of those coming and going through a juncture of lanes to George's trailer—right now that just meant carny rats seeking dust and forming small hit squads to find it. Jamie said to Shalice after a minute or two of silence, "How do I know I can trust you?"

She laughed. "You don't. If you cannot trust me, it is already too late for you."

"You know what we're trying to do, don't you?"

"I know enough. It may ease your fears to know I am not quite who I was, when last we met. Circumstance took from me many of the pleasing lies and blind spots I had to cultivate, when I was a willing part of this . . . enterprise."

Jamie reviewed his memories of the fortuneteller and found them faint—he did not have much to do with her last time, other than JJ stealing her crystal ball, and of course her lies when he first arrived, to make it seem he was better off here. "You know what we want to do. Will we succeed?"

Her eyes never left the alley that led down to the Funhouse. "Suppose I knew you would succeed, but if I told you so, it might make you complacent or overly bold, and thus you would overlook important things, and fail. Or perhaps you succeed at incredible

179

personal cost, so much that you'd fear to try what would otherwise work. Or suppose I knew you would fail, but that your attempt would unlock a door for others to try, at some future point. Do you see why I will not say all that I know?"

"Yes. Although frankly a little encouragement really wouldn't hurt."

"What happened with the last usurpation? The house's occupants were hurt, its furniture was ruined, and a frightful mess was made. The house still stands, and now the occupants are back. Nothing has changed. You will need to do more than last time."

Jamie said nothing. He followed her gaze as a group of terrified carny rats sprinted down the path, away from the Funhouse. "It's coming," one of them called to a friend over by George's trailer.

"Hush now," said Shalice. "If it looks this way, do not look into its eyes or it will know you."

A quiet fell over the showgrounds. Faintly came a sound like chains being dragged over hard dirt. Jamie felt the thing coming well before he saw it. It was like a winter wind that blew fear and malice instead of cold, and there was hate and envy for everything living in a body with warm blood, and other things it could mimic but never be. The shape imposing upon the dark alleyway between stalls and games was taller than any man, though effort had been made to cloak itself in garments: a black coat and cape, and to fashion for itself limbs which stiffly carried it in awkward lurching strides. It was darker than the night behind it, hobbling slowly, each step a battle like someone in sinking sand. Its thin arms shivered with anger; Jamie glimpsed bone-like talons in place of what had seemed moments before a hand in a black glove. Two red flames burned in its face. A hissing rasp whispered, "George, ahh . . . George, sss."

It did not look their way. He saw in its face twisted and chewed husks of bone, scale, skin, all wound together in shuddering lumps. Then it passed from view, moved toward the trailer. Ahead of it, screams pierced the hush, and then were quickly silenced. A stampede of footsteps beat across the ground; everyone near the trailer fled, the newer carnies gone pale, frightened, once more hit by rekindled doubts about their new world. JJ ran ahead of the others. Gonko they did not see in the fleeing rush.

They heard the split and crack of the wood barricading George in his home. They heard George's scream, and the sudden quiet falling like a blow when it stopped. Slowly, awkwardly, the creature came back the way it arrived, George dragged by a foot clutched behind it until, finally, it passed from view and the hush cautiously lifted. The distant murmur of carny folk resumed—awed whispers telling each other what they'd seen.

Gonko strolled past them, whistling happily. He paused to cast his gaze after the thing, sighed in contentment, then walked off toward the freak show.

"Now do you see?" said Shalice after a long while of neither of them speaking.

"How many are there like that, below?" Jamie asked.

"Fewer than you might expect. There are some lesser types than the one you saw, in greater number."

"It seemed sick, the way it moved. And it seemed like it . . . didn't like being up here." They were poor words for what he'd seen; especially on its return to the Funhouse, its outlines had wavered, and at times it almost looked like the air would soon dissolve it. Jamie had seen parts of it blur into something like pixels, swirling clouds of black dots held together by an irritated twitch of its hand.

"It does not belong here," said Shalice. "It comes from somewhere, or some*when*, never revealed to any of we slaves. What we might call magic is a kind of instability in reality that its presence causes. An instability much study and labor has learned to shape—to control. These showgrounds are a halfway point between its world and yours. *This* place borrows the laws of reality from both places, mixes them in ways they should not be mixed. You saw that it did not enjoy the solidity even of this halfway point . . . it cannot yet handle the physical realm. In the same way, you could not live on the ocean floor or in outer space. You are not built for those places, and they are not built for physicality. All my alterations of history, done on their instruction, may have been to change your world so that one day, they can survive your world and do there as they like." She caught his eye. "A little physical matter, in its presence, it could handle. Just as you could stand waist deep in water; not comfortable, perhaps, but easily enough. Too much physicality would harm it. Even kill it, if death is an apt term for the ruin of something not alive, as we understand the word."

Jamie shivered. "What are we going to do, Shalice? Can you help us?"

"I'll not promise anything more than this. Gonko and the other clowns are your greatest danger and impediment—not the only one, but the greatest. I can, when the day comes, keep them from interfering. You must survive until then. As for what you will do, it is not for me to tell you."

"Why not?"

"I do not see everything. The illusion that I do has served me well. Scraps of the future come to me in little flashes, that is all."

When the day comes. As the fortuneteller walked off without another word, Jamie found for some reason that those words sat heavy in his mind, more than all else she'd said. The day was indeed coming, he knew, and coming soon.

He went to back to the loose fence plank, mostly unseen on the short walk, and wrenched it back. "Dean?" he called to no response. Reluctantly he slipped out, sidled onto the narrow rock shelf, trying not to look down, then *making* himself look down and not care about the empty abyss. If he was to get rid of JJ, this was the obvious way: one quick wrench after luring him here on some pretext. The JJ who'd tried to drive him insane last time, ultimately tried to kill him . . . the JJ who tonight had maybe saved his life.

The thicker platform was an empty slab of sand-colored stone island—Dean was not there. If he'd slipped and fallen, naturally there would be no trace.

Most of the GEORGE IS WATCHING signs were already smashed and defaced. Gonko took a couple as souvenirs—he'd never been happier to see that face in all his life. "Let us go and put the final icing on the grandest suck up cake ever made," he told his crew, minus one of the J's. He could hardly tell the pair apart, but they seemed to be getting along this time around.

Goshy however was all riled up about something; he'd been doing that thing where he'd walk back and forth about three meters at constantly increasing speed, to a point he'd become a colored blur and maybe even set the ground on fire. Usually Doops could chill him out, but it was taking a while, this time. When Jamie returned, the clowns were on their way out, and his presence set Goshy off again: one stiff arm pointed an accusing finger, the mouth flapped mutely, a puff of steam from the ears—the whole shebang.

"Whatsa matter, Goshy?" said Doopy, pawing his brother's shirt. "He's tryna tell us something, Gonko, something real important." They all watched, waited. Jamie began to sweat. "C'mon Goshy, tell us!"

Flap flap, the lips smacked the gums with little *plop* sounds. Squinting, Doopy translated: "Jamie's gonna . . ."

Flap flap.

"Jamie's scheming to put an end to . . ."

"Come off it, this is silly," said Jamie, edging backwards.

Flap, flap, flap. "You was hiding out, and you heard Jamie say . . ."

Goshy's accusing finger shook, jabbed the air.

"Oh wow!" Doopy screamed. "Wow wow wow! Boss, boss, we gotta talk, you just gotta hear what Goshy says, it's *reaaaaal* important . . ."

"Spit it out!" Gonko said irritably.

"Jamie's gonna buy us all a present! A super duper present! Ain't it the bestest thing you ever saw? It's gonna be shiny, and pretty, and tasty, and it's gonna make us forget we ever hurt real bad."

"Jamie's going to buy himself a new pair of pants first," Jamie said.

Gonko snapped, "Knock it off, you jiggling tits. We're gonna set Kurt loose, then we're gonna bask in his gratitude from now til eternity. But he's a funny one. Just got a hunch it's best not to talk about the ol' secret upstairs show thing. Got it?"

They got it, and Goshy walked very close behind Jamie as the clowns headed for the freak show tent, a puff of steam now and then whistling out his ears.

"Why, good evening clowns," said Kurt from the glass case, his thick lips pulling their corners up through rosy cheeks. "My, hasn't it been an interesting day. I hear George has got himself in a spot of bother with . . . upper management."

"We're all just flabbergasted, boss," said Gonko. "Who woulda thought, eh? But someone's gotta run this joint. What say we let you out of there?"

"Hm! Well, why not. If it's no great trouble."

"None at all, boss." Though it was trouble disassembling the cage's ribs of metal and wood, under the pensive gaze of Dr. Gloom. It took an hour before Kurt could finally be dragged out, by which time they all got pretty sick of the tune he was humming.

Kurt's human flesh had regrown, though he was thin and looked brittle. He stood naked, smiling serenely at each of the clowns as Gonko retrieved one of his old business suits and helped him dress. "It will take some time to regain the strength in my legs," said Kurt, taking a few experimental steps. "Ah! There it is, that's better. Now, if you'll pardon me a moment, I must find something to eat a touch more substantial than fish flakes." Kurt sprinted away, and they heard no more from him for a while, unless the hideous shrieks of pain that soon followed were of his making.

Gonko, a touch irritated, led them back to their tent for a game of cards. Rufshod said, "Boss. Wasn't he meant to be, you know, a bit more grateful and shit?"

"Give it time," said Gonko, but the way he dealt the cards, ripping most of them in half, showed he felt the same way.

Bright and early the next morning word got around (via George's therapist, now apparently Kurt's secretary and minus a couple of teeth) that a Special Meeting was to occur in the acrobat stage tent. All performers gathered there, as did about half the carny rats, who looked no less edgy and murderous than they had yesterday. Kurt was five minutes late, after which he spent a further five minutes apologizing for it and lecturing them all on the importance of punctuality, as well as striving for excellence.

"In other news, my beloved performers (and assorted other no-less-valued staff), it appears that I, Kurt, am again the proprietor of the circus." Kurt waited expectantly. And waited. Gonko figured out why, stood and applauded gustily, followed by Rufshod, JJ, and Doopy. Kurt blushed, swished a paw at the air. "Now, now, remain calm. So, a few new ground rules. One, the clowns are officially Management's favorites. Be advised that in any inter-performer conflict, the clowns shall be default beneficiaries of every judgment call and or property dispute slash damages claim, until further notice. Two, should the clowns require any remedial massage treatment and or sexual favor from any other employee, it shall be given freely and with good cheer, with any who break this protocol answerable to me—Kurt Pilo—and my horrendous punishment apparatus. Three, if it would amuse any of the clowns to see other performers inflict self-harm, the clowns may request this service of any employee, and it must be delivered within twenty-four hours, provided it does not impact upon one's ability to perform on show day. Four, general groveling toward the clowns is henceforth encouraged, with the added proviso that should a clown snap his fingers, all within earshot must at once provide said clown a sincere compliment—sarcasm shall be punished. Any questions?"

Goshy stood up and screeched like a barn owl til the others wrestled him down.

"Very good," said Kurt. "Oh! I had a phone call. Surprise, everyone! Today is a show day." A groan passed through the audience. Kurt remained smiling, but his eyebrows angled downward. "Now, now. Turn those groans to moans. At once. There have been difficulties of late. Today, we strive for excellence! You must all remember what brought you into circus work, and recapture that spirit of enslavement. I expect the utmost professionalism. Do it in memory of my dear brother George—a fine show is just what he would have wanted." Kurt wiped away utter dryness where a tear may otherwise have been. "Which brings me to one final point. There has been some mischief of high order. George's show was sabotaged! This must shock you as much as it does me. Be strong! We must get to the bottom of what happened to George's show. A thorough investigation will be launched in the coming days. Every employee shall be interviewed at length. Large rewards and amnesties are offered for squealers and tattle-tales. If you have a suspicion, rumor, or conspiracy theory, you must tell my secretary, and she will compile a list for my perusal. A large 'culprit cage' will be constructed to prompt the guilty into a state of increasing terror.

"Thank you all for your warm welcome back to the Pilo Family Circus. I shall now end the meeting and stalk out."

With that, the meeting ended and Kurt stalked out.

Somehow Gonko managed to keep his poker face on til they got back to their tent. Rufshod was in his ear the whole way: "What the hell was all *that*? Didn't he *know*? He musta known! You said he knew, right?"

"Gosh, I'm mighty confused," said Doopy while Gonko paced back and forth, shaking his head in bewilderment. "'Cause, see, the boss says we're super duper, but then says we done did bad! Which what did we done do what that was bad good, Gonko?"

Gonko stopped pacing, eyed the card table. "Just when I fucking think . . . that I *understand* that big sack of weirdo dog shit . . ." The card table was then severed into several much smaller card tables. Rufshod dashed off to find a replacement.

"Gee-whiz," said Doopy.

"I like the sexual favors part," said JJ. "Does that apply to us? I mean, if I said to Doopy—"

"We gotta find out what gives here," said Gonko. "I'm gonna go see Kurt. The rest of you rehearse an act for today and make it good."

❀

The culprit cage construction was already begun—a group of nervous carnies had found a platform and were measuring for cage bar holes around its edges. Kurt was gnawing on a human-looking femur when Gonko entered his trailer. "Come in, come in," Kurt said cheerily. "Mandible? They're fresh." he shook a jar one quarter full of yellow teeth—some of them still attached to chunks of pink gum.

"New collection, boss? Looking good," said Gonko, taking one out of politeness.

"What can I do for you, Gonko? Has a sarcastic compliment been given?"

"Nah, boss, it's just . . . I had to ask . . . you see . . . hate to look a gift horse in the mouth, but . . . why exactly are we clowns getting the royal treatment?"

Kurt sighed. "I did not much enjoy my time in the freak show, Gonko. It was a pleasure to watch Dr. Gloom's exemplary conduct, but the worst part was being poked with a stick. There were also several hurtful remarks. Tell me, Gonko, do you think I am an 'ugly ass butt?'"

"Crazy talk, boss."

"Hm, yes, but that's what one freak show guest called me, right after three very firm pokes. Although it was under George's instruction, every employee poked me. But not you, Gonko, nor your underlings. I knew that should I ever manage the circus again, the clowns would be my temporary favorites for a good while."

"Aha. I see."

Kurt linked hands and leaned forward over his desk. "Isn't life funny sometimes, Gonko?"

"What d'you mean exactly, boss?"

187

"I remember when we were together below. And you asked a rather prescient hypothetical question, about what may happen if George failed to cut the mustard. And lo and behold! No mustard was cut."

Gonko swallowed, turned his poker face thoughtful. "I guess life just *is* funny sometimes, boss. But it looks like fishy business to me. Got any leads on the sabotage case yet?"

"Mm, several! My secretary has been meeting with dozens of eager performers, taking down notes. I shan't have time to review them today, for we're doing a show—how exciting! Tomorrow perhaps, or perhaps after I conduct the first wave of interviews."

"Good thinking, boss," said Gonko, edging to the door. "I'll keep my eyes peeled too. So anyway, I better go rehearse. See you, boss, it's great to have you back."

"Catch you later, Gonko."

The rehearsal did not go well, mainly because Goshy refused to join in on any sketch or gag. Instead he kept one stiff arm pointed at Jamie the whole time; from his mouth came mute gum flaps, kettle sounds, sharp tropical birdcalls, and phlegmy warbles. Each outburst seemed to get him more worked up. "What's that, Goshy?" said Doopy. "Jamie's secretly planning to what? Jamie and Deeby's gonna destroy who? Jamie's gonna . . . he's gonna . . . he's gonna fetch us all a bowl of popcorn?" Doopy crash tackled Jamie, apparently from sheer gratitude, crawling over him til they were nose to nose and Jamie's world filled with stale hotdog breath. "That's so neat," said Doopy. "I just can't wait to taste it, Jamie. You really shouldn'ta."

"Anytime," Jamie whispered, nerves frayed near to breaking. He had to get out of there. An hour remained before the tricks were due in; by now the ticket collectors would be at their location. He could only hope Dean was with them, that he'd not slipped in the abyss when edging around the fence. Also of concern was

JJ's enjoyment of Kurt's new rules. He wasted no opportunity to snap his fingers on a stroll through Sideshow Alley, provoking a chorus of "Nice shoes, Mr. Clown," "Looking good, sir," and "Handsome devil right there," all the while with an ear cocked for sarcasm. A dozen Sideshow Alley inhabitants had already been ordered to present JJ with a variety of entertaining injuries, from phallic burn marks to stapling accidents making temporary conjoined twins. Jamie could see it all too clearly: JJ was fast losing interest in any idea of rebelling against the show. And that was not a small problem.

When Gonko returned, it was clear that whatever had happened with Kurt had him very nervous. He said only, "We're fucked. We need to frame someone and frame 'em fast. Rufshod, get upstairs and bring down the rest of my stash."

Jamie slunk around the less populated places now, waiting for the tricks and for Dean to come in with them. At last, that transpired: Dean, Curls, and two others followed the last group of people into the showgrounds as the circus music began its song. The crowd was not made of train commuters this time but people headed for a day out in some local fair, somewhere on the surface world. Near their wits' end, the exhausted carnies somehow did their thing: *Step right up. You sir, you look pretty lucky, care to play a game of dice? Clown show in twenty minutes folks, you won't want to miss it* . . . And their collective mood picked up to no small degree when, lo and behold, whatever curse had kept the dust from falling was lifted, and the ground was soon sprinkled with a glittering carpet.

Jamie took Dean by the arm. "Man, I thought you'd died. Look, we have to hurry. Whatever idea you have, we need to do it tomorrow or today. Goshy knows about us, and he's trying to tell the others."

"Tomorrow it is. But we're going to need Jodi's help for what I have in mind. Are they making her up today?"

"I haven't seen any kissing booth. She's staying with the fortuneteller. Who is also on our side now, Dean, or at least I hope so. What's your idea?"

"Just meet me tomorrow, early. And don't get killed in the meantime."

He didn't get killed during the clowns' act, but it was a near thing. Goshy had it in for him in a way beyond normal slapstick, and often as not would interrupt a sketch to charge him, either with some ear-splitting screams or an actual weapon in hand. Gonko seemed too distracted by his own worries to care, and besides, it got the crowd laughing. But sooner or later, Jamie knew, the others would look closer into all this, or Goshy would succeed in taking him out or communicating what he knew to the others.

The tricks left at the act's end, leaving behind a healthy glimmering spread of dust, which the collectors began to bag at once. Gonko beckoned Jamie over with one crooked finger. "Got a job for your trick friend buddy pal, Deeby."

"What kind of job?"

"He's gonna help us frame some chumps to take the heat off. And tonight, we get busy. Understand? Put away your morals, 'cause if this goes bad, you are just as fucked as me. There's a bunch of carnies who *know*. Gonko is feeling the heat and getting paranoid, edgy, horny, and pissed off. Tonight we bury the hatchet, and the axe, and lead pipe. Jamie the so-called clown, you capered up a storm onstage. You capered oh so pretty and convincing and made the tricks all go giggly. But answer me this, for you also *know*. Are you *in*, sport?"

"You mean, will I help you tonight?"

"I mean what I mean when I mean it. *Are* you in?"

Gonko stared hard out of narrowed eyes. The other clowns peered at him from their deformed and made-up faces. "Course he's in, boss," said JJ. "He's so in, he's in over his head! Way over."

"Course I'm in," Jamie said. "Let me at 'em."

Gonko's mouth tilted sideways. "Pretty ear music you dribble, young Jamie. Now bring me your trick friend buddy pal. And hustle."

190

Jamie found his friend buddy pal standing by the exit gates as the last of the tricks were shepherded out. The relief about the show-grounds was palpable: rumor said Kurt was very pleased with the show and there would be no rampage through a blood storm this evening, and better yet, a day of rest tomorrow. The carnies would be paid a full wage at long last. Perverse gleams of anticipation came to many eyes as lustful wishes beckoned. Jamie noticed a distinct easing off of anti-clown sentiment as he made his way to Dean. "You have to be careful," Jamie told him as they headed back to the clown tent. "Gonko is going to do something tonight, maybe to everyone who knows about his rebel circus. Which includes you."

"And you."

"And Jodi. I'll be safe, if I help him kill the others. I think."

"So you'd better help him."

"Now I've got to kill people. Great."

"Get it through your head. What we're doing tomorrow might kill everyone here, along with you and me. These aren't people, bro. They're enemy combatants, and we're fighting a war. Got it?"

"I know the theory. Picture it though, standing there with Gonko and the others watching, an axe in my hand, and I'll have to swing the thing down and . . . man, I don't know if I can physically do it. You're right, I know. Just be ready to hide, after this job, whatever it is."

Back in the clown tent, Gonko handed Dean a sack and a Polaroid camera. He said, "The mission: you are a huge fan of the acrobats. You simply gotta have a picture of them, while they are holding this here sentimental sack—your prized possession. Get 'em to autograph your sack, take a happy snap while it's in their hands. Then off to Mugabo to do the same. The lion tamer too, while you're at it. They must be holding the sack when you take a picture. Get it?"

"What's the point of this again, sir?" said Dean.

191

"This, pal buddy friend, is a frame up. Note, the sack is empty. It will later be filled with stolen powder, the whole stash from our secret show, and then discovered by the boss. It's what we in showbiz call a skin-saver, yours as much as mine. Right now, a handful of dirty snitches who were up top have had a chance to squeal. We, however, are gonna uncover a massive powder theft and smuggling ring so Kurt has someone to punish. Dig it? The sack gets buried in the acrobat tent. Kurt's secretary gets a little note and some happy snaps mysteriously emerge. And Kurt will dine that night on acrobat, lion tamer, and Mugabo. Do we follow?"

"Yes, sir," said Dean. "Only, I'm not too clear on where all these performers live. Maybe Jamie can come and supervise?"

"Only if he stays out of sight. *You* are taking the photos so the accused will not point fingers at the clowns for framing them. Do we further follow? Get busy, chumbo." Dean saluted and went on his way with Jamie following.

Gonko watched them go, muttering to himself. "Tricky tricky tricks. They're lucky I'm already paranoid and suspecting everyone of everything, or I'd swear they were planning a crooked little scheme right before my eyes. *Catch you later*, says Kurt. Not *see you later*, but *catch you later*. Hey JJ, a little job for you too. When Deeby gets back here, you know what to do."

"Make him become not quite so alive as he currently is?"

"Yep. But don't do it in front of Jamie. We'll say his buddy pal ran away or something, and if he makes any noise about it, he's next."

"Excuse me, just wondering if I might have your autograph?" said Dean, extending the sack to the acrobats. They were flattered; it was the first time anyone had asked such a thing, and in truth, this was long overdue. Dean got a good shot of them all examining the sack between the three of them, slightly puzzled that such a thing would hold such value for this (rather attractive) fan. The camera's light fired like a gun's muzzle flash (only adding to the acrobats' excitement), and Jamie had to admire Dean's ruthlessness—there was no one in this circus he'd extend any mercy to, if he had his way.

Dean and Jamie left them to preen amongst themselves. Claudius said, "It's like all our hard work has paid off. Finally, some recognition."

Mugabo snarled and growled at the same request, sensing a trap. "Treek!" he bellowed, wagging a long finger. "You treek me! Spill it! What now? For truth!"

Dean backed up, not sure what to say. Jamie jumped in. "All right, sir, you saw through us. The truth is, we need the advice of a great mystic. We believe this sack has been cursed, bringing its bearer bad luck. Can you lend us your expertise?"

"The day I help clown, is the day of not help at all!" Mugabo raged. He grabbed the sack and shook it menacingly. "Take you stink sack, take ever thing and run, opposite!" The camera flashed and Dean got a good shot of Mugabo, sack in hand and teeth bared, but they had to sprint away as ozone filled the air—the Polaroid flash was interpreted as some kind of attack. They made it out as lightning struck within the tent, after which the magician collapsed, weeping.

The lion tamer—a diminutive, miserable-looking man with a curled black moustache and sad drooping eyes—was having dinner with his tiger, which was remarkably adept with a knife and fork. It was clear he'd not believe the autograph hunting story for a second, so Jamie (ignoring again Gonko's directive to stay hidden) said, "Sir, sorry to trouble you, but I have OCD. I need you to hold this sack for the count of three or I will be unable to bathe this week, for fear the water may turn to acid."

"No one wants that," sighed the lion tamer, getting slowly to his feet. He opened the empty sack, glanced in, which made a nice picture. "Terrible condition," he said, handing it back. "Best of luck to you, young man."

They left, not without a touch of remorse on Jamie's part—both the lion tamer and the acrobats seemed halfway decent sorts. "Now we have to talk about JJ," Jamie said. "I've got a really bad feeling he's going to give us up."

"So, do you have the balls to take him out, or not?" said Dean.

"It's not that so much. It's that I'm not *sure*. He's already helped me out a few times. And if we do this thing tomorrow, maybe we can get it done before he turns on us."

"Jamie, this is our one and only chance at this. We will probably die doing it, win or lose, and no I won't tell you yet, just in case something weird happens to you and they make you talk. What I have in mind, he'd be useful for, but not *essential*. You tell me, is he a risk or an ally?"

"Both, it seems. I just don't know."

"That means he's a risk. What's your gut tell you?"

"That we're in deep shit either way." Jamie sighed. "He's having a lot of fun with these new rules of Kurt's. I think he's a danger of reappraising how he feels about us at any second."

They both fell quiet as the clown in question appeared up ahead, shouldered his way through some carnies, and ran to them with big goofy knee-lifting strides. "Amigos! You'd better not go back there. Gonko gave me an order to make Dean be dead."

"I wondered about that," said Dean.

JJ took the Polaroids and the sack. "I'll deliver these to our boss, how about it? I'll concoct lies as to Dean being waylaid by someone and needing to dispose of this stuff. Don't you sweat it, trusted comrades. JJ's got your back."

JJ smiled proudly at them, waiting for praise. Jamie tried to hear his gut and warning bells sounded there. "JJ, you've been a great help to us. Come meet us by the loose fence post, near the popcorn seller, out where Fishboy used to meet his gang. There's something we need to show you."

"Sounds like a plan! See you there, pal." JJ bounded off, snapping his fingers as he went, provoking volleys of compliments from carnies along the way (who glowered after him and spat.)

Dean met Jamie's eyes and nodded. It was the safest thing to do, Jamie knew it, but it didn't make the deed sit any easier with him . . . in fact, he felt like the world's biggest shithead.

JJ was gone for nearly half an hour, plenty of time for wretched internal debate and self-doubt. Dean watched it all play out inside Jamie without much comment. "Here he comes," said Dean. "Game on. Man up, quickly."

So Jamie manned up, which he found a funny way to describe lying to lure someone into a trap. Nonetheless, he said, "You remember the platform out here? The little path and platform, where Fishboy used to hold meetings?"

"Sure," said JJ, a puppy's eagerness on his face that broke Jamie's heart.

"There's someone out here you should meet." Jamie pulled the loose board back and edged through.

"Okie dokie," said JJ, "although might it be easier if they come here?"

"He can barely walk, this guy," Dean said smoothly, edging through the gap after JJ. "But he's got some stuff to say you need to hear."

"Sure, that passes muster," said JJ, mollified. They climbed through the fence gap, JJ following Jamie. They were a few meters around the jutting dirt ledge, with a drop to oblivion just beyond their shoes. Jamie had his back to the fence. He felt dizzy. JJ faced the other way, his belly to the fence. The main danger, of course, was JJ grabbing hold of him as he went down. It would need to be quick, and yet his hands did not want to obey their orders. Here they were now, at the thinnest part of the turf ledge, the very spot he had in mind. It had to be now, but he couldn't . . .

"Go!" Dean screamed, startling Jamie so much he almost fell himself. "DO IT!"

He did it. One hard pull at the back of JJ's collar, then quickly shuffling to his right, as far out of reach as he could get. JJ stood poised for moment on the points of his toes, arms wind-milling fast in a doomed quest for balance. "See ya later, fucker," said Dean.

JJ toppled forward. "I guess disappointment and surprise are what I feel the most," he said as he dropped, arms and legs thrashing just like a swimmer. They watched him fall, watched as he blinked out of sight after around four seconds, swallowed by nothingness.

"Did you have to say that to him?" Jamie said. "I mean, did you really?"

"It'll be the least of his problems," Dean said, heading back toward the entrance. "Pardon me if I'm not the nicest guy to know right now. I've been through a lot."

There was just the scuff of their feet on the flat turf, and the ripping sound of clothes scraping the fence boards for a while. Dean said, "Just a random thought here, but . . . you've seen anyone jump or be pushed off the edge before?"

"Uh, no. Why?"

"Well . . . where's the drop actually lead? How do you know it actually goes anywhere? I mean, he didn't keep falling like I expected. He fell a little then . . . poof, vanished. Kind of weird."

"Guess it was. You suggesting that void might be some kind of illusion?"

They heard the noise at about that second as JJ crashed through a caravan roof, punching a neat JJ-shaped hole in it as he plunged through to the mattress of a bed below. "Motherfuckers!" his scream reached Dean and Jamie as they put the fence post back in place.

"Hide," said Dean.

"Hide where? Shit! We can't hide out there anymore. And I can't hide in the goddamn clown tent. We're screwed. Completely. There's nowhere to go."

They looked at each other for a second in total helplessness before the idea came to them both at once: "Fortuneteller." They ran.

"Something's off here," Gonko muttered, pacing. His fingernails were gnawed to the quick. Now and then he'd lash out with his boot at anything in range or crush to powder some Chinese stress balls.

"What d'you mean, boss?" said Rufshod, dodging a kick.

"JJ just fibbed to me. Said he'd offed Deeby, but he didn't."

"Say, boss, don't take it wrong, but you're kind of paranoid. Remember five minutes ago when you pulled a gun on your own shadow?" Rufshod pointed at the bullet hole in the ground. "Maybe JJ did it after all."

"And what's Goshy so stirred up about?" said Gonko, as if he hadn't heard. "He's got some beef with Jamie, and he ain't cooling down about it. Maybe he heard something we need to know."

Rufshod saw no way to answer this. He said, "Good photos, hey? They look so guilty."

"You took 'em to the therapist like I told you?"

"Course I did, boss, along with the note. And the stash is buried out behind the acrobat tent like you said."

"Just one thing left for us to do then. Pity about Curls, I really don't mind him so much. Grab yourself an implement of bodily destruction, Ruf. We're going snitch hunting."

Kurt's face expressed no anger, only delight as he peered at each of the Polaroid snaps for the thirtieth time. "Oh my," he whispered. "It's so very exciting." The anonymous note, which by some quirk of cosmic coincidence looked rather like Gonko's handwriting, said that the illicit stash of stolen powder could be found behind the acrobat tent. Delicious! Kurt basked in anticipation for just a moment longer, sucking on a wisdom tooth. Then he lifted his frame from the desk and loped outside.

Jamie and Dean tried not to be noticed on their way to the fortune-teller's place. Thankfully most of the population was asleep or whacked out on wish powder—only the occasional curtain parted with evil eyes glaring out through lamplight. There at last, a familiar caravan connected to Shalice's hut, a familiar trace of strange perfume threading through the air. The window was dimly lit. Jamie knocked very gently at the window. Footsteps within; the hut's door opened.

"You have to hide us," Jamie whispered. "We're in deep shit. We messed up."

She hesitated. "Did anyone see you come this way?"

"No one important."

With a sigh she moved aside, hushing them at once as they began to thank her. "This arrangement cannot last," she said. "You must do your task tomorrow. Or tonight. Any longer and I will have to turn you in to save myself."

"Some ally," said Dean.

She laughed. "Oh, I am. And yet I have only one useful way to help you."

"I'll bet there's plenty you could do," said Dean. "I've heard what you're capable of."

"My powers are *their* powers, don't you see? They will not cut their own necks. I will not let myself become a Funhouse plaything if you find you lack the courage to do this thing. Stay here tonight, if you need to, and for some of tomorrow. But no longer than that."

"It's okay, we get it," said Jamie.

Jodi emerged through the curtain and down the three steps that led from the caravan to the hut. She did not have her makeup on. She embraced Dean and then with a moment's hesitation put her hand on Jamie's shoulder. "So, I'm one of the good guys now," he couldn't help saying. And she was about to rise to the bait until Shalice said, "Shh! Quickly now, tell me what happened to bring you here."

In whispers they told her about JJ. She listened without comment or question, but a grim humor seemed to sparkle in her almond eyes . . . maybe at their foolishness, or at the certainty of their doom, Jamie could not tell. She stood, pulled a shawl about herself, and said, "Do not touch the crystal ball while I am gone." She stepped out into the night, a slight, slim, young-looking woman rubbing her arms against the cold, her hunched back making a lie of her mask of youth.

Jodi rushed to lock the door behind her.

Rufshod and Gonko prowled through Sideshow Alley, each taking one side of the lane, knocking on doors or breaking them down when there was no answer. Gonko shined a flashlight in the face of a sleeping gypsy who did not stir. Across the way there came a *thump-thump-thump*, indicating Rufshod had found someone from the show above.

They met outside. "Was it Curls?" said Gonko.

"Nope. His pal, the half bald dwarf who worked the gates with him."

"Dead?"

"Proper dead."

"All right. Keep looking."

They went further up the laneway. Gonko kicked down the door of a caravan with a newly broken roof. He cried, "JJ!"

On the mattress, JJ rolled over and groaned. The face paint had turned the fall from a certain fatality into mere extreme pain. He blinked up at Gonko, taller than death in the doorway with a lead pipe in hand. "Boss," JJ whispered. "If I come clean, promise not to rough me up too bad?"

"I guess it depends. There's a good chance you're gonna be washed off them sheets come morning. But I'll try to be restrained."

JJ sighed, tried to stand, fell back. "Deeby's not dead. Him and Jamie are trying to pull a Fishboy and bring the whole place down."

"You're shitting me."

"No, boss."

"How? They doing the ol' upstairs show routine?"

"They don't have a plan yet, but they're trying to think of one. They asked me to help 'em. I said I would, but just for a lark. Didn't think they'd actually have a chance to do it. I was about to tell you all about it, I swear."

"And that's why Goshy's pissed? He heard 'em scheming and he's been trying to tell us?"

"Yeah, boss. You going to splat me into soup now?"

"Nah. But you could be fibbing. I'll talk to Jamie first to get his take on it. If I smell a lie from you, soup's on. Ruf!" Gonko fished in his pockets, and pulled out several useless items til he found what he wanted: a compass with the letter J on it. Rufshod came in, new blood dripping from his axe. "Got one, boss. I don't think he actually *was* on our list? But he kind of reminded me of someone who was."

"JJ says Deeby still lives, like I thought," Gonko said. "We gotta get 'em before they blab to Kurt. Curls can wait. Let's go."

They turned to leave and found Shalice in the doorway. She said, "Gonko."

"Oh Christ, what do you want?"

"It's time for my favor, Gonko. If you still honor our bargain. If I may advise you? It would be wise."

"Lady, threat time is long past. You are talking to Kurt's personal hand-picked suck up favorite."

"Yes, I was at that meeting, Gonko. And you recall there were other things said, too. Some unanswered questions."

Gonko appraised her, bluffed: "All talk, just for show, toots. You didn't hear the private chat between me and the boss, where maybe all was revealed and met with approval and gratitude. So how much should I care about the bargain? You tell me."

She met his gaze and matched his smile. The gypsy jewelry around her neck, in her ears, gleamed to share her humor. "Is Kurt the highest authority in the circus? Do you suppose *others* may have an interest in how their pleasures and needs were deprived, for what must have seemed a very long time?"

Gonko's poker face broke like a dropped plate. He snarled and raised the lead pipe quite involuntarily. "Not this way," said Shalice with annoyance. "You think I made no provisions and precautions, should I happen not to return? Be sensible."

With some effort Gonko splayed his hands; the lead pipe clanged to the floor behind him. Shalice shuffled inside, shut the door, and lowered her voice. "I'm calling in the favor now. What I want is for you to leave the showgrounds for exactly twenty-four hours. Take Rufshod, Doopy, Goshy, and JJ with you. Twenty-four hours, then you may return and we are again on level terms with no debt owed."

Gonko's face twisted, grappled, like someone trying to understand the incomprehensibly stupid. "*What? Why?*"

"It is a subtle thing," she replied, "to do with the interplay of events. And in truth—though you would never see it—I am saving you a good deal of trouble."

"You got some *real* iffy timing, lady. So happens, I may have uncovered a treacherous plot, carried out by certain ne'er-do-wells, whom I happen to be in the process of hunting down."

"Oh please," she laughed, dismissing it with a wave of her hand. "I know what you're referring to. And what they intend will not succeed."

Gonko watched her, thinking. "Feeling tired, Shalice?" he said quietly. "Sick of it all? Yearning for greener pastures, mayhap?"

She watched him back, narrowing her eyes in a show of impatience. "Gonko. Under George's leadership, who wouldn't be tired? That time has passed. And I know who to thank. All I need now is the honoring of a bargain between friends, for reasons I can better explain to you tomorrow when events have concluded. It was you who raised the lead pipe, not me."

He sucked his teeth, looked away, and then nodded. "All right, goddammit. All right. We're out. Give us half an hour to finish some business."

"*Now*, Gonko. Go now. Please. It's important."

Curls, as it happened, was spending his pay in customary fashion beneath that very caravan, and he'd heard every word and every thump as Rufshod murdered his friend. His first instinct was to run away screaming, til he found Mr. Pilo and claimed the amnesty that had been offered to squealers. But who knew where the other four clowns were at that moment? Maybe keeping a close eye on the route to Mr. Pilo's trailer . . . maybe scouring the showgrounds for him with some bribed lookouts to help them . . . maybe the safest thing was to keep Gonko and Rufshod in sight while they hunted down everyone else who knew their secrets . . .

So he did, creeping out from what had just before been a love nest in the dark dusty space and shadowing their movements as close as he dared, flitting behind garbage cans, crawling beneath spare piles of canvas, into pools of alley shadow. He watched the fortuneteller approach, and edged closer.

Curls heard only part of the exchange between Shalice and Gonko. He had over years uncounted developed a fairly casual attitude to death, and certainly would not have said the prospect bothered him. So he was quite surprised to find himself almost blind with panic as he sprinted for Shalice's hut. Death by act of violent clown was something he'd never pondered before, and now they were after him, his only thought was the crystal ball. He'd hide in a safe spot, keeping an eye out for the clowns with Shalice's ball, perhaps until morning. He'd then see when it was safe to make a run for Mr. Pilo's trailer and squeal his lungs out. He could even take Kurt up through the gates and show him the proof.

The fortuneteller's hut was locked, but one learned a few things with enough time—the lock was no match for his special tooth-pick, screwdriver, and quick fingers. No sooner had he rushed in before a rough hand grabbed his arm. Dean? It was. With Emerald. With a clown! They were everywhere! How had they known he'd come? He yelled and thrashed til a hand clamped over his mouth.

"You got one choice to make," said Dean, a light in his eye placing him in the ballpark of Gonko, in terms of mortal terror. "Join the team, or die right here and now."

The hand came off his mouth. He said, "I'm in."

Shalice returned nearly half an hour after she'd left. She was not pleased to see Curls in her hut, but asked no questions. "I watched them go," she said. "They went up the lift. How long they'll stay away I can't be certain. You have some freedom of movement, for now. Gonko suspects I am part of your plan. Just suspects it, he does not know."

"Good," said Dean. "Curls, go now and bring back all the gate pieces. Act casual."

"I dunno, some of 'em are locked away, but—" That look was in Dean's eye again, and in the clown's too for that matter. "But that's no problem. Sure I'll do it."

"Bring them here, go go go." When Curls bustled off, Dean turned to Jamie. "We'll have some help up there now, at least. I was worried we'd have to do this alone."

"Do what? Isn't it time you told me, for God's sake?"

Dean grinned and produced several sheets of paper. "I was busy when you were looking for me." He spread the world map with lift coordinates across the small available floor space. "It's all been done already. Times, location codes, distances, and direction we'll need to walk from the lift point to the bases. Maybe one base will be enough, but we get more if we can. As many people as we can get. Then we get back here to help kick things off."

"Bases?"

"Military bases." Dean gave him one of the lists. "This tells us which ones are doing drills tomorrow. Live combat drills. Do you get it yet?"

Jamie looked at the list, laughed. "I get it, but . . . oh shit. I get it."

"I thought an actual combat zone would be better. If we got some suicide bombers down here—some edgy soldiers who've seen recent action with hair triggers. But if we got hit by a stray shot or stood on a mine, it would be game over. So, we set up the gates in a place where the troops are getting ready for their drill. They come straight down here, tomorrow when there's no show on and no music box playing. Surely we can sneak through a military base at night. They won't see us, right? With face paint on?"

"I hope not. At night, we can hide pretty easily, you just have to kind of remember you're hiding."

"This one looks likely," said Dean, tapping a location code with his finger. "Urban combat training, marines. Get them down here, Jamie. As many as you can, a hundred is not too many. And then it's game on."

"But how did you get this info?"

Dean pulled from his pocket a bunched handful of empty velvet bags. "Curls told me about the powder, how it works, the limits and rules. All I wished for was information, and that was before all this was even strictly the plan to run with. If I'd wished for a bunch of marines to come down, it wouldn't have worked. But it looks like information is allowed."

Jamie nodded. "You said you never wanted to use the dust," he said more in admiration than to contradict him.

"I never wanted to join the circus, either."

They waited for Curls to return, which took long enough to make them nervous, particularly Shalice. She paced and muttered to herself then sought him out with her crystal ball, but could not find him.

"We're going to be too late," said Jamie.

"I got info for the whole week, don't worry. Drills are going on all the time around the world, if my info is good. Didn't know exactly when we'd be able to do this, so I made sure we'd have options."

"You're forgetting something, Dean. You can't come up there with me for this mission."

"Why not?"

"You'd need the face paint to be able to sneak through the base. But when you put it on, you're not Dean. You're Deeby."

Dean thought about this for a second, then slapped his leg. "Shit!"

"I'll go with Curls, if he gets back here alive. Curls can sneak through a crowd at a train station without being seen, so he'll be okay up there. You'll have to stay here."

Dean paced the floor. "Now, when these soldiers get down here, how does the show respond?"

Jamie said, "They rush to turn the music box handle, put them all to sleep."

"Right. And what can we do about that?"

Jamie thought about it for a minute. "That could be where you and Jodi come in. Jodi, you have the veil?"

She pulled it up around her face. "I look like Emerald, right?"

"You do," Jamie said. "Dean, correct me if I'm wrong, but wouldn't Deeby the clown do just about anything to prove himself worthy of this fine piece of—of womanhood?"

Dean laughed, getting it. "He would indeed. He'd even trash the music box and use his big muscles to keep the door jammed, so no one could come in and fix it."

Shalice had been listening in silence till now. Her voice and expression showed none of the growing confidence slowly infusing the rest of them. "Jamie, make sure you return. You will need to be here with wide-open eyes. For, so far, we are discussing a plan to mess up the furniture and injure the house's tenants again, if you succeed even in that much. Nothing yet convinces me the house itself will come to any harm."

Their mood dampened. "What should I do about that then, Shalice?"

"Keep your eyes open and your wits about you. You will know."

They waited mostly in silence until Curls finally returned, panting, burdened with several lengths of curved iron. They explained the plan to him, saw his eyes fill with fright. "This is just our way of getting rid of the current clown group," Jamie lied. "You want that, don't you? Don't worry. The fortuneteller has seen the future and knows it'll work out fine."

"It is true," said Shalice. "Your future is bright, but you must help them."

"Ready, Curls? Let's head up and get this over with."

19. ABOVE

Arizona, early evening. From the lift, they stepped out to the small iron ladder leading up to a manhole cover. Traffic passed above, but they heard no voices, and chanced pushing away the cover—to hell with it if someone saw it move, or saw them emerge. With some difficulty they maneuvered the gate pieces through the gap, Curls spitting curses nonstop, certain he was being set up for yet another fall. Jamie fought the urge to clobber him so he could concentrate—they had left plenty of time to find this place, or so he thought.

A lot of faith was needed in the scrawled note that read *Northeast, half a mile* until road signs pointed them toward the base. The regular street blocks gave way to wide open fields, tall fences, and the occasional roar of craft cutting across the sky. "This is it," Jamie said.

They threw the gate pieces over the tall fence topped with barbed wire, and though cameras pointed their way, they could only hope they weren't seen. They prowled through acres of parked jets, helicopters, armored jeeps, until they found through sheer luck their way toward a barracks, guided in part by the sound of distant shouts. They stood near an open window where a briefing was underway to some uniformed cadets. They listened for a minute or two but heard nothing relevant, ran through covered walkways, hiding now and then behind hedges as people passed by. Finally they found a group in full uniform, bulky with helmets and Kevlar vests, long guns in their arms, chatting and laughing as they walked. They followed, still unseen, for about half a mile out into the fields, where now and then a distant bark of fire could be heard. Curls stopped cursing and stared about himself like one who has stumbled onto a new planet.

They saw a mass of buildings ahead, what seemed a kind of adventure course of imitation apartments, with only empty rooms, doors, windows. There came the *crack* of doors being kicked in, shouting voices. The group they'd followed went off to the side, waiting their turn for urban combat simulation.

Jamie and Curls snuck past, climbed another fence, and then watched for a gate or door where all the soldiers seemed at one point to pass through.

"Delta six, do you copy?" The unit commander looked at his apparently broken hand radio. It hissed static at him, as did his headphones. "Sir, we seem to have lost contact with Delta six."

"Lost contact how? Are they not with you, Delta nine?"

"They are in shouting distance, sir; they just entered domicile one and went in, but are not responding. Radio is dead, sir. No shots fired, but something is, uh, something is wrong, sir. We can see no sign of activity in domicile one." *Unless my fucking binoculars are broken too*, the marine thought. Eight men in that small apartment and none had yet passed by a window . . . ? Some of the little surprises they threw into these drills . . .

The order came through: "Send in Delta four. Delta one will split to sweep the back door."

"Copy that. Delta four, do you read me? Proceed to domicile one; tell us what you see." He wasn't supposed to say this kind of thing—they were to treat all this as seriously as the combat they were soon likely to see in a few weeks' time, but a strange feeling had come over the marine, one that put his hairs on end. It wasn't like a military base had never been infiltrated or attacked before, even on home soil. "Take care in there, Delta four; this is live ammunition in an enclosed space. Safeties on. You better not need me to tell you that."

When Delta four went through that same door and failed to respond, or even to walk past a window just like the last group, naturally the other teams were sent by an increasingly nervous mission coordinator. "Stop the drill," he shouted into his radio. "Stop the fucking drill. We have an incident here."

Hidden in the dark, crouched low as possible in fear of a stray bullet, Jamie whispered, "How many have gone through now?"

Curls began a finger count but couldn't get past nine.

"Must have been thirty at least," Jamie said. "Is that going to be enough . . . ?" It was hard to think; unnerving, to say the least, when so many large heavily armed men had seemed to stare *right at him*, one after the other.

Curls groaned. "You said this was just to take out the clowns, these gun having tricks. How many more you need? I'm being set up!"

"Can never be too careful, Curls. But they need us to get back there and help." He looked at the list again, struggling to concentrate while shouts rang out and boots pounded past them. He wanted more than thirty, but it had been mostly luck that had gotten them here in the vastness of the base, and he didn't like the odds of finding another base, somewhere else in the world. A vision came to him: right now, the guns being pried out of the docile hands of sleepwalking tricks, lured under by the carnival's song. Maybe Gonko had returned early and found Dean . . .

Alarms began to blare, the electronic howl rolling across the base. Garbled orders crackled from speakers and echoed nonsensically. More boots pounded the pavement, coming this way.

"Gettin' hot," Curls observed. "I'd say we kicked an ants' nest."

"This could be good," Jamie said. "Give it a few more minutes . . ." but Curls had already dashed through the doorway where they'd set up the gate pieces, leaving Jamie alone. Pretty soon they'd probably have all the armed marines below they'd need and then some, as long as no magic below won the day. Why not just leave the gates where they were? The more who came through the merrier, and there was no point in sneaking back and pretending they were loyal carnies any more. JJ would know just where to point his accusing finger, and if it failed from here . . .

Jamie dashed through the doorway, back to the showgrounds.

20. BELOW

A sad business, what had happened to the lumberjacks—inconvenient too, for there were few left strong enough to pull the culprit cage along after Kurt's loping strides. Inspiration struck: "Wheels!" said Kurt, slapping his paws together in delight. "Put wheels on the bottom of it." He watched with glowing pride as the dozen or so summoned minions rushed to do just that. Kurt remembered the pokes from each one of them, and sought deep within for patience, forgiveness.

Kurt wore a tie-dyed muumuu. A woven band of flowers hung around his neck. Christianity had begun to bore him; it was time for a New Age phase. He would send the clowns up soon to capture some real live hippies for research.

The wheels were now on. With much greater ease, the cage trailed along behind until they came to the acrobat tent. A little earlier, he'd come out here with a shovel and found the stash buried there, just where the anonymous tip-off had said it would be. It was all so stimulating, this detective work! It got one's juices flowing, especially after the long confinement. "Knock, knock," Kurt cried at the acrobat tent door. "And, oh, ho ho, that's not one of those jokes where one replies, *who is there?*" It was just before dawn, but the acrobats were already up rehearsing, painting the image of ideal enthusiastic employees. Clever devils! Criminal masterminds. Kurt's eye fell on the GEORGE'S FAVOURITES sign, and his smile pulled wider.

"Mr. Pilo!" one of the acrobats cried. The three of them rushed over, bowing and groveling most pleasantly.

"Hello, chaps," said Kurt, and here came his cunning plan. "I need three brave volunteers to test the structural integrity of my culprit cage. Care to do the honors?"

They could hardly wait to. One after the other they climbed in. "Very good," said Kurt. "Now just sit patiently while we find some more brave volunteers."

"Happy to help, Mr. Pilo," said one of them, bowing. "Any luck with the real culprits?"

"Aren't you clever!" said Kurt, but said no more. The acrobats glanced at each other uneasily.

Kurt pulled the same routine at the lion tamer, who gazed for a while at the caged acrobats. They looked just a touch wary now. Kurt's smile was serene. The lion tamer weighed the situation up, sighed heavily as if he knew just what was up and had long expected something like this. Into the cage he went, where he sat in the corner, his face in his hands.

Mugabo put up no more resistance than the others. "Cage treek now, new magic, pff," he muttered, but he went right on in. Kurt himself locked the door and loped off, gesturing for the cage to be wheeled behind him to the middle of the showgrounds for maximum public shaming. Only then did Kurt let on. "Your plan was bold, your wits were sharp. But your one mistake was posing for incriminating photographs!"

The acrobats looked at each other in confusion as Kurt loped away. "What the hell is he talking about?"

Kurt took a pleasant stroll during which he contemplated punishment—those performers had also poked him, albeit rather gently. For starters he would sit by the cage, staring at the guilty parties, studying treachery itself til he knew its every nuance, facet, and protestation of innocence. Til he could spot it from across the showgrounds before it reared its head, perhaps develop a preemptive punishment system. Then, he supposed, they'd need to be executed rather brutally—flesh eating ants, perhaps, or maybe via lawnmower as a message to the others.

And what was this? More excitement! Shouting—yes, panicked shouting, and the voices unfamiliar! Kurt prowled towards it to see. His smile slowly went flat, his brow furrowed in confusion. No show was scheduled for today, and yet, why, here were several tricks. Rather nervous looking, physically fit tricks who, breaking usual conventions, looked to be heavily armed with automatic weapons, grenades, pistols, protective gear, night vision goggles, and an unmistakable air of can-do spirit.

"Hm," said Kurt. How had this come to pass? Some mistake of the ticket collectors? And no one was turning the music box. Why, half the circus was still asleep. Kurt wrung his paws together, a touch unsettled. The tricks were in a rather impressive formation they'd clearly rehearsed, and were shouting orders at each other. Their guns pointed in all directions, with little beams of light from mounted torches, though none of them had fired a shot, not yet. "I had better turn that music box myself," said Kurt, at once proud of the idea. He went to do just that, breaking into a jog and a sweat.

Several minutes prior, Dean stood panting with his hand at rest on the sledgehammer. Deeby may have done it without this much exertion; the broken parts of the music box were scattered around his and Jodi's feet. This was one hell of a leap of faith in Jamie and Curls. He felt certain they'd messed it up, but there was no choice: they had to proceed as planned. "Check the veil," said Jodi. "Can you see through it?"

"Nope."

"I look like Emerald?"

"Yep."

Anything else in the small cramped space that looked like a spare part was also shattered, but Dean had seen these carnies fixing things and knew they were far from safe. In a couple of minutes, they might have the music box repaired.

He lit a match under the glass beaker, melted the powder within, drank it. "I wish, once my face paint goes on, to forget the past week spent with Jamie and to be filled only with a desire to impress any female I see. I wish when the face paint comes off, to have the memories returned." To Jodi he said, as he began to smear on the face paint Jamie had stashed for him, "You know what to do?"

"Yes, but your friend had better fucking hurry."

"I'm not going to argue with that."

Jodi held an ear to the door. "Something's going on out there . . . I hear shouting . . . I think they're here! Hurry up, go!"

The face paint was on. Dean looked into the hand-held mirror they'd brought, and Deeby gazed at his beloved. "Sup," he said coolly, popping a bicep.

Jodi swallowed, tried for Emerald's distant composure—she'd done a little acting in school plays but this, naturally, was a whole different assignment. "My love, there is but one way into my heart, and I will be yours eternal. Let none pass through this door. Prove to me your strength."

Debby spat on his palms, rubbed them together. "That is probably one of the weirder ways into a woman's heart that I have ever heard of. Wouldn't you rather hear some shitty beatnik poetry while sweat drips down my pecs and I promise you a whole bunch of stuff that's just never going to happen?"

His response was not quite what Dean had predicted, but she stuck to the script anyway. "It can only be this way. This is the only way into Emerald's heart. You want to impress me, don't you?"

"Whatever floats your boat. By heart you mean pants, right?"

"Whatever you like," she said, nervously listening to the sound of approaching footsteps. Deeby's shirt ripped as his torso inflated. Someone twisted the door handle; he snapped it off, crushed it in his teeth, glanced to see that Jodi had witnessed the display, then threw himself against the door. "Bring it on," he said.

"Hm! How puzzling." Kurt's voice. "To which employee have I the pleasure of speaking with? What might you be up to in there?"

"Shut up," Deeby explained.

"The situation is rather urgent," said Kurt in firmer tones. "We rather pressingly need the music box. Be a sport and let me in."

The door pushed an inch or two. Deeby let it give that much, then shoved it back. He screamed like a Viking, again checked Jodi for any sign of approval. She feigned a yawn.

A slow, "Oh, ho ho," sounded outside.

At first the marines whispered to each other that this was part of the drill, some kind of computer simulation—no other explanation was possible. Some virtual reality thing, like they did with pilots, though what in God's name the point of it all may be, none could guess. "Why do we bring *live ammo* for a computer simulation or VR?" someone asked, which pretty much shot that theory to death and made each of them realize, with slowly dawning understanding, that they were in a very weird place and, just perhaps, just possibly, in real trouble. One by one, safeties on their guns were snapped off. Weird faces began to peer out at them from doorways and windows.

"Freeze! Get down on the ground. Get down, now!"

When Jamie returned to the showgrounds, four groups of marines stood in a roughly circular formation. The lights mounted on their guns pointed out in all directions. He counted twenty-two of them, but maybe others had ventured deeper into the circus. They were shouting but not shooting—probably a good thing for the moment. Someone yelled at him to freeze and get down, which was jarring since he'd gotten used to not being seen. Down here, where the troops were made a part of the circus reality, it would not be so easy to hide.

He did not freeze or get down—he dashed away as fast as he could, bounding in a few floating clown jumps defying physics, in part to show these guys they were not in a normal situation anymore. No shots followed—only various cries of "What the fuck was that?" and a clearly growing tension.

"OH, HO HO!" came a familiar booming voice rolling across the showgrounds and stirring awake the last of the sleeping carnies. Then, a thump. Kurt attempting to break down a door? Deeby had to be holding him out this very second. The troops meanwhile just stood there, unsure what to do. Some looked outright paralyzed. An apparent leader tried and failed to make radio contact with his superiors. Equally perplexed carnies watched them from doorways, struck dumb and mute by the bizarre sight. Heavily armed tricks? That was a new one. Only the newer circus recruits understood what they saw, and in one or two of them stirred previously dead hopes of rescue from the show.

But the armed tricks had not quite figured out they were in a war zone yet. Jamie ran to the clown tent, not sure what he'd have to do to kick things off. He went to Gonko's room, opened a chest and dug around inside. Plenty of useless junk, one or two weapons . . . an antique pistol. Perfect! An old bottle of reeking moonshine. Flammable? He spilled a small puddle, lit a match, and up went a tiny ball of fire. *This*, he thought, *will do nicely.* He stuffed a rag in the bottle's neck, ran back to the shouting marines, aimed the pistol above their heads . . . *Click, click.* The damned thing didn't fire. He lit the rag, screamed a war cry and hurled the Molotov cocktail at the nearest formation.

One of the marines stopped, dropped, rolled as a lick of flame crawled up his pants. Jamie cursed; he'd not meant to actually hit them—just scare them. Two others opened fire in his direction, and it kicked things off better than he could have hoped.

In teams of four the marines ran through the showgrounds. Their shouts rang out from inside huts and caravans. Doorways were kicked down. Most carnies were too startled to fight them, but several had booby-trapped their homes once word had spread of Gonko's murderous trip through the neighborhood. A few marines fell back, clobbered by falling axe heads rigged by string webs to the tops of doors. Thus, the massacre began.

Over at the music box hut, Kurt had (as he'd have put it) "lost his temper." He did not look human any longer—sharp scales and ridges tore to shreds his tie-dyed muumuu. Yet he could still not push the door in—Deeby held it firm, muscles bulging absurdly, calling out taunts. "That all you got? Bro, you clearly lift . . . like a total bitch!" Kurt rammed the door so hard the whole hut shivered, but Deeby held it. He said, "Give it up, this is just going to embarrass you. For some reason, my girl is impressed by this kind of thing. Give me something to work with here."

Kurt swung his head toward the firing guns, screamed so loud the ground shook, then charged. He tore through a team of four marines before they had time to shut their flabbergasted mouths. But the team behind them saw what had happened to their friends, and opened fire. Bullets peppered Kurt's hide, knocking off bloodless chips like they'd shot at stone. He held a marine's corpse as a shield and backed quickly away, til he was hobbling toward the tunnel to the realm beneath.

Mugabo helped to heat things up quite literally. When a marine found the culprit cage, he yelled at those inside to freeze, and get down. The acrobats and lion tamer obeyed, but Mugabo resented it. "You freeze," he retorted, already short tempered by this latest outrage, "you geddown."

A warning shot was fired over his head. "Freeze! Get down!" a nervous marine screamed at him.

"Freeze? No thank," Mugabo snarled, splaying his fingers. "No freeze. How bout BURN!" And he did just that, unleashing a torrent of fire. The troops who saw it no longer seemed to care about who, or what, they fired upon. Their formations lost order; they screamed and fired at anything moving. A thunderstorm of gunfire, and the lightning flash of muzzles engulfed the showgrounds.

Jamie hid on the roof of the clown tent, looking down on the scene through a growing cloud of smoke. His every impulse told him to flee to the surface for safety, but Shalice's words played in his mind. Even if these guys shot everyone down here, it would change nothing in the long term—the clowns would return soon enough, and Kurt had already escaped below. So he tried to watch and make sense of the confusion. By now, all the carnies were aware of their danger. A great stampede broke out, scattering all over the place, but since the way to the lift was blocked by marines (and most of the carnies had no pass-outs anyway), the crowd generally headed toward the Funhouse, just as Kurt had done. Jamie supposed that made sense—maybe it was the only place to hide. Maybe the marines would follow them down there and blast away the big bosses, the demonic things that could not stand solid reality. Would that wreck the house, as Shalice had put it? Could bullets even hurt those things?

Maybe, maybe not, but too much physical matter in their presence? Like a flood of panicked carnies, and the marines, if they followed them down there? Maybe that would hurt them . . .

And what would they do about it, those powerful but frail entities? Maybe they'd fly into a blind panic, maybe they'd run. And if they ran, maybe they'd come up that tunnel, up here into the showgrounds. In which case . . .

In which case, Jamie suddenly knew what he had to do.

"Am I done yet?" said Deeby. "Has your heart been won over by my ability to prevent this particular piece of wood from moving too much?"

A bullet tore through the wall. Jodi yelped as pain bit her arm, but it was just a graze from a ripped piece of wood. She had no idea what to do. Stay and hide? Run for it? Call for help? Dean might know. He'd told her what to do to bring him back. It was not easy staying in character, but she took a handkerchief and said, "Yes, my love. Let me wipe the sweat from your face."

Deeby swept her up in the crook of one arm, checked his watch impatiently as she began to rub off the makeup. He said, "Easy! You're rubbing a little hard there. Hurry up with the smooches, then we can kink it up. Whatever tasty treats I got coming, I think we can agree I've earned it."

"You have," she said, and cleaned the last of the face paint off him.

For several minutes Jamie tried to spot a fallen marine—it would do no good to wander around dressed as a clown. There were a few lying inert, possibly dead, but in each case their team stayed with them. Finally a group of them rushed off, chasing some fleeing carnies, white fire flashing from their guns.

He leaped, floated down, dragged the body to the shadows of the freak show, ignoring Dr. Gloom's "What'sss all thiss ruckusss?" He stripped his clothes, stripped the dead marine and put on the poorly fitting uniform, which left his navel and shins exposed. He looked more like a Mardis Gras parade marcher than an actual soldier. It might save him from any long-range fire, but up close it would be clear he was an imposter. Reluctantly he wiped off the face paint, removing the protection and power it granted him.

He ran to Shalice's hut, where Dean had left the gate pieces. Along the way bodies were slumped on the ground, torn by gunfire, and some of the homes had begun to burn. The fortuneteller's bullet-ridden body was draped over her table, and the crystal ball had been knocked to the floor. The sights barely registered. He took the gate pieces over his shoulders, and headed to the Funhouse. Some gunfire barked out, but it was muffled, which he knew meant some of them had probably dropped down the tunnel in pursuit of fleeing carnies. Others waited at the tunnel's top.

"Get down there!" the apparent commanding officer yelled, followed by a string of numbers and letters Jamie could make no sense of. A burst of black smoke wafted up the opening. "Go!" the leader screamed. Down went the rest of the marines, their leader taking the rear. Cries and gunfire carried up soon after.

Jamie ran in, lay one part of the gates flat on the ground on each side of the tunnel, the arching piece on top, not needing to physically connect this roof piece to the rest, as Dean had explained. Jamie was amazed at how serene, calm, and easy he felt. JJ had done him a favor, back in the clown tent with the axe held high, showing him death and making him face it. It was not new. Otherwise maybe his hands would forget the angles and numbers on the gate pieces' dials. How he admired the fearless, competent little machines his hands had become.

And it was done, and Jamie was once again completely useless down here. What more was there to do? He could not affect what happened down that tunnel; if he jumped down he'd be shot or maybe killed by something demonic. If the "upper management" fled through the tunnel, the gates would send them out to the physical world, up to the campsite where, like a man held under water, the environment would destroy them. If it worked, it worked; if not, the world had made its choice. Jamie decided to leave, and let the world decide for itself.

Except Dean had the pass-outs. Maybe he'd have to take them off a corpse.

"Dean?" he called, unable suddenly to remember where the music box hut was. So he wandered randomly through the smoke and ruin. "Dean? Jodi?"

It seemed a long time before two lonely figures trudged through the wreckage towards him. "Dean," Jamie's voice was dreamlike. He noted he was probably in some kind of shock. Jodi's blank stare said she was the same way.

Dean patted his back. "It worked, bro. I think it worked. Good job."

"We probably got all those soldiers killed."

"Hear that? They're still shooting down there. And they're better equipped for all this than we are. Yeah, maybe they won't make it out. We can't change that now, and if they die, they'll die saving God knows how many people. Okay? Deal with guilt later. Let's get back home and work out what the hell we're going to tell everyone."

21. ABOVE

Gonko paced back and forth through the campsite where the remains of his secret show stood like grave markers. The other clowns watched him pace from safely out of kick range. Goshy stood by the remains of the baby Goshy JJ had killed, the shovel blade still wedged in its head. "I just couldn't stop Jamie from killing it," JJ said. "He was, like, possessed by lust for blood."

A clown tear of fluorescent green dripped down Goshy's cheek and bounced around where it fell. His belly gurgled with sad hunger.

"Something's *up* I tell you," Gonko raged. "It's a mighty bad time to be AWOL with Kurt on the hunt. We better be on our toes when we get back."

"We should maybe go back now, boss?" said Rufshod. "Sneak back, check it out?"

"Maybe we oughta. Bury all this gear first. C'mon, you sad pack of jizz tissues, dig!" Then a ripping sound rent the air. The clown heads all slowly turned, just as the rotating clown-head game in Sideshow Alley was now turning for the last few times. Their mouths all opened wide enough for ping pong balls. Then a dozen large shapes, followed by twice as many small ones, burst out into the afternoon and looked about in shock and confusion. Gonko alone knew what he saw, but he was too stunned to do more than stare. In that instant, these things from beneath the Funhouse would know all about the secret traveling show.

However, that looked to be the least of their troubles. A sizzling noise arose, as the entities howled in pain, staggered, and groped blindly in the morning sun.

Millions of consumed souls burst from each of them in small explosions of white light, fading from visibility as they soared skywards. The entities' outlines wavered to flickering, fast-bending lines as they twisted and folded to wretched, writhing shapes.

All their works and deformities, all the things their knowledge and willpower had held together, now bent, withered, and broke apart just as they did. Doopy said, "Gee, golly, I don't feel so good . . . it kinda sorta hurts, guys." His skin began to melt and slide from his face. His ears and eyes sucked back into his skull and smoke gushed out the gaps. Goshy's kettle scream went full blast as his skin turned to bubbling liquid, slipped from the fat and muscle beneath. "Mr. Bigbad's comin', Gonko. It ain't no fair, I wanted to taste the sky pretties, Gonko, I wanted to be a super duper clown . . ." Gonko, JJ, and Rufshod fell to their knees, clutching their throats. Their bodies lurched and quivered on the grass. There was a pop and crack as bones broke. Ooze and sludge poured from ruptures in Gonko's skin. It was over, *he* was over, and in that moment he knew that, somehow, his own scheming had brought things to this. As had the fortuneteller. One furious surge of anger held him together longer than the others. His quivering bones, in a melting pile of flesh, shuddered and shivered, tried to pull themselves back together, the white gloved hands reaching in vain to scoop liquid flesh back about the bones. Then Gonko joined his fellow clowns and lay inert. Their clothes—like a deflated balloon's skin—spread across the grass.

Below, as the unfortunate marines screamed and fired through their nightmare, all that was the showgrounds began to crumble. Great swaths of nothing were torn into the place's fabric. The tunnel collapsed, trapping and dooming those inside. They were people who at least had this much: they had understood and accepted that not every heroic deed is known and praised by those rescued, and that one day they may die in war.

Like the tents below, the traveling show's campsite tents deflated and faded in sunlight that seemed, just now, to pour down a little more brightly. The air filled with birdsong. Soon, all that remained of the clowns was the scuff marks their shoes had made in the dirt, and the memories left in three people's heads, where the memories would be forced by a skeptical world to remain.

The tenuous links holding the circus and its nether world to the world we know buckled and snapped at last, were closed off. The realities split and parted, and the foreign thing dropped away like a parasite forced by death to finally release its fangs.

The three of them—Jodi, Dean, and Jamie—surfaced not knowing that the marines would not survive, nor how close the timing of their escape through the lift had been; a few minutes longer, and they too would have been trapped. About them the city bustled through its usual throes of morning. It was noisy, yet somehow seemed eerily quiet. Angry men in hard hats chased them off the construction site.

They looked around like strangers to the world, seeing it all through new eyes and, each in their own way, realizing that the *normality* around them was a lie.

Dean took from his pocket a little velvet bag that was half full. "So this is what you did last time," he said to Jamie. "You made yourself forget. How about now?"

They all stared at the bag. Jamie didn't know whether he wanted to forget or not. But as they stared, the bag seemed to shrink and lose color until it was gone altogether. They looked at each other, and Jamie broke a stunned silence. "I think that means it worked. Where I set up the gates, at the tunnel . . . the big monsters came up here and died. I think it worked!"

Jodi's veil faded to nothing. So did the rest of her clothes, as did Dean's—clothes the carnies had made for them. Only Jamie remained dressed in his ill-fitting marine outfit, which he quickly stripped off. They sat on the park bench naked and laughing. Wolf whistles and cheers fired at them from passing cars. "It worked!" Dean screamed, jumping atop a parked car. "How long were we gone?"

"Not much more than a week," Jamie said.

"A week! Man, we may not even have lost our *jobs*." Dean whooped at the sky, blew kisses to a passing police car, which was, luckily, otherwise occupied.

Still laughing, they ran most of the way back to the apartment, broke out all the liquor they could find, and celebrated. Their old lives, or something resembling them closely enough, stretched out ahead in their minds. A few bad memories and a few bad dreams, it seemed to them then, was not too high a price to pay.

Will Elliott is the author of *The Pilo Family Circus*, which won five literary wards including the Golden Aurealis. He was named as one of the Sydney Morning Herald's Best Young Novelists. His novels has been published in the UK, US, Germany, Italy and Sweden.

Will lives in Australia.